CONQUEST

Also by Nina Allan

CONQUEST

Nina Allan

riverrun

First published in Great Britain in 2023 by

riverrun

an imprint of

Quercus Editions Limited
Carmelite House
50 Victoria Embankment
London EC4Y 0DZ

An Hachette UK company

A CIP catalogue record for this book is available
from the British Library.

Hardback 978 1 52942 077 7
Trade Paperback 978 1 52942 078 4
Ebook 978 1 52942 080 7

10 9 8 7 6 5 4 3 2 1

Typeset by CC Book Production
Printed and bound in Great Britain by Clays Ltd, Elcograf S.p.A.

Papers used by riverrun are from well-managed forests and other responsible sources.

For Helen Marshall

But who may abide the day of his coming? and who shall stand when he appeareth? for he is like a refiner's fire, and like fullers' soap:

And he shall sit as a refiner and purifier of silver: and he shall purify the sons of Levi, and purge them as gold and silver, that they may offer unto the LORD an offering in righteousness.

Then shall the offering of Judah and Jerusalem be pleasant unto the LORD, as in the days of old, and as in former years.

Malachi 3: 2-4

CONTENTS

PARIS

THE BEING FREE WAS the thing, that and knowing the truth. Frank didn't get a high from breaking rules for the sake of it the way some of his friends did. Frank saw rules and laws as strands of opinion, some right and some wrong. Those that made sense he'd go along with no problem, those that didn't (in the words of Karl Marx) were part of a system of oppression that should be opposed. A law is a line in the sand Frank thought, a stripe of red thread like that game the girls in primary school used to play with a piece of elastic, a game that was really a set of rituals you had to memorise, the elastic creeping higher and higher up the legs of the girls with each new move.

Like the Goldberg Variations (BWV 988), the longer the game went on the more complex it became, the more highly charged. Frank remembered how one of the teachers had yelled at him for watching the girls: Frank Landau come away from there at once haven't you got anything better to do? Mrs Webster (aka the spider) thought he'd been staring at the girls' legs, trying to see up their skirts probably, though in fact Frank had been admiring the patterns they made, the way the elastic crossed and uncrossed in a kind of slow fractal. No one even noticed he was watching until the spider yelled at him, until his cheeks and neck burned red and his insides churned as if they'd been injected with a hot greasy liquid.

He went to hide out in the locker room, the elastic patterns still folding and unfolding inside his brain like the coloured chips of glass inside a kaleidoscope. He remembered the first time he'd heard the Goldberg Variations, almost exactly two years (six hundred and ninety-eight days) after the spider yelled at him for staring at the girls, and how the patterns in the music made him think of the patterns the girls had made with their strip of elastic.

The record (Peter Serkin RCA 1965) belonged to his gran and on the day Frank first heard Bach he was twelve years old and it was summer, the tall French windows of his grandmother's living room thrown open to the garden. In the years since, Frank had listened to the Goldberg Variations hundreds of times. He could not say exactly how many, he wished he'd kept count. Sometimes it really bugged him that he hadn't but it was too late now no good no point thinking about it really but he knew it had been hundreds. The Goldberg Variations were imprinted in his memory like a blueprint like code. Frank liked to think there was a part of his brain that only became fully engaged when he listened to Bach.

What if Bach was his trigger his activation meme an attraction that had been implanted, like with his dad? Frank thought about this a lot worried about it sometimes but there were some things you couldn't know for sure which meant it was probably safer to pretend you hadn't noticed. Frank owned fourteen different recordings of the Goldberg

Variations. His four favourites in ascending order were András Schiff (ECM 2002), Glenn Gould (Sony 1955), Angela Hewitt (Hyperion 1999), Peter Serkin (RCA 1965). Serkin would always be his favourite because it was the first recording he had heard. There was a limit to what you could do with pre-digital recordings but Frank didn't mind the bumps and crackles, they gave the sound depth.

Frank wondered more and more about the possibility that Johann Sebastian Bach had never existed, that he was an artificial construct planted in the historical archive to rationalise the existence of his music. That Bach's music was not simply music but an alien code. There was a friend of his friend Eddie named Janet Glass who was sometimes on the forums who was converting the whole of Bach's oeuvre into computer graphics. Sound maps she called them. No one really knew what they meant yet but Eddie had people working on it. Janet Glass wasn't related to Philip Glass she said though it was an interesting coincidence.

The Voyager space probe was launched on August 20th 1977 which was ten years almost to the hour before Frank was born. On board the Voyager was a disc of sound recordings called the Golden Record which included three recordings of music by J. S. Bach: Brandenburg Concerto No. 2 in F major BWV 1047 second movement (Munich Bach Orchestra/Karl Richter), Partita for Solo Violin No. 3 BWV 1006 Gavotte en Rondeau (Arthur Grumiaux) and the Prelude and Fugue in C major BWV 870 (Glenn Gould). The programme for the Golden Record had been chosen by a committee of academics from Harvard University chaired by the astronomer and cosmologist Carl Sagan. In the case of Bach most of all Frank found their choices curious even suspect, all three of them in major keys and when you listened to them together as a group they lacked depth they lacked significance like grazing the surface of Bach instead of diving deep. Frank thought this was probably down to the influence of Carl Sagan who everyone on LAvventura agreed had been an FBI stooge.

The n-men were back. Frank first noticed one in Superdrug, a guy in a herringbone jacket with a brown leather briefcase. His facial features were so symmetrical they seemed to vanish in the crowd, the kind of guy you'd find it hard to say afterwards what he looked like, the kind who if he were in a police line-up you'd never pick out. Frank wouldn't have noticed him if he hadn't been on the lookout. The n-men started appearing about a week after he first posted on LAvventura which might have been a coincidence except it wasn't. LAvventura was where he'd met Eddie. Frank felt the connection between them at once, like the lines of magnetic force between binary stars.

When Frank told his girlfriend Rachel his connection with Eddie was preordained, that Eddie understood the propensity of the avant-garde for uprooting conventional thinking for mounting a defence against hostile mind control she said I know you believe it Frankie and I believe in you.

He and Rachel met when they were both fifteen. Frank remembered those crappy roller skates he had back then, the kind that buckled on over your shoes with the metal sliders. Right through the summer evenings weekends holidays he and his brother Michael and a load of other kids used to skate all over the estate down the back alleyways the concrete ramps that led to the garage blocks the avenues the crescents the drives. The sound of roller blades on tarmac was the sound of summer, the constant rumbling along dustbin alley fringed with nettles and brambles and cow parsley and chain-link fencing the lane that led from the good estate to the bad estate.

Kids shuttled between the two estates all the time especially in summer in spite of the parents of the kids from the good estate trying to put a stop to it. The two estates were sometimes at war though more often they joined forces climbing on the roofs of the garages chasing each other across the prairies of their neighbours' back gardens.

Rachel was from the good estate. Her dad was a sales rep for Bovril, her mum was a radiography nurse. Rachel had no brothers or sisters. Rachel's parents seemed to hold back from Frank to begin with but in the end they got used to him being around. You've become part of the furniture, haven't you? Rachel's mum Ricky said to him once, Ricky short for Frederica though Frank never dared call her either he called her Mrs Gabon.

Frank was from the bad estate but the good part of the bad estate. Frank's mother Emily had bought their council house under Thatcher's Right to Buy scheme. Frank didn't remember Thatcher not really not from when she was in power though he'd seen videos of her from afterwards, going to the shops in a headscarf that was meant to disguise her but didn't. Thatcher was definitely one of them, but she was over now, she had outlived her usefulness and Frank had the feeling she'd probably been abandoned. That's why she went mad later, because she couldn't remember who she was any more. Frank might even have felt sorry for her if Emily hadn't hated her so much because that's what they did with people, used them up then threw them away like dirty dishrags.

At least we got the house out of her, Emily always said (meaning Thatcher) it's not a bad place to live.

Frank's brother Michael was five years younger than him and their sister Faith was five years younger than Michael. Frank liked to think of them as three fives are fifteen because five was a good number thank goodness a number that gave them some protection against the n-men. Michael and Faith's dad Gavin still dropped round occasionally though Frank didn't feel comfortable around him and made a point of being out if he knew he was coming.

Frank's dad's name was Adrian Skeaping. Frank remembered him less than he remembered Thatcher though when he was younger he'd used to send him stuff, postcards Christmas cards badges, photos he'd cut out of magazines which he'd post to the last address Emily had for him which was in Bristol. Frank never told anyone he'd tried to contact his dad, not even Rachel and he'd never received a reply because Dad had been shipped out most likely that's what happened with people in the program they were always being reassigned and moved away to avoid discovery.

Adrian Skeaping was keeping out of sight in order to protect his son.

What was he like? Frank had asked Emily when he was ten.

Emily sighed folded her arms shook her head. He was young, she said. We both were. I'm sorry Frankie but you're best off letting him go.

Letting him go, like releasing a balloon string, or donating a jacket to Oxfam because it no longer fitted. When he was younger the thought of his father out in the world fighting to keep them safe made Frank feel less anxious even hopeful though the more he discovered about the program the harsh reality of it the more Adrian Skeaping seemed to recede from him, to become lost, something you couldn't do anything about like closed-down pubs and fake news and his friend Jayden Lotz who he used to hang about with on the estate. Jay was arrested for possession (ten grams) then got stabbed to death by some Britain First thugs while he was on remand.

Jay usually came top in maths. Jay had an old-fashioned Dictaphone he'd bought on the market he used for recording street sounds for his rap compositions. Britain First were part of the old order, that's what Eddie said, intellectual dinosaurs headed for extinction but for now they were a fact of life.

A fact of life, like Frank's love for Rachel. A fact of life, like the war.

Their house had four bedrooms, an open-plan kitchen and dining room and (because it was on a corner plot) a massive garden. The good part of the bad estate backed on to a parcel of overgrown wasteland they called the copse. Frank liked being on the copse especially in summer liked the long grass the stands of foxgloves and dandelions the brown stream flickering with tadpoles they called the Amazon. You found all sorts of stuff on the copse: old pram wheels and broken radios and shards of pottery, glass bottles from before World War Two. Frank liked to collect the bottles and the pottery especially, the edge of a plate with a pattern of daisies half a teacup with a golden rim a green (salt-glazed) pepper pot with its stopper missing. Digging around on the copse made him feel like Red Schuhart the stalker in Roadside Picnic the novel by Arkady and Boris Strugatsky (1972/1977).

The copse was like the zone in Roadside Picnic: a patch of land where strange things happened where you could go sometimes to think about the world a territory people thought they understood but actually didn't. Roadside Picnic was important because it proved the Strugatsky brothers had understood what was really going on.

Frank remembered seeing Rachel at school sometimes but he had never spoken to her. He knew girls thought he was weird but he didn't really care. He could look at girls online if he wanted but mostly he didn't bother. The first time he spoke to Rachel was on the copse. She was sitting by herself on the part of the copse called the meadow where kids sometimes played football. Frank could taste the dryness of pollen at the back of his throat and in his nostrils, smell the perfume of warm grass. Rachel had long pieces of grass stuck to the back of her legs also a heart-shaped yellow leaf and her feet were bare, her trainers on the ground beside her with her socks stuffed inside. Frank wondered what she was doing there and why she was alone. Normally it was Frank who was alone, and when Rachel looked up suddenly it was like a camera going off, freezing the moment in place before the present fell into the past and was gone forever.

Hi, Rachel said.

I can go if you want, if you're busy.

I'm not busy, just thinking. I like it out here.

I do too, Frank said. He felt amazed he had even spoken and maybe he hadn't maybe he just thought he had, I do too, a stupid sound like a bird sound like a pigeon cooing. He sat down on the grass. He wondered if this was how future kings felt when they realised that one day they'd be actual kings. He and Rachel talked about school stuff (which classes they were in which teachers were OK and which were idiots) and none of it mattered at all except they were together.

Then Rachel asked him what kind of music he liked. I like David Bowie, she said. Ziggy Stardust is my favourite album ever.

Frank had heard of David Bowie but he had never listened to him. I like Johann Sebastian Bach, he said. I like the Goldberg Variations.

That's cool, Rachel said. Bowie's into classical he likes all kinds of weird music. Sometimes I think he might actually be Ziggy, you know, like an alien from Mars or somewhere. She laughed. I saw Mars once, she added, through a telescope at the space centre in Florida. We went there on holiday two years ago. I'd love to go again.

She leaned back on her hands. Weren't you ill or something last year? she said. You were off school for ages.

I was in hospital, Frank said. Generalised Anxiety Disorder, which meant no one knew what was wrong with him, and how could he describe the terror that came in waves and that stopped him from sleeping? The terror had been his awakening, he realised that now, the first sign of *them*. He knew because his father had told him in a dream. Frank's heart rate leaped from resting to racing as he asked himself how he could answer Rachel's question without telling her a lie because he knew if he lied to her now (there's nothing going on here you moron she already thinks you're a weirdo so just say you broke your leg or something no one knows why you were in there except Mum and Michael) this moment would end.

I was having problems digesting food, he said, which was true so far as it went, at least it gave him a breathing space more time to think.

That must have been awful, said Rachel. I hate hospitals. I had to stay in overnight once when I had a tooth pulled and it freaked me out.

And that seemed to be that at least for now no further questions ladies and gentlemen of the jury as if his breakdown at the age of fourteen had never happened. Frank felt light as spider silk light as tumbleweed.

You could come to ours for tea, if you want, he said. We could listen to some music. He felt amazed at himself for having spoken for having dared to think of himself even for a second as someone she would want to see again, and in the nameless echoing interval between his speaking the words and the thing itself happening Frank went into town to the second-hand music store Boomtown Records. There was an HMV in the mall but the staff there (college kids punk kids) made him feel nervous not like Mr Hannigan in his glasses and cardigan who let him browse without saying a word unless Frank asked a question.

Frank looked in the David Bowie section and found a second-hand CD of The Rise and Fall of Ziggy Stardust and the Spiders from Mars (RCA Victor 1972) for £3.50.

An unusual choice for you said Mr Hannigan when he took it to the counter.

It's a present Frank said for a friend. He felt panicky out of his depth but Mr Hannigan only nodded and said good choice Bowie's a great artist which made everything all right again. Frank paid for the CD then went straight home and up to his room where he played Ziggy Stardust and the Spiders from Mars three times in a row through his headphones because he didn't want anyone to know what he was listening to until he worked out how he felt about Rachel's music.

The album cover showed Ziggy Stardust who was also Bowie standing on the lighted doorstep of a club called K.West (pronounced Quest not Kay West Rachel told him later) under a violet twilight sky somewhere in London. There were cars pulled up at the kerb which looked like spies' cars, their outlines distorted by a crack in the jewel case Frank hoped would not grow any larger because that was what happened sometimes with second-hand CD cases they got brittle and broke.

The music was a part of his life now whether he liked it or not and for those first three times he played the album he honestly didn't know if he could get used to that kind of music though he found it easier to imagine liking it when he thought about Rachel sitting on the floor of her bedroom holding the CD case in her hand, unfolding the liner so she could read the lyrics along with the music.

In the end and after five play-throughs Frank felt able to say he liked the song Five Years best something about the harmonic progression and because the music was in ¾ time which was a comfort zone for him. He copied the lyrics on to a separate sheet of paper so he could study them properly and found he couldn't get the images out of his head after that, the crying newsreader especially he could not forget.

Is the song about an alien invasion? he asked Rachel three days after when they listened to the album together for the first time. Emily hadn't batted an eyelid when they came in together just said oh hi you must be Rachel. She asked if Rachel liked spaghetti Bolognese then went back to studying her OU module papers spread out on the kitchen table the same as always.

Your mum's cool, said Rachel, later.

She's studying for a degree, Frank said. Politics and sociology.

I'm not sure what the song means, Rachel said. I've always thought it's more like the aliens are coming to save us, because we've made such a mess of the world. You like it, then? she said, resting her back against the side of the bed just the way he'd imagined and Frank said he liked the way Bowie used science-fiction imagery, the way he mixed it up with ideas about rock and roll, he found it more interesting each time he listened. The way he uses musical form, Frank said, grabs hold of it really.

Rachel laughed but only gently then punched his arm and said what are you like?

A week after buying the CD Frank began to think his favourite track might actually be Rock 'n' Roll Suicide which was also in ¾ time and used a similar set of harmonies to Five Years but the song's meaning, mood and direction were practically the opposite. It wasn't until much later that Frank realised hearing Ziggy Stardust for the first time marked the moment he became properly switched on to what was happening, that the album was not just an album but a private message. The first fall had been his awakening but now they knew he was ready to learn the truth. Bowie's lyrics had been listened to by millions of people all over the world but only a few of them would come to realise they were about the war.

If Frank had not met Rachel he would never have heard Bowie which meant Rachel was part of the message though it was better she didn't know that because not knowing would help keep her safe.

Love you're not alone, Frank thought, and the thought was precious was everything was pure Rachel.

*

Frank knew the n-men would interpret his contact with Eddie as some sort of milestone. The day after they first spoke on the phone (Eddie was in Geneva he said at a film festival) Frank wrote him a letter care of his department at the university. Eddie said they should start using snail mail in preference to email unless it was urgent. Eddie wasn't keen on mobile communications of any kind, a nervousness Frank shared because the digital pathways were so easy to track to hack to record and even when you were being careful there would be lapses. Lapses were what the n-men depended on what they got off on.

The marvellous thing about snail mail was that no one cared about it. The small miracle of pen on paper, the slow passing of information of thoughts of ideas that would carry on being his until the envelope was opened yet at the same time belonged to Eddie from the second Frank dropped the envelope into the post box. Like sending an email in slow motion, the slow spray of data through the fabric of space, a burgeoning of spores like the vortex of midges that swarmed the copse at twilight or after rain.

For Frank the anxiety of knowing he was under surveillance was less than the anxiety of being spied on in secret. You could even say there was something energising in knowing for sure, a sense of forward momentum even of power yet he knew he should be careful not so much of them as of himself of the ceaseless careless unspooling of his unguarded thoughts.

The first fall when it finally happened had come upon him quickly, overwhelming his senses with their senses, his thoughts with their thoughts, that intolerable hum. A hum like a swarm of bees like a pinpoint diamond drill against human bone. Three months in Woodside

View that seemed to pass in an instant that lasted forever. Sometimes when he couldn't sleep Frank found himself circling the idea that he might still be in there, the impregnable fire door marked Admissions the iron bar that slid across with a thunk as they led you inside.

I was fourteen, Frank wrote in a letter to Eddie. Michael wanted to visit but they wouldn't let him.

When he finally told Rachel about his breakdown his teeth started chattering. Rachel took hold of his hand. She seemed utterly calm.

Tell me about the war, she said. I want to understand. When will it begin?

Frank shook his head. No one knows exactly. This isn't a normal war with bombs and bullets. Some people think the war has started already. He closed his eyes. It's not schizophrenia. I don't hear voices. I know that's what the doctors think but they don't know because they don't listen. They think they've got me sewn up and that's the problem because they don't pay attention. What I hear is more like a sound, he added. A kind of vibration.

Like white noise?

He nodded. Like electricity. Or like a magnet. Like I can feel the force in my body. It's as if the Earth itself knows it's under attack and the hum is like an early warning system.

So there's still time to bring people together? Rachel said. Time to get more information?

Frank squeezed her hand. He felt breathless with relief light-headed flying like they both weighed nothing. Rachel had heard had listened and she was still by his side.

Ow, Rachel said. You're hurting. She laughed. It's OK Frankie I know you didn't mean to. She kissed him on the forehead then again on the lips. His chest already felt lighter his breathing less painful. He was beginning to think there was a chance the war could be won.

That girl is a wonder, his mother said when Frank was finally back at home after his second fall the year he finished college. He was inside for six months that time and Rachel had been in to visit him every day.

Yes she is, Frank had agreed and now in the Café du Nord the restaurant-bistro at 19 rue de Dunkerque pictured on the postcard Eddie had sent him confirming their meeting-place, now as the garçon brought him the steak sandwich with frites he'd ordered and as he kept watch on the street outside not through the window because that would be foolish but in the heavily ornate gold-framed mirror behind the bar he thought about Rachel and her being a wonder and how hard that must be. She had carried the weight of his fear and kept on loving him. Kept on loving him through the years, kept on loving him even now when it must be obvious even to her that he was powerless against the might of what was coming.

Frank gazed into the mirror so hard and so long he forgot about his food forgot he was supposed to be sitting there looking inconspicuous just a guy eating a meal while he waited for Eddie. The street in the mirror seemed less solid than it ought to be, its edges softer than the reality inside the café as if he and the café were in a film and the world outside the window just a fake background. He began to wonder if the mirror was not really a mirror but some sort of camera. He tried to concentrate on his sandwich, to hold panic at bay by focusing on familiar details as he'd been taught to do at Woodside then just as the panic started bleeding through again Eddie tapped him on the shoulder slid on to a chair.

You're early, he said, his smile relaxed and open and friendly as if they'd met many times as if they came to this café often which of course they never had before today. Frank had never seen Eddie before today except on a screen. His hair was blond and curly like an angel's on a Christmas card only his face wasn't an angel's his face was a poet's. He pushed his glasses up his nose, making them crooked. You looked really out of it just then, he said.

Frank stared at him blankly. He couldn't work out how he'd missed seeing Eddie arrive then realised he must have come in through the door at the back, which opened on to a different street. The explanation was simple and logical and Frank felt instantly calmer.

Eddie raised an eyebrow. You can never tell who might be watching, you know.

I'm sorry, Frank said. I was miles away.

More than a hundred, it looked like. Eddie laughed, and his laugh was good-natured and easy and went with his hair. Frank felt the briefest stab of regret that Eddie de Groote the angel-haired poet was as doomed as they all were.

We're going to Marco's, said Eddie. He glanced down at Frank's steak. Aren't you going to eat that?

I'm not hungry, Frank said. He stuck a ten-euro note under the ketchup bottle and got to his feet already regretting not finishing the sandwich because in fact he felt ravenous exhausted diminished as if he'd been travelling all day and all night although the journey from London to Paris had taken less than three hours. Frank had never been in a foreign country before. The feeling was overwhelming like an attack of vertigo like the feeling he'd had when he came out of Woodside the second time. He kept thinking about the way Eddie had appeared so suddenly and without any warning which was exactly like the n-men how the n-men came and went although Eddie wasn't one of them Eddie was his friend.

And yet he could not deny there was a knowingness about him, a quality of hardness beneath his friendliness Frank had not been prepared for.

And the way he had appeared, so suddenly.

No Frankie you're just tired Rachel said inside his mind and of course she was right.

I'm ready, Frank said. He nodded. Let's go.

Eddie was big on LAvventura because he made all kinds of connections. Connections between films and books and sometimes music, song lyrics mainly though he did know Bach quite well from talking with Janet and the Second Viennese School (Schoenberg Berg and Webern) who he called the brotherhood. Eddie's theory was that art was more important than people realised, that art was a secret history of the war. A coded critical commentary on the structure of power he had called it once, a manifesto of resistance.

Eddie had given Frank a reading list he was working his way through. Some of the titles had asterisks beside them which meant they were particularly important. One of these was The Tower.

You might have trouble getting hold of a copy, Eddie had told him. It's been out of print for decades. Once you read it you'll understand why.

Frank had managed to find a copy on the website of a bookshop in Cardiff (condition: acceptable/reading copy only/no dust jacket £40). He half-expected the book not to arrive but it did, the following day, mustard-yellow boards title and author name embossed on the spine in neat grey capitals. The book's pages were coarse-grained almost chalky and slightly foxed. Slightly foxed meant spotted with rust as if a fox had brushed its tail over the paper.

The story of the tower was set in the future. The main character was an American architect who was trying to rebuild his career in the aftermath of a war with an alien planet. He wins a commission to design a building that will stand as a memorial to the millions of dead. The architect wants to build the tower from a special type of rock that has to be imported from the alien world. The city planners say the project is too expensive but after a massive legal battle the architect gets the go-ahead and the conquest tower is built. What no one realises until it's too late is that the rock the tower is built from is partly alive.

The story gave Frank nightmares. He understood as soon as he read it that Eddie was right, that The Tower was a secret history of the war to come. A lot of the people on LAvventura the older members especially believed the covid-19 pandemic was part of the invasion strategy and Frank could see how they might think this although Eddie was sceptical. We're talking about something much more insidious much more subtle, he said like the rock in The Tower which isn't actually rock at all but a species of mould and the thing with mould, Frank said to Rachel when she asked him about it, is that you don't notice it at first because it starts in damp dark places (cellars and outhouses) and because it spreads so slowly.

And Eddie thinks this is what is happening to the Earth?

Frank nodded. It's like a preparatory stage, he said, to make Earth hospitable to alien life. The Tower was published in the 1950s. The guy who wrote it died years ago, he added, but he knew what was really going on.

I'd like to read it Rachel said. Do you mind if I borrow it?

Frank said he didn't because how could he not but even so he was worried because the book was like the mould it could get inside you. When Rachel returned the book two days later she said she'd found the story powerful, frightening even especially the last part but surely it was just a story, like The Day of the Triffids.

There's no such thing as just a story, Frank said. You have to ask yourself where stories like that come from.

From inside a writer's head Rachel said from their imagination.

Yes but ideas don't come out of nowhere, they come out of what you see or think or feel in real life. The imagination is a way for writers to translate their experience, to show people things they wouldn't notice or understand otherwise. The Day of the Triffids is the same story as The Tower, if you think about it, he said. People being blind to what's really going on, the whole world changing around them and they refuse to see it.

Words were slippery, Frank thought. So unlike code, or music, which had to be rendered perfectly or it wouldn't run.

The first thing you see is a river, Frank read, the long green strips of water weed weaving to and fro in the underwater current. A small brown leaf is swept downstream and the weather is changing. Kris

Kelvin stands alone on the riverbank. A layer of white mist drapes itself like a gossamer veil above the fields. Kelvin walks through the trees away from the river and towards a house. The doors leading to the veranda are open to the outside. The opening scenes of Tarkovsky's Solaris have a mesmeric quality. Events, such as they are, play out almost in real-time. There is a darkness hanging over the scene that Kelvin does not see yet but that we the audience intuit as a vibration, a sub-audible hum of unease. Even before the storm breaks we understand that the wheels of an alien clockwork are already in motion. Most film students are not interested in Solaris within the context of alien intelligence. They talk of metaphor, of nostalgia, of political satire. When Stanislaw Lem wrote his original novel he was interested in all of these things. Yet many choose to forget he was also obsessed with alien language systems and coded modes of expression. As a science-fiction writer, Lem was genuinely open to the possibility of alien contact. There are few who choose to pursue these lines of enquiry as a part of Lem's genius; Tarkovsky himself professed a complete lack of interest in science fiction. None of which takes anything away from the fact that as both film and novel, Solaris is the story of humanity's first, overwhelming contact with an alien intelligence . . .

Reading Eddie's essay was like experiencing the movie again but in a different way. Each time Frank watched the opening of Solaris he found himself thinking the same thoughts: this is the beginning. The river so clear and so glistening Frank knew exactly how it would taste if he bent to drink from it: cold and heavier than tap water and flavoured faintly with green. What scared Frank most about this opening sequence was the idea that none of it was real, that Kris Kelvin was actually on the spaceship the whole time, that his childhood home was no more than a memory and a series of photographs. A fire in the snow, a horse whinnying in a thunderstorm, a teacup filled with rain.

The music Tarkovsky had chosen for the opening titles was Bach's Chorale Prelude in F minor BWV 639 Ich ruf' zu Dir, Herr Jesu Christ. A supplication, said the sleeve notes, in times of despair, the music slow and gradual and patient as raindrops thumping against the windows on a wet afternoon. There was no way this choice of music could have been an accident. Against the background of the black-and-white title cards the melody seemed old and faded and crackling, the last music you would ever hear.

Marco's flat was on the third floor of a modern block. Council flats Frank supposed if there was such a thing as council flats in Paris. They took a train from the Gare du Nord to a station north of the city. Frank had already forgotten what the place was called, its name reduced to a trace memory, black letters on a flaking signboard half-covered with graffiti. From the station they walked for twenty minutes or so through a neigh-bourhood of vacant lots and tatty strip malls, washing lines strung between the balconies of concrete apartment blocks, football fields cracked and balding from lack of rain the deeper into the zone the nearer to heaven.

They crossed over a bridge spanning a five-lane highway, traffic speeding between Frank's feet like clockwork mice. He knew he would not be able to find his way back to the station now even if he wanted to. The knowledge veered and butted against the walls of his mind like a crane fly trapped in his grandmother's loggia in early October, drunk on the dregs of sunlight and too stupid to realise it could be swatted dead in less than a second. Frank hitched his rucksack higher up his shoulders. It felt heavier than when he'd got on the Eurostar yet Frank found himself numb with horror, overcome by the creeping conviction it contained less than it should, that he had forgotten to pack his travel plug, that he'd be unable to charge his phone to speak to Rachel.

Eddie will have a travel plug he assured himself, there's nothing to worry about. He wondered what Rachel was doing at that exact moment, though the idea of her seemed dreamlike, part of another universe altogether. I am removed from space and time Frank thought stop panicking.

The guys will be here already, Eddie said. He was walking with his hands in his pockets dragging his feet slightly against the potholed tarmac his hair casting a tangled shadow across the pavement. They are eager to meet you in person, he added. You can never be sure, you know, when you've only spoken to someone online. If they're serious, I mean, if they are for real.

I'm serious, Frank said. He swallowed. His throat was bone dry and yes he thought that was probably all it was, he was hungry and thirsty, tired too, and Eddie was right, you couldn't always tell what people were like or who they were working for. He'd been nervous himself when he and Eddie first got talking on LAvventura, and remember there's no such thing as too careful, as too much information. He thought about what Rachel had said to him the evening before, about him not being strong enough to make this journey alone. He was still too vulnerable she'd insisted but he'd told her she was wrong, he had to do this, his future maybe their future depended on it.

You can't keep taking the weight of the world on your own shoulders, Frankie. You can't go on like this or you'll end up getting ill again.

Ill again she'd said, as if illness were a recurring nightmare a beast of prey. He might keep ahead of it for a time but in the end it would run him down, leaping from overhead branches to bring him to ground.

I thought you believed in me, he said. He saw the hurt in her eyes but he had no choice. He took both her hands in his and they sat like that for what seemed hours, the two of them side by side on the bed just holding hands.

I do believe in you, she said at last. I'm worried that's all. I wish you'd let me come with you.

It's too dangerous Frank had said, which should have made things worse but that was the thing with him and Rachel, in the end they always came back together because that was who they were. Rachel was still sort of crying but she was laughing at the same time because that was who they were.

What are you like, Frankie, she said, and Frank had wanted to tell her how he saw everything all of a sudden, how his mind was like a kite like a paper aeroplane so high and so light he could fly on the wind he could soar above everything feel the G-force in the pit of his stomach see the world as it truly was the new world he had discovered the further into the zone the nearer to heaven. How in those moments of brightness and clarity he could see beyond what the doctors believed of him their falsely smiling hopes for him their insistence that he could be normal that he could *fit in*. Not realising even for a second how that was the problem how like death their innocent visions could sometimes be.

And Rachel was like an anchor like the rain in Tarkovsky's teacups like mica sparkling in the pavements like alien gems. If Frank could fly he could fly too far sometimes too near the sun but Rachel would always always always bring him back to safe ground.

They climbed the stairs to Marco's flat, the open metal treads clanging with every step the same as the stairs in the block where Michael and Faith's dad Gavin lived. Frank had walked past the block a thousand times but he had never been inside, not inside the flat anyway though he'd waited in the lobby for Michael every now and then.

Frank could hear music coming from the open door its bass notes shadowing his heartbeat putting him on edge.

We leave the door open because of Tilda, Eddie said. She's scared of being trapped.

Claustrophobia?

Eddie shrugged. Something like that, I guess. It isn't the size of the room she is in though, more like having to be sure there is a way out. Hey guys, he called out, we're back, raising his voice to make himself heard above the pounding music, some kind of rap Frank thought some kind of French hip hop. Eddie pushed the door wide, its grey surface rubbed and stained, reinforced glass in the top half, again like Gavin the Grunt's place but so what there were millions of flats like Gavin's clammy with the stink of Campbell's meatballs tomato soup or oxtail just about managing in every town in every city all over the world so what did it matter if it looked like Gavin's place or not?

They stepped inside. A figure loomed in the darkened entranceway, punched Eddie on the shoulder.

I'm Marco said the figure bright eyes glittering in the semi-darkness so I guess you're Frank?

Let's talk inside guys Eddie said. He bumped fists with Marco gave him a push a playful push Frank thought though with the light in the hallway so dim it was difficult to tell. Marco made space for them to enter and then they were inside. All's cool, Marco said, the twang in his voice suggesting he had learned his English from American sitcoms.

The flat's main room was large, larger than Frank would have expected, a long rectangular sitting room with an archway leading through to a kitchen area. Three windows overlooking the rear, scrubby grass a row of rotary driers and beyond them a parking lot, guys leaning against the cars you could see they were dealing quite openly but no one seemed to care.

The walls of the room were covered in maps: one huge map of the world surrounded by at least twenty smaller maps of individual cities, territories Frank couldn't identify without moving closer. The maps were covered in coloured push-pins some standing alone others grouped together in clusters. Were the colours of the push-pins relevant? Frank couldn't say.

Including himself and Marco and Eddie there were twelve of them. The faces seemed friendly Frank thought though the longer he stood and stared at them the more nervous he felt. For a room so full of people it was eerily quiet.

Well get the new boy some coffee, someone said finally, the youth looks exhausted.

She was sitting by herself in a black leather armchair, the kind you see in hotel lobbies or lawyers' offices, an older woman older than his mum Emily for sure though not as old as Gran sixty maybe sixty-five? She was wearing combats and a black long-sleeved T-shirt, her grey hair falling loosely over her shoulders her wrists heavy with bracelets gold and silver bangles. Posh blue-framed spectacles designer probably if you knew about that stuff. Slightly tinted, as if her eyes required protection from the light.

She held out her hand. Jeanne-Marie Vanderlien she said, Jeanne-Dark, and immediately Frank found himself blushing because JeanneDark was not how he'd imagined her from the forum not at all. He'd thought she would be younger which was just stupid when you came to think about it because why should she be, a realisation that made him blush harder.

JeanneDark was one of LAvventura's most respected posters and she seemed to know everything. Every book every idea every new theory and the way she thought the way she wrote was so powerful it lifted him excited him scared him every time.

It was as if she never went to sleep was always working.

I didn't know you'd be here, Frank said. He felt sick with his own stupidity but JeanneDark was smiling. Of all the eyes in the room turned towards him JeanneDark's were the most intelligent welcoming questioning the most alive.

Coffee would be good, he said and found in spite of his dizzying heart rate he was smiling also. I never finished my lunch.

They cleared a place for him on one of the sofas. Moments later a woman brought him a basket of bread some cheese and salami. The coffee is being made she said. She was young, skinny jeans bright red hair shaved close to her skull a tattoo curled around her wrist a frond of bracken. Frank wondered if this might be Tilda because she looked like a Tilda. He took a piece of bread. He felt shy of eating in front of them because no one else was eating probably but the scents acting on his empty stomach were overwhelming. He bit down on the bread and chewed. Saliva flooded his mouth and his muscles relaxed. For the first time since leaving the station since the hike through the desolate streets Frank thought yes he had been right to come here there was no harm done.

The work you have been doing, JeanneDark was saying. It is most impressive. All of us have felt the benefit of your insights.

Frank glanced up from his food saw Eddie the young woman with the shaved head (Tilda?) another woman beside her with brown skin and braids. A lanky guy with mended specs an older guy sitting with what looked like a tape recorder on his lap, Marco standing with his arms folded, eyes on the door.

I like working with code, Frank said. It relaxes my mind and then I can see things. The solutions come easily.

The way you are able to interpret patterns in data is quite remarkable. You have helped us to make progress, to show us where we would be best to concentrate our focus. We are happy to have you with us. Your contribution to our cause is already making a difference. We want you to feel welcome here.

Frank nodded. Talking about the work always steadied him. His facility with code his ability to see connections these were things he knew he was good at. Like Bach they made him feel more confident and less vulnerable. Less vulnerable in this landscape of parking lots, less nervous around these strangers who Eddie was always referring to as the war cabinet. And he saw they too were serious, they believed in the war. They understood the insidious terror the three-dimensional nature of the beast. He looked down at his feet. His backpack was gone which meant someone must have removed it while he was eating. A new wave of panic swept through him, younger cousin to the first wave and with twice as much energy.

Where's my bag? he mumbled. His face and hands felt numb.

Ed put it in the bedroom, Marco said. He unfolded his arms. A bracelet dangled from one of his wrists steel links the chain secured with a padlock his eyes were narrow and hard. You're bunking down together tonight. I made you up a camp bed. I hope that's OK.

Fine, Frank said quietly and there was no reason to think it wasn't fine except he hated being separated from his phone which he couldn't charge in any case, he remembered, making his stomach lurch, he'd forgotten his travel plug.

Could I use your loo, he said, I mean toilet, because it was the only way he could think of to get out of the room. As he stood there in the narrow cubicle the walls covered with photographs clipped from magazines and stuck down with varnish (all of them Frank realised with a sick feeling were of people being arrested) he felt blankness overtake him, a mute calmness that was like a drug, like the tranquillisers they'd given him at Woodside View. This was his body trying to protect itself he realised because even if Frank didn't admit it his body knew damn well there was something wrong. Not just wrong that was a copout that was bullshit because he knew the people in the other room, Marco and the guy with the tape machine especially, the whole war cabinet even Eddie were not going to had no intention of letting him leave.

You don't really know these people, Frankie, Rachel had said to him the evening before. You're not always great at reading people you can be too trusting.

Eddie wants me to be there. He says they need me. They're expecting me.

So you keep saying. I don't really see the point though. You being there in person, I mean.

We have to meet, to organise. This is a war, Rach. We have to get the word out. He swallowed, his throat jam-packed with words dry and brittle and stuck in his gullet like toast crumbs like thistle heads. He felt breathless, jittery. I thought you understood.

Rachel grabbed both of his hands pressed them together. I'd do anything for you Frankie you know that.

Frank nodded, panic rising in his chest compressing his lungs and when he tried to take a breath the air tasted thin and sour like breathing through a snorkel through a rubber tube like the time he'd gone into the sea at Pett Level Michael his butt in the air swimming swimming swimming like a little water rat but Frank had almost thrown up inside his mask he was so terrified of drowning.

You really do believe Rachel was saying that there's an alien spacecraft?

Artefact.

Something buried in the ground somewhere up in Scotland that it's leaking dangerous chemicals into the earth?

It's not just the one in Scotland though. There's also Roswell everyone knows about Roswell but there are others no one's discovered yet because they're so deeply buried. There needs to be more research. A worldwide effort to explode the cover-up. That's what we're fighting for. I thought you understood. Frank's palms were sweating. The thought that Rachel could doubt him that she'd only been playing along while really she thought he was crazy he couldn't stand it.

He took a long shuddering breath and it was like whatever she said in the next few seconds would decide his future because how could he go on without her without what they were?

I would rather die now, he thought, and afterwards he couldn't remember if he'd spoken the words aloud or just inside his head. A single tear spilled from the corner of his eye, traced a curve down the wall of his cheek like an image in a manga so eerily perfect a symbol for sad and Frank found himself thinking of that song Faith liked, The Tracks of My Tears by Linda Ronstadt, belting from her bedroom window the whole summer long. You could hear it all the way up on the copse and if you stopped what you were doing and listened carefully you could hear Faith singing along. She had a good voice, Faith, though he had never told her so, never really thought about it. She liked old vinyl records. She said they made her think of summer think of cars with all their windows open picnics on the grass.

Don't cry, Frankie, Rachel said. She put her arms around his shoulders drew him close. I'm scared, that's all. Scared of you getting ill again. I couldn't bear it if anything happened to you. And now it was Rachel who was crying, her tears the tracks of her tears warm and wet against his neck her breath coming in sudden gasps like she was measuring it out.

Rachel, he said. He loved saying her name aloud and always had done because saying it was like holding her, like holding her completely. I'm not ill, he said. I feel good. Better than I have for ages because I feel like I'm doing something. There's beauty in numbers, Rachel.

He pushed his fingers into her hair, moved his lips across her eyelids tasting her tears their salty wetness and as they kissed he felt her spirit lift towards him. The lightness of it was the lightness of birds, and as he kissed her throat and the blades of her collarbone Frank touched the narrow boundary between her presence and the threat of her absence and for a blissful shining moment he thought about how if he had the courage he would let her go now. Better to know she was safe, safe from everything and high above him in spite of his own bereftness his own dereliction.

They made love, and afterwards they lay on the bed and listened to Space Oddity all the way through. Space Oddity was Frank's favourite Bowie album and Cygnet Committee was Frank's favourite Bowie track ever.

You have a beautiful soul, Frankie, Rachel said. No one cares about things the way you do. That's part of why I love you.

Do you want to stay over? Mum doesn't mind. Have some supper with us at least.

I should go. She pushed back her hair. You'll be needing an early night and anyway, she said, the sooner I leave the sooner you'll be home. Sounds silly but it's true. She kissed him on the forehead and then again on the mouth. Look after yourself, Frankie. If you find yourself getting worried – about anything – you call me straight away, OK?

They went downstairs together, Frank pulling on his jeans. Rachel left by the back door like always, moving away from him round the side of the house, she didn't look back. Never look back was one of her sayings, only forward. He closed the door softly behind her, went through to the living room. Emily and Faith were in there watching a Bond movie.

Hey said Emily come and join us. Is Rachel staying over?

She had to get back, Frank said. Where's Michael?

Out with some mates, I think. He said he wouldn't be home for supper. We're having lasagne.

Great, Frank said. Budge up, then.

They made room for him on the sofa, Faith shifting sideways resting her head on their mother's shoulder and it was like so many other evenings, evenings when he'd been well when he'd felt free from the restless ceaseless anxiety that had come to govern his life, to define who he was.

Generalised anxiety is often a manifestation of insecurity said Dr Browne his psychotherapist at Woodside View. Do you ever think about how your view of the world might have been affected by your father's absence?

I never knew my dad so how could I miss him?

That's what I'm asking you, Frank – do you miss him?

All I know about my dad is that his name is Adrian and he was in the army. He could be dead for all I know.

Do you ever think about your father? Wonder where he is?

Not really. Sometimes.

And would you say your feelings towards your father are positive or negative?

I don't have any feelings. I hope he's OK, you know, whatever he's doing. That he's settled in his life.

Have you ever felt anger towards your father for not being there for you?

Frank shook his head.

Not even when you were younger?

Frank shook his head.

And your siblings – they still have contact with their father?

Gavin's a tosser, he's a waste of space. Faith's still a kid really she deserves better.

Would you say you feel a sense of responsibility, Frank, for your younger siblings?

Frank sat silently counting his heartbeats to counteract panic to remind him not to reveal what he was truly thinking.

To consider his words to count the weight of each.

To consider who might be listening and if it mattered.

To stand his ground to not give in to questioning to protect his father's identity. Dr Browne's questions seemed innocent but they were designed to break him, to harvest information on the program, which meant whoever was speaking through him was probably an n-man.

It's my job to look after them, he said carefully. The world's a dangerous place. You only have to turn on the TV to see how bad things are. He gazed at Browne steadily trying not to blink. They loved it when you blinked. It told them they were winning.

And would you consider your perception of risk to be average, below average or above average?

I know what you want me to say – that it's above average.

I don't want you to say anything, Frank, just to answer honestly. There are no right or wrong answers.

There are, though, aren't there? If I want you to believe I'm getting better?

And are you? Getting better?

I feel much better, Frank said, I want to go home, and as the words passed his lips he had felt the truth of them as if his brain was signalling yes and his gut agreed.

What are we watching? Frank said.

Moonraker, said Faith. It's only just started. We can put it back to the beginning if you want.

It's fine, Frank said, I've seen it before. He rested his feet on the coffee table thinking this time tomorrow he would be in Paris. He wished Michael was here because now he wouldn't get to see him before he left. When Michael said he was out with his mates what he meant was he was with his boyfriend Rafik, which meant he wouldn't be back till the morning or even later.

Frank and Faith chatted constantly when they were together yet their lives were separate. Frank and Michael talked hardly at all, but they were close in the way only brothers could be, yet hardly ever were. Thick as thieves you two as Emily was fond of saying right through their childhood. Always up to something.

You feeling OK for tomorrow? Emily said. Everything packed?

No worries, Mum. Frank spoke quietly eyes on the screen. They ate their lasagne on their laps watching Roger Moore eject Michael Lonsdale out through the airlock. One small step for Drax, one giant leap for mankind. The laser battle aboard the space station had to be the most disappointing fight scene ever, so relentlessly wooden Frank found it comedic, almost calming it was so far from the truth, so far from what was actually happening out there in the world.

This is the way the world ends not with a bang but a whimper. He imagined himself falling through space, tumbling through the blackness bright as an ember.

He jerked awake as the credits were rolling. You missed the best bit, Faith said. Her hair shimmered ghostly in the bluish light from the TV.

I know what happens I've seen it before, Frank repeated. I'm going to bed.

It's nine thirty.

He's got an early start tomorrow don't forget, said Emily, hands folded around her Captain Birdseye coffee mug, the one Faith was always threatening to smash for being so hideous. Emily was pleased he was going to Paris, that he was making friends that he was getting himself out more gaining his independence finally and Frank's love for her for the three of them was both anchor and millstone. He watched it sinking into the depths, dragging its chain behind it like the barnacle-encrusted spine of an iron plesiosaur.

See you Friday, Frank said.

You've got your passport?

Yes Mum, he said, like a kid in a family sitcom, the same bored familiarity the same overacted tolerance the same predictable groan that hid a bottomless love. The kind you could never confess openly because nothing was more vulnerable to danger, the line between a thing taken utterly for granted and a thing gone forever so faint so microscopic like a crack in porcelain you could only see from a certain angle, the fine line between the visionary and the diseased.

He threw himself down on the bed, the sheets still tumbled from him and Rachel, her scent green as nettles as pondwater both bitter and comforting. He leaned over towards the CD player ejected Bowie (one small step for Dave) and slotted in Bach, the sonatas and partitas for solo violin, disc 2 the partita in D minor BWV 1004 (Nathan Milstein Deutsche Grammophon 1972) which aside from the Goldberg Variations might be his favourite Bach work of all time.

Frank dream-slept until track 5 which was the chaconne, 13'55" long and the most important and difficult work in the violinist's repertoire. A chaconne was a musical invention based around a Spanish dance rhythm from the sixteenth century set in ¾ time. In the hands of Bach the chaconne became a musical odyssey a phantasmagoria an LSD trip journeying through a sequence of variations (like the Goldbergs) each more complex and more beautiful than the last until eventually you ended up back where you started with the original tune.

The way Bach used the violin in the chaconne reminded Frank of the way Bob Dylan (Bob the Slob was Emily's hero) used the harmonica on his most out-there blues tracks, as if it were bigger than itself saying more than a wooden box strung with catgut had any right to say. Partly this came down to the double-stopping which had a raw almost primitive sound that was nothing like how you expected a violin to sound and that some people (he'd seen them on the music forums) thought was ugly but people like that they didn't get it they just weren't listening properly.

The ache of it, like a wolf's cry, as if for the time the chaconne was playing that single lonely violin became the centre of the world and all its troubles. Frank had listened to all the recordings (there were more than thirty) but Milstein's was special because Milstein seemed not so much to be playing as transmitting a signal. Acting as a conduit for code the way a lightning conductor acts as a conduit for an electrical charge, a charge that has been swirling about in the aether since before the big bang. And Milstein just taking the lightning, not flinching not even once just letting it burn.

Milstein's downstrokes were like scaffolding, the upright iron structure on which the whole thing hung. Milstein never lingered never tried to milk it because he didn't have to, Bach's notes were enough. There was something naked about his performance something austere. Frank lay still in the tangled sheets in the smell of Rachel trying to become nothing, to become like Milstein, just a space a human tube for the music to pass through. To convey music through the rhythm of his breathing and the deeper in he swam the deeper his inhales the deeper into the zone the nearer to heaven.

Code could not lie and neither could music. For the invaders, Earth was the alien planet in all its glory and terror. The strangeness of its sounds and the light of its stars and the error of our ways. Listen and watch because the truth is out there the truth is Bach the truth is Rachel the truth will set you free.

In the vastness of this universe does it matter where we came from or where we are going?

If they are here among us already what am I running from?

If the worst thing has already happened why am I afraid?

ARIA

Rachel's address is difficult to find, a one-bedroom flat above a laundrette located on the borders of Catford and Hither Green. Rachel grew up round here, from the sound of her. When Robin asks how she can help her, Rachel says she's worried about her boyfriend, Frank Peter Landau.

Frank went to Paris nine months ago, Rachel says, to visit some friends of his. I've not heard from him since the day he left. The police aren't interested.

Robin asks how old Frank is.

Thirty-four last birthday, Rachel says. She frowns and looks away. Robin nods, tries to seem encouraging. She knows Rachel Gabon will have been asked this question before, not just from her expression but because it's the first question any DC would ask. A day over eighteen and the cops aren't going to do jack shit unless you can offer them something more to go on, some proof that the person you're looking for is actually missing as opposed to taking a time-out from family and friends.

Do you have any reason to suspect foul play? She's beginning to sound like something off a TV cop show. You think Frank is in trouble, that he might have come to harm?

He must have. There's no other explanation. Frank would never do this – go off like this. Even if he wanted to leave, he would have called.

This is what they all say, but there's no point telling that to Rachel. Like the question about her guy's age, she'll have heard it before. She is thin, light brown skin, long crinkly hair tied back in a scarf. Turquoise nail varnish, berry-coloured lipstick, dark blue mascara. Late twenties, early thirties, same as her missing boyfriend, probably. Robin is about to ask if she has a photograph of Frank – to put her at her ease mainly, they're nowhere near the photo stage, not yet – when Rachel folds her arms across her chest and says she can't afford to pay her.

Not all at once, I mean, not in advance. I'd have come to you sooner otherwise. I had to call you, though. I'm desperate.

What is it about her that makes Robin resist the urge to terminate the interview? She gazes about herself. Rachel's place isn't much: rust-coloured carpet, dralon-covered sofa, glass-topped coffee table. Nothing of distinction, and that tangible air of sadness seeping into everything, as familiar to Robin from her own life as from anywhere else. Hanging on the wall above the G-plan sideboard is a small framed print of Caspar David Friedrich's Winter Landscape, one of Friedrich's most frequently reproduced works and often seen on Christmas cards, though Robin has always wondered why, because there is something creepy about it, the way the pine trees in the background form a mirror image of the church in the foreground, a kind of ghostly echo. The painting isn't romantic so much as eerie; different from what you think it is, different from how it appears. Robin wonders if Rachel has chosen the painting for what it really is or for how it seems on the surface, whether she has chosen it at all. More likely it was here already when she took on the rental, part of the flat's inventory, like the sideboard and the glass-topped coffee table.

Old things found in junk shops, a cheap way to furnish a flat like this, a flat over a laundrette on the far edge of Catford. Rachel sees her looking. She says she keeps meaning to take the picture down because it scares her a bit but she hasn't got round to it.

I'm almost used to it now, she adds. I think I might miss it. She laughs for a second, dries up.

Tell me about Frank, Robin says. We can discuss the money later.

The hard set of her mouth, the small crease between her eyebrows. Prepared to be disappointed but nursing hope. Robin wonders who recommended her, how long Rachel has forced herself to wait before calling her number. These questions are interesting, because learning the answers will tell her more about her client, more about the case. People speak about idle curiosity but there is no such thing. Curiosity is never idle. Details matter.

Rachel draws in her breath, as if the subject of Frank is too big for her to tackle suddenly, and then asks Robin if she would like a cup of tea.

I'd love one, Robin says. Better to give her an occupation, a familiar routine task, something to calm her. The kitchenette is cold and dark, overlooking the laundrette's back yard with its cracked concrete and collection of wheelie bins. Robin sits down at the breakfast bar, dumps her backpack on the floor, takes out her notepad. The notepad is mostly a prop – Robin remembers things without having to write them down, not a photographic memory but in that ballpark. The notebook is useful though because the clients like it, like seeing her scribbling notes with a half-chewed biro. It fulfils their expectations, makes them feel they're getting their money's worth.

What does Frank do? For a job, I mean?

He's a computer programmer. He writes code.

Who does he work for?

He's a freelance. He's done jobs for all kinds of people.

Good money in that?

Rachel shrugs. There would be, but he's not always well enough.

Well enough?

To work. Rachel turns towards the kitchen counter, spoons sugar into her mug. She is bending forward, hunching over slightly, uncomfortable with the question, which again is interesting, a clue possibly, but Robin decides to let it lie for now. What she wants is for Rachel to keep talking, to tell her about Frank, to give her the picture behind the picture. As in Friedrich's painting, she thinks and the comparison surprises her with its resonance. So does Frank live here with you normally? she asks. Her choice of tense is deliberate and comes straight from Alec Dunbar. Keep the missing alive for as long as you can, until you know for a certainty they're no longer breathing. You'd be surprised what gets brought to the surface, on both sides of the equation.

Frank lives with his mum. In Eltham, Rachel says. I moved in here six months ago. I've been wanting us to get our own place for ages but it never quite happened. I know how it sounds, a man of his age, but Frank needs security. Places he knows, people around him he can trust. Emily – that's Frank's mum – was always encouraging him to branch out more and every now and then we'd go and look at some flats but Frank was scared to make that leap. He worried about getting ill again, about ending up in hospital. Frank was terrified of going back there.

Robin resists the urge to tell her to slow down, to back up, to start from the beginning. She has learned that the way people tell their stories is a part of the story, that chronology is almost as important as the story itself. Dunbar used to talk about a statement's hidden architecture, which had little to do with content and everything to do with focus and with emphasis, with what Dunbar called order of service and with point of view. Rachel Gabon has been speaking for less than ten minutes but she has told Robin a lot, more than she realises, probably.

You say Frank went missing in Paris. Did he travel abroad often?

Rachel shakes her head vehemently lips pressed together. Frank had never been out of the country before. This trip – it was a really big deal for him. He tried not to let on because he knows how much I worry but I know he was nervous. Scared to death, really.

Do you know what he was afraid of?

She laughs. Everything. Buying tickets, catching the Eurostar, finding his way in a strange place. Mostly he was scared he was being followed. Frank isn't like other people. His mind moves so fast sometimes it's hard to keep up with him, but in other ways he's like a child still. He finds ordinary life difficult. But he felt he had to go to Paris or he'd be letting his friends down.

And who were these friends?

People from the UFO forum. That's all I know, really. I'm angry with myself for not asking more questions, for not finding out exactly where he was going. With Frank the way he is I've always thought it was better not to let myself get too involved with his beliefs. I thought I could look after him better that way, keep a sense of perspective. You can imagine what it was like, trying to explain all this to the police. I know who the main guy is because Frank showed me an article he'd written once, in a film magazine. His name's Edmund de Groote – Frank called him Eddie. The police tracked him down pretty easily – he's a lecturer somewhere in Paris. He told them he posted on the forums occasionally – that's where he and Frank met. He said Frank had emailed him a couple of times after that, about films they were both interested in – he even showed the police the emails. He claimed he'd never met Frank in person and didn't know anything about him coming to Paris. The police seemed to think Frank had imagined the whole relationship, made out it was more than it was. But I know this Eddie is lying. I tried emailing him myself but he didn't reply. I've thought of going over there – to Paris, I mean – but I don't know where Frank was staying, just that Eddie was supposed to be meeting him at a café near the Gare du Nord. I feel like such a fool.

Edmund de Groote – you're sure that's his name?

Rachel nods. It's on the film article. I can show it to you if you want. Frank said he was Dutch.

Robin jots down the name de Groote on her notepad. Not that she needs to. It is a common enough surname, she supposes, though anyone would have to admit the coincidence is striking. She feels disorientated and vaguely nauseous, the same way she'd felt in the days leading up to her final disastrous confrontation with Alec Dunbar. She experiences a strong urge to be outside, in the open air, yet she can hardly leave, not if she intends taking on Rachel Gabon as a client that is. There are things she needs to ask. Robin realises there is no question of her not taking the case, not now, with or without the client's dodgy finances. The de Groote connection has made it impossible to say no.

She asks Rachel a few more questions – Frank's home address, where he went to school, any previous partners – then tells her she will call to arrange a second meeting once she has drawn up an outline. An outline for the case, she explains, preliminary findings. It's all routine, she says, though it is not; normally the preliminary interview would be twice as long but the urge to regroup, to collect herself is too pressing to ignore.

Is there anywhere I can get lunch round here, she asks.

There's a Turkish place. Just down the road, Rachel says. She looks surprised that they seem to be through so quickly, bewildered almost, as if she suspects she's been short-changed in some way.

I'll be in touch soon, Robin says, hoping this will be enough to reassure her, and as they pass back through Rachel's living room she glances once again at the painting above the sideboard, Friedrich's Winter Landscape in its chipped gilt frame, a window on another world. She imagines the squeaky crunch of snow beneath her boots, the scent of pine cones and woodsmoke, like stepping into Narnia through the back of a wardrobe.

Robin still thinks about the conversation she had with Ashley when she resigned from the force. Ash kept insisting she should think about it

some more before pressing the eject button, that she was letting Alec
Dunbar ruin her career.

Forget V. I. Warshawski, she said, most of the work you get as a
private investigator is basically dustbin-rummaging. You'll be bored
shitless.

Turning up evidence of tax evasion or insurance fraud, spending
hours across the road from some scuzzy hotel while she waited to snap
a photo of someone's husband or someone's wife on their way in or
out. Freezing her arse off more often than not, and all in the name of
proving the glaringly obvious. Robin knows she is supposed not to
like the work, that she is supposed to feel contempt for its drudgery,
but she has come to appreciate its rhythms, to find satisfaction in such
pinpoint observations of the mundane. In the systems she has put in
place for herself, the cellophane-wrapped pack of index cards she opens
to mark the beginning of each new case. The rituals and thought processes induce a sensation that resembles the sliding-together of pieces
in a complex jigsaw puzzle.

Robin's father Derek loved jigsaw puzzles; thousand-piece monsters featuring the crowd scenes from old black-and-white movies
were his favourites, complex fantastical landscapes by Breughel and
Bosch. He claimed he found them relaxing. Robin used to help him
sometimes, or try to, the two of them working silently together in a
state of concentration that, Robin supposes when she thinks about it
now, was not unlike enchantment.

After lunch at the Turkish restaurant she heads back to Leyton, to
the one-bedroom ex-council flat that happened to come on the market
the day Ashley finally told her she was leaving. The flat is on Hainault

Road, five minutes' walk from the tube in one direction and from Leyton Midland overground in the other. The traffic runs twenty-four seven but London's background hum has never bothered Robin, she finds it difficult to sleep without it.

There are days, more and more of them now, when she barely thinks of Ashley at all. She considers cracking a beer then decides against. She dumps her backpack on the floor by the door then puts on a CD, Bach's Goldberg Variations played by András Schiff, not the prissy 1983 Decca recording but the ECM New Series from the early 2000s with its warm and limpid sound production and increased artistic confidence.

Not long after they moved in together, Ash asked Robin why she had so many CDs of the same piece of music.

I don't think of them as the same, Robin said. They're completely different records. The Goldbergs are like the master key to Western music, she added. They're a rite of passage for pianists, the same as Fermat's conjecture is a rite of passage for mathematicians. You know you're never going to solve it but you have to try.

It goes on a bit though, doesn't it? Ash said. I can't really tell the difference between one recording and another.

She claimed afterwards that she'd been joking, and Robin laughed along with her, said she couldn't care less if Ash liked Bach or not. It was only after Ash moved out that Robin realised it was true, she didn't mind, in fact she preferred it that way and maybe that was part of the reason Ashley had left.

The first recording she'd owned was the Rosalyn Tureck from 1957, the same recording she'd heard on the radio the summer she had pneumonia. Tureck sets forth the aria like a philosophical treatise, with each of the variations a responsive argument. She plays more slowly than anyone, every rhythm to the metre as written and almost entirely without ornament, like a piano teacher demonstrating the rudiments of textbook counterpoint. Robin cannot listen to Tureck now though, because Tureck is for the endgame. Tureck gets beneath her defences every time, and the case is still too new.

There is always Glenn Gould of course, Gould who mumbles over the aria as if questioning its provenance before launching into the body of the piece like a lion, like a keen March wind, like the Assyrian coming down like a wolf on the fold and fuck, Robin thinks each time she hears him, fuck he's good. She finds it hard to choose between Gould and Maria Yudina, Yudina the miracle freak with her initial stuffy insistence on correct ornamentation, that swooning thing she does with the mordents before tearing into the first variation. Not as fast as Gould but getting there, the turns catching like thorns are stabbing her fingertips, her rubato so wild and so unorthodox she sounds as modern and as daring as Angela Hewitt.

For teasing out the intricacies of a case though, for thinking things through Robin chooses Schiff every time. More disciplined than Yudina, less flippant than Gould and with a purity that challenges Perahia's but feels edgier. Back when she was on the force, when she finally got home after the initial briefing and no matter how late, Robin would pour herself a whisky and put on Schiff. Some of her colleagues carried personal talismans or used lucky pens but for Robin it is Schiff and the Goldbergs every time.

Those first slow notes, like raindrops falling into a puddle the morning after the apocalypse. People who work with computers say that code is beautiful and Robin wonders if this is what they mean, a version of it at least, the abstract beauty of numbers. She thinks about Frank Peter Landau, who was or is a computer programmer, who is or might be missing or even dead. Frank was scared he was being followed, Rachel said, words from a cheap spy movie, words rarely spoken aloud in the real world, though in this case Robin believes they were spoken in earnest.

Robin believes Rachel was telling the truth when she told her story, though Frank believing he was being followed does not make it true.

Robin likes to begin with empirical facts and work forward from there. The only certainty she has to go on so far is that Rachel has not seen or spoken to Frank since she left his home on the evening before he went to Paris. A cursory police investigation carried out at the time confirmed that Frank Landau did indeed board the Eurostar at the time and on the date stamped on his ticket, but where he went and what happened to him afterwards is unknown.

Which leaves Robin with two possibilities: either Frank has absconded by choice, or Frank has come to harm. Whichever of the two possibilities turns out to be correct, the procedure for discovering the truth is broadly the same: first, find out everything she can about Frank Landau – who he knows, what his interests are, everyone he spoke to or had contact with in the weeks leading up to his disappearance. Second, try to discover more about his contacts in Paris, the people on what Rachel Gabon referred to as the UFO forum, and in particular Edmund de Groote. Third, stop listening to the voice that insists de Groote is the key, because Robin doesn't even know yet if de Groote is who he says he is.

Rachel has given her five hundred pounds on account, promised she'll give her more as soon as she can get it. It's laughable really, Robin should have told her not to waste her money, should have doubled down on what the cops said, that Frank's gone off with someone else most likely, too much of a coward to tell her the truth but there you are, what can you expect, all men are bastards.

Robin likes Rachel, though. She wants to see her again. She wants to help her find Frank, if she can.

She thinks of Caspar David Friedrich's Winter Landscape, hanging over the sideboard in its shabby gilt frame.

She hears Rachel speaking the name de Groote and her skin prickles, like a shadow from out of her past just stepped over her grave.

RACHEL, FOR THE TAPE

ALL FRANK KNOWS ABOUT his dad is that his name is Adrian Skeaping and he was in the army. He and Emily were just kids when she got pregnant. Emily told me she and Adrian had already split up when she found out. She liked Adrian a lot – loved him maybe – but she didn't see herself becoming an army wife. She was still at school, studying for her 'A' Levels. Her parents weren't mad keen about her keeping the baby but she never had any doubts on that score and in the end they came round. Emily's father died when Frank was still a toddler but Frank was close to his gran. I think not having a dad around affected him more than people realised. I don't mean that whole not having a male role model crap. I mean in the way he felt responsible for Michael and Faith. Frank can't stand Michael and Faith's dad Gavin. I don't know if that's because he was afraid Gavin might try and take them away, get custody or something, or whether it was because their dad was still around when his wasn't.

*

I think it would have done Frank good to try and find out more about his father – to try and get in contact with him even. I said I'd help him, if he wanted me to, but he wouldn't consider it. Frank believes his father Adrian is a supersoldier. That the real reason his parents split up was because they wanted to keep Emily's pregnancy secret from the supersoldier program. He thought the best thing he could do for his dad was to stay away. Ever since Frank went missing I've been wondering if I should do what I said, try tracing Adrian myself, but what would be the point? Hi, Mr Skeaping, I'm here to tell you your son has gone missing and the cops won't help me find him? I don't like to imagine how that would make him feel, if Frank's dad is still out there that is, if he's still alive. You never know with army guys, do you? He might have been killed in Iraq or somewhere. Or died of a heart attack, or cancer. Or maybe he has a family of his own now who don't know Frank exists. He's not my dad, I don't have the right to make that kind of decision. The last thing I want is to make things worse than they already are.

The online community around the supersoldier program is massive. There are even supersoldier conventions. I had no idea. I'd never even heard of the program before I met Frank. Frank believes that supersoldiers are part of an elite military taskforce that is being pre-pared to fight a war against alien invaders, that their brains have been genetically adapted so they can exist in the real world whilst at the same time becoming alive to a deeper reality. There's a whole bunch of people who are convinced we've been infiltrated already, that most governments are run by aliens, all the big corporations, the banking system, the energy firms, everything. You ask me whether I share any of Frank's beliefs and all I can say is I don't see the world like he does, but I can understand how someone might come to think that way, especially someone who suffers from anxiety, like Frank. Reality is scary, especially with climate change, especially since the pandemic. Believing in aliens is like believing in God: suddenly there's an explanation for everything that's gone wrong with the world. Suddenly there's a cause you can believe in, a ready-made family.

Frank says information is corrosive, like acid – once you touch it, you're changed by it, you find you've been burned. Not long after Frank went missing I spent most of a week online, hanging out on the forums. I thought I might be able to make contact with the people Frank had been talking to, or that I might stumble across some useful information. I spent so long staring into a screen the outside world began to seem less real, like a stage set, like it might crack into pieces. I remember thinking the colours were too bright, like they were fake, painted on. I started wondering if my movements were being tracked, if the simple act of looking at certain web pages had marked me out as dangerous. I knew I was being ridiculous but at the same time there was a part of me that was convinced I was on the brink of a major discovery. As if everything in the world had meaning, suddenly.

My parents were never thrilled about me going out with Frank, and after he was in hospital the second time my mum said it was pointless to keep sacrificing myself, that it was time for me to tell him it was over. We had a terrible row. I still hate thinking about it. They don't understand that I love Frank not because I feel sorry for him or because I've got some sort of saviour complex but because he's gentle and thoughtful and would never hurt anything or anyone on this planet, ever. I love him because he has the most original, imaginative mind I've ever encountered or ever will again. I believe Frank is a genius. It's as if he experiences intelligence as a physical sensation, as if he's on fire with a deeper knowledge. He trusts people way too easily though, oh my God yes. He sees danger everywhere except where danger is. It's like he's on the edge of a precipice, constantly at risk of falling because he's too busy gazing up at the sky, at the stars, at the mountains in the distance.

Frank and I spent our first date listening to David Bowie. He'd never heard Bowie before, can you believe that? But he got it immediately, what Bowie was doing, more than I did probably. Frank gets music on a deep level. He can never just have an album on in the background the way most people do. He has to give himself over to it completely, almost like he's dancing or swimming or playing football. I once asked him if he'd thought of learning an instrument himself and he said there hadn't been the money, not back then, and in any case he'd never wanted to be a musician. What he wanted was to write code, which was a kind of music anyway.

These are the things that make Frank happy: code, music, the Fibonacci sequence, constellations, atomic structure, geological timelines. When Frank is happy and in his element he's a different person – confident, excited, the way all human beings would be maybe if they weren't so greedy and scared. Frank is anxious around other people because they don't behave logically. The thing that upsets Frank more than anything is when people tell lies. It's not even that he believes lying is morally wrong – it's like he doesn't understand it, why someone would say something is true when they know it isn't. The contradiction doesn't make sense to him. I told you before, Frank's not like most people. He can't switch his brain off. He becomes more and more emotionally exhausted and in the end he blacks out.

Frank first spent time in hospital when he was fourteen. He was in for three months, then again for six months five years later when he was in college. He was OK for a while after that, seemed to be doing well but then he had a relapse. He was only in for a month that time but I know he was scared, more so than before because he'd thought he was over it. When he came out that last time he told me he was done with hospitals for good. He said the worst thing about doctors was that they pretended to believe you, but didn't, that they'd mostly decided what was wrong with you before you opened your mouth.

There's this book called The Tower that Frank is obsessed with, a science-fiction story about an architect who builds an apartment complex out of alien rock. The rock turns out to be alive – some sort of fungus – and all the people who live in the apartment building start changing into aliens, including the architect. It's a good story and parts of it are scary. The guy who wrote The Tower was an accountant. He was born in a town in the north of Scotland, Frank says, a place called Tain. The town isn't named in the book but someone on the LAvventura forum worked out where it was, said that when you knew the town yourself it was obvious. I don't see anything strange about that — writers often base their stories around actual places. Frank says yes, that's true, but in the case of The Tower it's also about the author sending a coded message to the rest of the world.

Frank believes The Tower is a sacred text. He goes on and on about the way the pages are numbered, about certain key words that keep repeating, like a piece of Morse code. How if you could translate the book into binary you'd find a set of equations to calculate the location of the alien planet. He believes this is the mission he has been assigned.

I haven't told anyone this, but I travelled there — to Tain. I suddenly got hold of the idea that this was where Frank had run off to, that he was waiting for me to join him. The train journey takes twelve hours. You have to change trains twice — once in Glasgow and again in Inverness. Scotland always looks so small when you look at it on the map but you forget how maps can sometimes distort reality. It was September when I went. In London it still felt like summer but north of Glasgow it was autumn already. The slopes of the Cairngorms were purple with heather, the banks of the Tay were swarming with trees, huge oaks and beeches in their autumn colours, reflected in the water like golden galleons, like circus tents. I couldn't stop staring out of the window at the mountains, at the narrow stony tracks leading into the hills, the sheep and the barns, the Highland streams like shiny blue ribbons where the sun shone on them, thinking about Frank and wondering if he'd come this way before me.

I started to cry then, I couldn't help it. The woman in the seat opposite asked if I was all right, if I needed help, and I told her I was fine, it was just that my grandmother had died recently and I was missing her. She came from round here, I said, she was born in Perth. The woman nodded and smiled and said she was sorry to hear that, so sorry. I felt awful because I'd told her a lie – my gran is alive and well and living in Maidstone – but it seemed more believable than the truth, less complicated. I'd never see the woman again, so what did it matter?

The train finally pulled into Tain at around six o'clock. It's a hard little town. As I stepped down on to the station platform I felt a long way from home. Later, when I asked the woman on the hotel reception desk what it was like living there she laughed and said it was like anywhere, once you got used to it. Her name was Mandy. The winters can be difficult, she said. The wind is terrible sometimes, like wolves are tearing your hair out, but when I asked her if she ever thought of moving south she shook her head at once. Not for me, she said. I guess this is home. It gets into you, this place, she added, and I know you'll laugh when I tell you this but I found myself thinking of that architect, the guy in The Tower.

I always wanted to be a maths teacher. I'm not good with numbers the way Frank is but I'm not bad. I used to help out with remedial maths after school sometimes. My maths teacher Mr Bennett said I was good at explaining things and I think maybe that's because I always understood I'd never understand the language of numbers the way Frank does, that hardly anyone is like Frank, but I could catch a tiny glimpse of what he saw. I liked the idea of helping kids make sense of numbers, especially those who believed they would never master them. The main thing to know about maths is so long as you don't panic there's always a way of making your sums add up.

There was a girl I met at college, Claris. She was studying electronics and engineering. She was into cars, she wanted to work in the motor industry, and she loved David Bowie and Elvis Costello, The Smiths before Morrissey went crazy, the same as me. We were friends, or we were becoming friends, then Frankie got ill again and I dropped out. I always meant to go back and finish my course but the time was never right. I took the job at Tesco's to tide me over and kept not leaving. Because I was scared, mostly, and that's something else I've discovered – that it's easy to get scared. Scared you won't have enough to live on, scared you were never good enough in the first place. Scared to change even one small thing in case everything else comes crashing down around your ears.

These past couple of months I've started to wonder if it's not too late, if I could study in the evenings or something. I can't afford to give up my supermarket job but I could do college part-time. Anyway, after I got back from Scotland I looked Claris up on Facebook and sent her a message. I thought she probably wouldn't remember me, or wouldn't want to be in contact because of the way I'd dropped her suddenly but she replied straight away, asked if I wanted to meet for a drink.

I was so nervous about seeing her again I almost chickened out. I think it was only then I realised how isolated I'd become, how I'd fallen out of the habit of doing normal things. How I'd fallen out of the world, almost. I ended up telling Claris everything. Not the aliens and not the war but the rest of it: Frank falling in with a weird crowd and then going missing, me sitting on my arse for a year waiting, shuffling in and out of Tesco's as per usual and not having a clue how to move on with my life because I couldn't begin to think what life might be without him. Afraid to move forward because that would mean I'd accepted Frank wasn't coming back.

Claris was amazing. She said I shouldn't try to forget Frank, that I should live my life as if he was coming home tomorrow. It sounds simple but no one had put it like that before or even tried to. Claris said I should find out what qualifications I still needed to train as a teacher and take things from there. You're probably already qualified, she said, or nearly. You can learn on the job these days. You need to get on the college website and find out.

I still love the idea of teaching maths, the calm and certain pleasure of it, the way you can see someone's mind go click when they finally get something. I think I could be happy doing that. I might even be good at it. But I can't give up on Frank, not yet. The cops don't think he's important enough to waste their time on – just one more loser who can't hack his life so he fucks off to Amsterdam or somewhere but I know that's not what happened.

I went into every shop in Tain, every pub and every café. I showed Frank's photo to everyone and anyone who would talk to me, asked if they'd seen him, but no one said they had. On the train journey back to London I listened to Handel's Messiah. I could never admit this to Frank, but I've never really liked Bach much. I've tried, but there's something about his music that leaves me cold. There's an indelible pain at the heart of it, a sorrow that can't be shifted. It's there even in the pieces that are meant to be joyous, like the Brandenburg Concertos.

I can't say what made me try Handel instead, just that I remember my mum telling me she was in a choir at university and they used to perform Messiah every Easter. I'd never heard it before, or only the Hallelujah Chorus, but around a month after Frank went missing I bought a CD recording and started getting into it. At first I listened because I found it comforting – I knew Frank would be chuffed that I was interested in classical all of a sudden. But then I realised I liked the music anyway, better than Bach, because there was life in it, there was excitement. Messiah is a human drama with real characters, a story of betrayal and intrigue that anyone can feel excited by, whether they believe in God or not. That's why the stories in the Bible have lasted so long, I guess. Why directors still want to make films of them. Why people spend entire lifetimes arguing the toss over what they really mean.

*

I stared out the window at the Cairngorms listening to Emma Kirkby singing But Who May Abide and seriously, it was like her small true voice was the most powerful sound on Earth, like it could hold back a storm – or release one. Like a firefly aloft on the wind. And the joy she found in singing was something you could feel. She ran up and down the scale like quicksilver, like it was no effort, like Handel's music was a message she was delivering, words she had to utter or she would burst apart.

There were the mountains, blazing gold, and that music. Frank was not there in the carriage with me and yet somehow he was, we were there together. We could not touch, but we could coexist. And it was as if I could hear him trying to tell me something, as if he was speaking to me through the rapture of Kirkby's voice. There are bombs in that music, if you choose to listen for them, the sounds of people running and screaming, like there are in The Tower.

The war, I thought. So we're back here again? And I could feel Frank say yes.

SCARBOROUGH

THE COPPER IN HER keeps insisting there is no case. She imagines Alec Dunbar leaning his elbow on the edge of the bar and
laughing through his teeth. Laughing through his teeth, knocking back
his shot of Macallan then calling for another. Hearsay, lassie. Hearsay
and a load of blether that's all you've got here. If you weren't so soft
on this woman you'd tell her to save her money, buy herself a week
in the Seychelles instead, whatever. Time to put the lid on it, pull the
plug, cut your fucking losses, you tell me, you're the one with the
silver tongue on ye, you tell me.

Patronising pig. Robin is frustrated with herself, angry at the way
she continues to filter her thoughts and reactions through the distorting
lens of Detective Chief Inspector Alec Dunbar. What he would make
of the de Groote connection for instance – she'd love to have seen his
face when that name came bobbing up from the sewer. Still no case
to answer then, *laddie*? And tempting though it is to go chasing off
to Paris (even the cops were able to track down this Eddie de Groote
to his *domicile* so how hard can it be?) Robin knows it would be a

mistake, at least to begin with. De Groote has denied all involvement, which can only mean he is confident his connection with Frank Landau cannot be traced. If Robin goes after de Groote without ammunition she will meet with more denials. More significantly, de Groote will be wise to the fact that she is making inquiries.

She needs a sideways approach, an oblique angle of attack, as Dunbar might have said if he was in a piss-taking mood, which was practically a given. Robin telephones Rachel (a work call, strictly a work call) who picks up sounding distracted, as if her mind is elsewhere, as if she has barely thought of Robin since their meeting a week ago. Then her focus seems to narrow and they are together again. She says hello and her tone is guarded enough, self-protective enough for Robin to understand the effort she has to make, not to ask the question that will always pop up on her phone screen alongside Robin's number: have you found him yet?

Just a quick question, Robin says. She reminds herself again this is a work call. I've been wondering if there was any press coverage at the time Frank went missing. I think you mentioned Emily had been in contact with a journalist?

There was one guy, Rachel says. She sounds disappointed, as if Robin's question is so much less interesting than she hoped it would be. He contacted Emily saying he wanted to write an article – a feature on Frank for one of those UFO magazines. I never spoke to him. Michael did, though.

Frank's brother Michael?

Yeah.

Do you know what happened? Did the journalist ever write the article?

Michael went to a conference he was at, in Scarborough, spoke to him there. The guy—

Do you still have his name?

Miles something. Miles Shipley? He asked Michael some questions, said he'd be in touch to do a full interview only Michael never heard from him. I thought that was typical – the police weren't interested and neither was this reporter. But then Michael tried to contact him, to find out what was going on, and it turned out he'd died in Scarborough, the same weekend Michael met up with him. He had a heart attack in his hotel room on the Saturday night. I remember Michael was upset – because it happened so soon after he spoke to him, I suppose. I was upset too, but mostly for Frank. Another door slammed shut. I didn't think about Miles Shipley much, but then I'd never met him.

This is all really helpful, Robin says, thank you. She swallows and her throat is dry suddenly.

I don't see how. He's dead, isn't he?

Yes, but. Robin hesitates. She doesn't like to share her thinking with clients, not at this stage, but she feels she owes Rachel something. If I can find out why this Shipley guy was interested – what he knew about Frank, or thought he knew, it might turn up something. A new way into the case, she says, trying to steer a path between sounding too upbeat (we're halfway to cracking this) and too desperate (we've got fuck all else to go on) and grounding herself in the no-man's-land between them. She is trying to picture Rachel, to imagine where she is standing, what she was doing before Robin called. At any rate, she adds, it's a fresh way of looking at things.

Do you think so?

Yes, Robin says, I do. She ends the call soon afterwards, because the hope in Rachel's voice is difficult to listen to. She switches her phone to silent and turns her attention to Miles Shipley the journalist. At this moment in time his most distinguishing feature is the fact of his death. Shipley died while in pursuit of the story Robin herself is pursuing, a coincidence that seems striking but might not be. Coincidences happen and journalists die from natural causes, especially male journalists, especially from heart attacks.

In the line of duty, as Dunbar might say. But at least she has something new to occupy her mind, a name to focus on other than de Groote's. It is not much but it is at least, as she insisted to Rachel, a fresh way of looking at things.

Miles Shipley studied chemistry at university. He wanted to go into R&D but his grades weren't good enough and so he ended up in sales, an agricultural pesticides business called Nonesuch Chemicals. Shipley worked in key accounts marketing for almost a decade before resigning his position seemingly out of the blue. It turned out he'd been approached by a journalist asking questions about neonicotinoids and the dangers they posed to bee and other insect populations. This was before the impact of pesticides on biodiversity was widely known or publicised, and Shipley referred the matter upwards, requesting that the issue be discussed at departmental meetings. Shipley's initiative was rebuffed. His bosses let it be known his manner was becoming obstructive, hinting that any further activity in this area might become a pretext for disciplinary action.

Shipley resigned on the spot and retrained as a journalist. His background in science was an asset and he had no problem landing commissions. He started out writing stories about the green economy, renewable energy and action on climate change. At some point he started to become interested in more esoteric subject matter: conspiracy theories, fringe groups, alien abduction cases, which is how he came to be looking into Frank Landau, Milan Harwicz supposes, though there appears to be nothing suspicious about Shipley's death.

Milan Harwicz is in digital forensics, a civilian like Ashley, though he was often around the squad room, did a brilliant impression of Dunbar when the coast was clear. Robin has always liked Milan. There is something reticent about him, something always held back, and she likes the pleasure he seems to take in his job, his genuine fascination for detective work. Because it mirrors her own, probably. There might have been something between them, only Milan's cautious nature seems to have stymied it. Not enough to prevent him helping her, fortunately, even when Robin asks him to hack into classified police files, an action that could see him suspended if it were discovered.

The paramedics confirmed Shipley had died at the scene; the hospital pathologist signed it off later as myocardial infarction. Death was instantaneous, apparently. Shipley was forty-five, prime age for heart attacks. There was one odd thing, Milan concedes, the hard drive of his MacBook had been wiped clean, restored to factory settings, right down to the background wallpaper. There was no evidence of a break-in though, no sign that anyone had been in the room aside from Shipley, either before his death or afterwards, so it had to be assumed he'd wiped the machine himself.

There was a folder of printed papers on the desk in Shipley's hotel room: press clippings, a series of photos of what looked like waste dumps, the programme of the conference he had been attending. Who wants to know? Milan asks finally. What's the story?

About Shipley? Nothing. Just a lead I'm following up, one of the stories he was working on. This conversation won't be coming back to haunt you, don't worry. Robin asks if he can email her copies of the papers and photographs from Shipley's hotel room.

Fine, Milan says, so long as this stays off the record.

Half an hour later they land in Robin's inbox: grainy snapshots of refuse tips, incinerator sites, waste skips and recycling centres. A row of cars parked beside a section of chain-link fence, a stack of fly-tipped fridges and other assorted gadgetry. Because the photos are photos of photocopies it is difficult to get a sense of where they originated, whether they were pulled from third-party publications or whether they are copies of actual photographs taken by Shipley as part of an assignment. Shipley was interested in environmental issues, after all – it was his concerns over bee-killing pesticides that had led to him becoming a journalist in the first place.

Sandwiched between a photograph of an unidentified gasometer and a stock library image of the biological weapons research station at Porton Down there is a photograph of Frank Landau, the same one Emily gave the police when she and Rachel reported him missing.

Robin feels her heartbeat begin to accelerate. She tries to repress her excitement, to remind herself that the photo is simply a confirmation of facts she already knows. Shipley was interested in Frank – check. Now tell me why. She scrolls her way through the conference programme, which is still online. A World at War? The rise of misinformation in the 21st century. The marquee name appears to have been Lars Pedersen, a libertarian agitator from Norway, and there are a couple of other names she recognises, including that psychic Jayney de Silva she'd seen on Breakfast TV, explaining how Donald Trump was actually a reincarnation of a Vandal warrior from the Dark Ages. Robin scans through the rest of the participants, the lesser knowns and the unknowns, the leaders of seminars on getting to know your Roman ancestors and growing your own vegetables for the apocalypse, of group meditations for alien abduction survivors, of discussion forums on 5G and the deep-psych influence of Big Data, and it's here among the also-rans that she clocks his name, Edmund de Groote, lecturer in Film Studies at the College International des Arts, Clignancourt, Paris: Film and the Subconscious Perception of Alien Influences in Public Life.

De Groote had been in the UK, in Scarborough, less than a year ago. He had been at the same UFO conference as Miles Shipley. What if Shipley had been at the conference to make contact with de Groote, to question him about the disappearance of Frank Landau? Robin knows she is going out on a limb here, but given Shipley's interest in Frank it seems a reasonable assumption.

The fact that Shipley wound up dead? Best not to read too much into that, or not yet. As Milan said, there was nothing suspicious about a forty-five-year-old male having a heart attack. But guests aren't in the habit of dropping dead in their hotel rooms, not every weekend anyway, and so there is a good chance that members of the hotel staff would remember the incident. Who knows what else they might remember.

Robin decides she will travel to Scarborough on her own account, not charge the trip to Rachel's expenses unless something comes of it. You're a fucking eejit then, she can hear Dunbar saying. It's a lead, isn't it? Call me old-fashioned but is that not what the lassie is paying you to find?

She's paying me to believe her, Robin thinks, though if Dunbar taught her anything it is that belief is less important than attention to detail.

Miles Shipley died in Room 236. Robin knows this already from Milan Harwicz. Her own room – 319 – is on the floor above. The room is L-shaped and rather gloomy, and overlooks the hotel's courtyard. The sea-facing rooms are substantially more expensive. Robin changes her shirt and sets up her computer then goes down to the floor below to check the position of Shipley's room. 236 also overlooks the courtyard. The possibility of gaining entry via the fire escape is practically nil. It is already pitch dark outside, a filthy night. Robin decides she will eat in the hotel restaurant. The guy on reception informs her that the current wait-time is half an hour.

Robin tells him she'll be in the bar. You're busy this evening, she says to the barman as he pours her Macallan.

We've got a dentists' conference in. His badge name is Dayton. Plus there's a big wedding party. Not all of them could get rooms, because of the dentists. The overspill's in the Grand. There's a conference here every week now, pretty much. That's where the money is.

Robin sips her Scotch and asks Dayton if he was on duty the weekend one of the guests died. I read about it in the local paper, she says. There was a conference on UFOs or something.

I was off that week, Dayton says. I was on holiday in Majorca with my girlfriend. Heard about it though. Like Fawlty Towers in here sometimes. They exchange a laugh. Robin takes her drink to a corner table. She is tired from the journey up, and Scarborough out of season turns out to be depressing. Wind and the cries of seabirds, that biting northern chill, someone drunkenly yelling they'd lost their wallet. Robin wonders about Shipley, who he talked to while he was here, how he'd passed the hours. By the time she is called through to the restaurant, she has half-convinced herself the trip is a bust, a waste of time and money.

Later in her room she watches a documentary about locust farming, then listens to Anne-Sophie Mutter playing Sofia Gubaidulina's second violin concerto, In Tempus Praesens, which she has recently recorded on to her hard drive. Robin bought the disc for the Bach it is coupled with, the A minor violin concerto, curious to see what Mutter would do with it and in this respect at least she was disappointed. She finds Mutter's approach too polished, too virtuosic, too easily digested. She prefers the older recordings, Stern or Oistrakh. The Gubaidulina though is a revelation, a forest of sighs and whispers trembling uneasily against the background of an approaching storm. Mutter's tone, shiny as resin, unspools a path through the branching undergrowth, Ariadne's thread.

Robin closes her eyes, exhausted. In the present time, the concerto is called, and perhaps this is its function, to awaken both performer and listener to their own present moment: the slippery brown bedcover, the inadequate lighting, the cheap reproduction furniture that is supposed to resemble the Georgian originals in the restaurant and lobby but in no way does, the black rectangle of the window glass, spattered with rain, the difficult progression across an unkempt landscape towards an unknown goal. A night-lit hotel bedroom as geometrical still-life: orange cube on black #319.

Robin gets up to close the curtains and check her phone: another missed call from Dianne and also unexpectedly a text from Ashley. *Your mother called says you're not picking up she sounded upset.*

Subtext: call your mum you selfish bitch what are you playing at??

Dianne and Ashley always got on like a house on fire, so it doesn't come as a surprise that they are still in contact. No doubt Ash has given Dianne all the gory details of their breakup. Whether Dianne has told Ashley why Robin has stopped answering her calls is less of a certainty. Robin doubts she would go that far, though it depends how upset she is, how out of her mind with worry. There is always a chance Ash knows everything now, and in that case they can just go fuck themselves.

Dianne is trying to call Robin because she wants to explain why she never told her the truth about Marianne Lees. She has said as much in all the messages she has left, messages that leave Robin feeling so wretched she wants to throw up, only she doesn't dare call Dianne back in case she loses it. She remembers the barbecue she went to at Stuart Vickers's place just before the weather turned, four days before Rachel got in contact and this whole mess kicked off. Vick is one of the few friends from the force Robin has kept up with, or who has kept up with her, one of the few who'd dared to say openly that DCI Dunbar was out of order.

Vick put away most of a six-pack then told Robin she was a moron for breaking up with Ashley. Ashley was a civilian on one of the SOCO teams so everyone knew her. Robin reminded Vick there was a spanner in the works, one cute DS name of Eric, spanner's the word.

You don't get it, do you? Vick said. She'd come back to you in a heartbeat but you never asked.

Robin was too fucking proud for her own good was what Vick meant, and maybe he was right, only Robin doesn't feel inclined to examine the causes of her passive aggression, not here, not now and especially not with Eric being a permanent fixture in Ash's life, the chances of removing him small and highly complex and not to be considered.

Robin and Ash are broken anyway, regardless. With Dianne she has a choice: she can leave off being a prick any time she likes. She hears the Gubaidulina through to its end, like flames billowing up, like roses blooming from burning oil, like a proclamation, like an augury, like the rising sun. The solo line rolling tossed and triumphant in the angry spray, Gubaidulina quoting Sibelius word for word. It is nine o'clock, the time Dianne always pauses whatever she is watching and goes through to the kitchen for her last cigarette of the day, or in the decade since she quit smoking to make herself a mug of Horlicks or hot chocolate. Robin can see it all like she's there beside her, the Formica-topped table where she used to do her homework, the 1950s units, the cream-coloured phone with its rotary dial, hanging on the wall beside the light switch.

The kitchen was where they did everything except watch TV. The kitchen was where Dianne had sat Robin down when she was eight years old and told her she was adopted. Robin remembers not feeling surprised because there was always something, something unspoken, and what she felt most of all was relief it was not something worse.

Your birth mum was a musician, Dianne says. She died when she was twenty. She would never have given you up otherwise, Bobbie, I want you to know that.

When Dianne's husband Derek was alive he and Dianne had worked as foster carers for the local authority, which was how they came to take in Robin and then to adopt her. That was the story Dianne had told her, and that story was true though as Robin later discovered there was stuff she wasn't saying. Dianne's husband Derek was a cop, a detective sergeant with the Metropolitan Police. When Robin was twelve, Derek was killed in a hit-and-run during an investigation his team were conducting into a jewellery heist. Your father died in the line of duty, Dianne was always saying, which means I get the widow's pension at least. Del would be pleased.

After Derek died it was just the two of them. Dianne gave up her job as a social worker and started doing contract cleaning for the council instead, because it meant she could be home in time for Robin getting in from school. Money was tight but they didn't mind, at least they were together.

I've always wanted to do right by her, Dianne said. By your birth mum, I mean.

This has nothing to do with Dad, Robin said when she told Dianne she'd decided to join the police. This is what I want to do, and Dianne said so long as she was sure then she should go for it. Robin loved her for that, for not trying to change her mind even though Dianne more than most people would have known how hard it would be for her, doing the job, getting on in the job when bigots and bullies like Alec Dunbar were still the norm. Men who said they were all for equality but there were ways and means of policing and where was the harm in a bit of banter, a bit of *locker room talk*?

Robin wonders if Dianne was also worried, then or later, about what Robin might discover about the death of Marianne Lees.

Robin knows she has to stop being angry, firstly because it's not fair and secondly because she's not even angry, not any more, she's using anger as an excuse to punish Dianne. She sleeps her laptop and picks up her phone.

Hi Mum, Robin says when Dianne answers. I'm sorry I missed your calls. I've been busy on a case. I don't know where the hours go.

True, but not the point, a fiction both of them can live with, Robin hopes. She can hear Dianne's breathing, rapid and light as if she's afraid to say the wrong thing or ask the wrong question, afraid Robin might put down the phone before she's said a word.

Robin has been selfish, callous, obtuse, as bad as Dunbar, well maybe not as bad as Dunbar but she's still been a bitch. I'm sorry, she says again. None of what's happened has been your fault. It was a shock, that's all. I'm fine now. I should have called sooner.

Bobbie, Dianne says and she is crying now, Robin can tell, that whispery intake of breath, the catch in her voice. You have to understand the last thing I wanted was to hurt you. I didn't know what to do, how to tell you. The more time passed the harder it became. I never meant to hide anything from you. I hope you can believe me.

I believe you, Robin says and this is the nub of it, the reason her behaviour has been so stupid, because she does believe her and has never not believed her. The rest of it – the silence, the umbrage, the leaving bloody Ashley to pick up the pieces – is her own toxic baggage.

No shit, Sherlock, no shit, *detective*, what was your first clue?

Do you want to come round? Dianne is saying. We can talk all this through. There's not a lot more I know, but at least you can hear it from me, I owe you that.

Not now, Robin says, then mentally kicks herself; she still sounds so angry. I mean, I can't at the moment. I'm in Scarborough. For a case. We can speak more when I get back. The main thing for now is not to worry. I wanted to make sure you were OK.

If you're sure, Bobbie. She's sounding better, thank Christ.

I'm sure, Robin says. I'm sorry to call so late. Go back and enjoy your programme. What were you watching?

Waking the Dead, Dianne says, and giggles. What am I like?

That's a shit show, you know that?

So you keep saying, says Dianne and Robin thinks of the way she puts her head on one side – the lopsided glasses, the mass of curly greying hair in its messy bun, the laugh she imagines has stayed the same since Dianne was in school.

Love you, Mum, Robin says. She waits to hear Dianne repeat the words back to her, then she says goodnight and puts down the phone.

I remember him, says the second-floor room attendant. Her badge name is Meral. He locked himself out of his room and I let him back in with the master key. It was on the Saturday. We're not supposed to do that – guests are meant to go to reception if they lock themselves out – but I could see he was telling the truth and he said he was in a hurry. He was really apologetic about it. She pauses. A lot of the guests don't notice the hotel staff but when this man smiled you could see he was for real. He seemed nice.

Meral has dark, wiry hair and a Manchester accent. Why do you want to know? she says. She straightens up. Are you from a newspaper?

Robin shakes her head. Not me. Mr Shipley was, though, he was working on a story while he was here. I'm following up some details.

You're a cop, then?

A private investigator.

Seriously?

I was hoping I could get a look inside his room.

You can't. It's booked. There are guests staying.

I realise that. How about if you went in there with me? I only want to look.

The woman thrusts her hands into the pockets of her overalls. I can let you see inside, if that's all, she says finally. They're out for the day, at the dental conference. But you mustn't touch anything. She hesitates. I was shocked when I heard Mr Shipley had died. He seemed perfectly well when I was speaking to him.

It wasn't you who found the body, then?

I was on lates that day. It was Doris who found him, Doris Akele. Doris was on earlies.

Would she talk to me, do you think?

Doris gets nervous around people she doesn't know. Anyway, she's not in today, she's on her day off.

Do you think you might ask her for me? Anything she tells me would be confidential, if that's what she's worried about.

I don't know. She's a private person, Doris. It was upsetting for her, finding the body I mean. Nothing like that's ever happened in the hotel before, not since I've been working here anyway.

How long have you been working here?

Eight years, give or take. She swipes the pass key, nudges open the door to 236. The freshly serviced room has the artificial, slightly spooky appearance of a film set. Robin steps inside. The patterned carpet, the faux-antique desk, the gilt-framed mirror – the room's fixtures and fittings are more or less identical with those in her own room. Hardly unexpected, yet she is taken aback nonetheless and the presence of the dentists' personal possessions make the effect still more unsettling: items of makeup on the shelf in the bathroom, a discarded handkerchief, a radio plugged into the socket beside the bed. As if she has blundered into a crime scene.

Do you know where he was found? Robin says. Mr Shipley, I mean. She can smell the woman dentist's perfume, floral and cloying. LouLou by Cacharel – the flacon is on the nightstand to the right of the bed.

On the bed, I think. I don't really remember. You would have to ask Doris.

Robin crosses to the window, looks down into the courtyard. No visible means of access, unless you were a seagull. If someone else was in the room when Shipley died, either they'd been lying in wait for him, possibly for hours, or Shipley had let them in of his own accord.

What happened after you opened the door? she asks the room attendant.

Nothing. Mr Shipley said thank you and went inside.

You didn't go in with him?

Why would I?

To make sure it really was his room?

How would I have known that, either way? Anyway, I believed him, I told you.

What time was this?

Around half-past ten? Quarter to eleven maybe.

Did you see him again after that?

Meral hesitates for a second then nods her head. I did, as it happens. In the lounge bar, just before lunch. I remember because I was coming off shift. He had his back to me, so I doubt he saw me and I wouldn't have noticed him if it hadn't been for what happened earlier. I remember he was talking to someone – a younger guy. They looked like they knew each other.

How come?

She shrugs. Just the way they were talking. They seemed deep in conversation. Not how you'd normally behave if you'd only just met.

Do you remember what he looked like, this young guy?

Stubbly beard, blond hair. He was wearing a denim jacket. I only saw him for a moment.

Could he have been a guest at the hotel too, do you think?

No idea. There are always loads of random people about when there's a conference on. Some have day passes, others sneak in without paying. There's supposed to be extra security but they can't be everywhere.

You've been very helpful, Robin says. Thanks. The room attendant reminds her a little of Rachel, not just the hair and the angular stance but the way there's no side to her, the way she says what she thinks, regardless. The woman looks puzzled, as if she is trying to work out what their conversation has really been about, what she might have given away and who it might matter to.

I don't see how, she says.

You pay attention to detail, Robin says. Not everyone does, and maybe it's this snatch of honesty, this admission of common ground, maybe the room attendant has doubts of her own about Shipley's death but whatever it is, when Robin sees Meral standing on the front steps of the hotel an hour or so later she realises the woman has been waiting there deliberately in the hope of running into her. Robin has been in the downstairs bar, grabbing a bite to eat and wondering about the bearded guy, the guy in the denim jacket Meral saw chatting with Shipley on the day of his death. Could this have been Edmund de Groote? The photograph on the university website shows de Groote with shoulder-length hair and John Lennon glasses, faintly shabby but self-consciously so, a kind of avant-garde hipster. He has no beard. Meral's guy sounds more like Michael Landau. Robin is wondering how come she forgot to bring a photograph of Michael, one she could show to potential witnesses, when Meral appears in front of her as if summoned.

I called Doris, she says. She says she's OK to talk, so long as I'm with you. Do you still want to see her?

That would be fantastic, Robin says, and she means it. Doris Akele was the first to see Shipley's body, presumably the first to enter his room after his death. Doris will have information to give her, whether she realises it or not.

Can you come now? Meral says. Doris lives close to town. It's not far.

No problem. I was going for a walk anyway. Are you sure you won't get into trouble, leaving the hotel like this?

It's not a prison, you know. It's fine. My shift ended an hour ago.

They walk up through the town, past the station and along the boundary line of the main A64 until they come to a pub called The Commercial. The pub marks the right-hand turning into Commercial Road, a mix of two- and three-storey Victorian terraces and 1950s local authority housing blocks. Doris Akele's flat (5C) is in one of the council blocks about halfway down the road, directly opposite the pedestrian cut-through to a large Sainsbury's. Not a bad road but not a good one either. Light littering, faded graffiti, neglect shading to absence, people passing through.

Meral rings the bell. They wait for maybe a minute then the glazed lobby door clicks open and Meral leads the way up the open-tread staircase to the upper floor. The downtrodden feel of the place, the Spartan communality is familiar to Robin from a thousand similar visits to similar locales. Lifts sometimes out of order sometimes not, stairwells sometimes stinking of piss sometimes not. Doris's block is a not, the inside of the building relatively clean and in good repair. Doris is waiting for them on the landing outside her flat, a short, solidly built black woman with cropped grey hair and spectacles. Deep creases around her eyes and at the corners of her mouth. Meral steps forward, takes hold of her hands, and Robin feels the usual backwash of guilt, that she has made this woman feel anxious just by being there.

Mrs Akele? I'm Robin Clay. Thank you for agreeing to talk to me.

Meral tells me you are not with the police, Doris says. Her eyes behind the gold-rimmed spectacles seem wary, but observant. Doris is like Meral, Robin can tell, she pays attention to detail. She says you are a private investigator, Doris adds. Like Philip Marlowe.

You're into Raymond Chandler? Robin cannot help smiling.

Doris loves detective stories, Meral says. Philip Marlowe, Adam Dalgliesh, she reads them all.

Robin is relieved to see that Doris is smiling too now. They go inside the flat. Two rooms plus a bathroom and kitchen, the living room cramped but comfortably furnished, the mantel shelf above the gas fire crowded with china ornaments and family photos. In the kitchen the appliances are dated, well used, but the work surfaces and vinyl flooring are spotlessly clean. A child's colourful crayoned artwork is displayed prominently on a cork pinboard, though there is no sign of the child itself, no toys, no scattered schoolbooks, no gym kit on the drying frame.

No spare cash whatsoever, but Doris has done her best with the place. In spite of the decades-old metal-framed windows, the Artexed ceilings, the thin partition walls the flat exudes warmth and calmness, a feeling of refuge. The tidiness, the silence, the sense of order – all seem to indicate that Doris Akele lives here alone.

I will make us tea, Doris says. She puts digestives on a plate, shaking them from a tin that is itself a larger replica of the packet it contains. Robin takes a biscuit from the stack and bites into it, thinking of Dianne – the kitchen, the biscuits, the same sense of self-reliance. Meral is sitting diagonally opposite at the small square table. She seems completely at home, as if she has sat to drink tea in this kitchen many times before.

I don't mind talking about him, Doris says. She places a teapot in a red knitted cosy on a laminated mat. I have seen dead people before. I was a nurse, she adds, in Zimbabwe. People die in hospital every day.

It's good of you to spare the time, Robin says again. Can you tell me what you remember about the morning you found Mr Shipley? Did you notice anything unusual – before you went into his room, I mean – anything at all?

Doris Akele is silent, her eyelids lowered. Her concentration is palpable. I remember the card was on the floor, she says at last. The Do Not Disturb card. It was lying on the ground outside the door. I noticed the card was ripped, which meant it would not stay on the door handle. I could not tell if the guest wanted their room serviced or not. I remember I knocked on the door before I went in, just in case they were in the bathroom or still in bed. There was no answer so I went inside. I knew the guest – Mr Shipley – was dead as soon as I saw him. I knew even before I went to him because he was lying so still. You think a sleeping person is lying still but they are not, not like a dead person. When you see a dead person lying still you begin to believe it is a miracle they moved at all. If you had seen him I would not need to explain because you would know. Have you seen dead people, Miss Clay?

Some, Robin says. More than she cares to talk about or think about even, and Doris is right, it is the stillness, that inimitable absence you never get used to. Interesting that Doris has alighted on this detail in particular. She is a nurse, Robin recalls, but even so her exactitude is impressive. How exactly was Mr Shipley lying, do you remember?

He was lying on his side on the floor, facing the door. His eyes were closed. The bed was still made up – he had not slept in it. He was wearing all of his clothes apart from his shoes. I remember looking at his feet, with his grey socks on and no shoes. He looked like a doll, lying there. It made me feel sad to see a man who had died so alone.

Can you describe the rest of the room to me? Did it look as if anything had been disturbed?

The curtains were closed, and there was a lamp switched on, one of the bedside lamps. I remember there was a glass of wine on the desk, next to the TV remote. Red wine. I was only in the room for a second. As soon as I realised the guest was dead I knew I had to fetch someone. Apart from the curtains and the light on the room looked normal. Just as I was going out of the door I saw his shoes were underneath the desk, next to the chair. As if he had come in and sat down and then taken his shoes off, to rest his feet.

Being a witness is a skill like anything else, a skill few people have, which makes Doris Akele's talent for observation all the more remarkable. Robin finds she can imagine the room in perfect detail, smell it even, feel her eyes adjusting to the hampered daylight through the curtained windows, note the oddness of that bedside lamp still being switched on. She can see Miles Shipley sprawled on the carpet like a department store mannequin, the outline of a human being no longer human.

Shipley had died sometime after he returned to his room for the night but before he went to bed. He had taken off his shoes, poured himself a glass of wine – or brought one up from the bar, whatever. Hardly the actions of a person who was on their guard, and if the casually discarded shoes were anything to go by, it seemed unlikely he had been surprised by a hidden intruder. Either someone had come to the room later on, or Shipley had died of a heart attack, as the autopsy said.

Forty-five-year-old bloke walks into a bar and there's your punch-line.

There is one thing I did not mention to the police, Doris is saying. Robin turns to look at her. I did not mention it because it was nothing you could see or touch, just a feeling I had. When women try to explain their feelings they get called stupid. Is this something that is familiar to you from your work as a detective, Miss Clay?

Robin, Robin says. What was it you felt, Doris?

Something bad about the room. As if there had been an argument. As if the anger in the room was still trapped inside. She folds her hands in front of her on the table. I felt sorry for Mr Shipley, for what had happened there. But I could not tell the police that, they would have thought I was crazy. A crazy, black, African woman who believes in dark magic. I have had enough of that, for this lifetime anyway. But there is something else you should see.

Doris gets to her feet and goes through to the sitting room. When she returns she is carrying a handbag – a bulky, rust-coloured handbag with a heavy brass buckle. She places the bag on the kitchen table, rummages inside.

Here, she says. The hotel brought in an industrial cleaning firm after Mr Shipley died. People like to complain, you see, about everything, and if a new guest found out there had been a dead body in their room before them there would have been a fuss made. But those people who came to clean, they did not find everything. The room was cleaned then left empty until the next weekend. The housekeeper asked me then if I would go over 236 once again just to be sure it smelled fresh and so I cleaned everywhere, even inside the cupboards, which we do not always have to do because many of the guests don't even use them. I found this inside the wardrobe. It must have been in one of Mr Shipley's pockets, and fallen out. They took all of his clothes away – the police, I mean – but they did not find this.

Doris hands Robin a small, brown envelope, the same kind Dianne uses to keep receipts in. There is a telephone number scribbled on the back, a mobile number in blue biro, above it a name in block capitals, RACHEL GABON, but Robin knows that already, she knows the number by heart.

Inside the envelope is a photograph of Frank Landau. Not the image Emily Landau showed to the police but a snap of Frank in a more relaxed mode, his head turned to one side, his arms hugging his knees, a broad smile on his face. He is sitting on the grass and the sun is shining. He is wearing a baggy grey T-shirt with a Möbius strip design on the front, the words *To Infinity and Beyond* stencilled beneath. He looks happy. Robin thinks it was most likely Rachel who took the picture. She feels a twinge of regret.

Stuck to the back of the photo is a yellow Post-It note, words scribbled in the same blue biro as on the envelope: *check F. Landau/E. de Groote. Frank possible sighting August Inverness?*

When a person is absent their image is holy, their only means of making contact with the living, of entering a plea.

I have not seen this young man before, Doris says. Do you know who he is?

Robin nods slowly. Do you mind if I hang on to this?

It was here for you to find, Doris says. I am glad you came.

Robin reaches for her teacup, downs the dregs, a stray tealeaf tickling her throat and bringing tears to her eyes. Doris's son was a doctor, Meral tells her as they walk back to the hotel. A junior consultant at a hospital in Leeds. He died suddenly about a year ago – something wrong with his heart. His wife moved back down south to be closer to her parents, which means Doris only gets to see her grandson once or twice a year. He's five now. Doris doesn't say much but I know she's heartbroken. She has no other family. Not living in the UK, anyway.

Robin thinks of the child's coloured drawings in the scrubbed-clean kitchen.

Did she speak to you about Miles Shipley? Before I turned up, I mean.

Not really. Just that it was awful to see a life cut short so suddenly. I'm sure it brought back memories of what happened with her son. I think it did her good, you know, to talk about it. Doris has worked at the Royal for more than ten years. She knows the place like the back of her hand, better than the housekeeper. She once told me that the building talks to her. I think she's amazing.

Me too, Robin says. Thank you for persuading her to talk to me. I think you being there made all the difference.

No worries. I hope you find what you're looking for. Is it about the guy in the photo? The photo Doris found in 236?

The guy in the photo is missing. His name is Frank Landau. I think the man you saw in the bar – the young guy talking to Miles Shipley – might be his brother.

And it must have been Michael who gave Miles Shipley Rachel's number, Robin thinks but does not say. The photo too maybe. Was it also Michael who told Shipley about a possible sighting of Frank in Inverness?

Shipley was going to write about the case, I'm sure, Robin says. Only he died before he could do that. I've been trying to find out what he knew, anything that might be important as a way of finding Frank.

Do you think Miles Shipley was murdered? Meral's eyes are wide with the possibility of what has only previously occurred to her as a species of fantasy.

It's a possibility. A remote one, but that's the thing with this kind of work, you learn not to discount anything until you can say for sure it didn't happen. Which means gathering evidence to prove it. She asks Meral if she fancies going for a drink somewhere.

On me, she adds. I owe you one. She thinks of Doris reading Chandler, and once again she is smiling. The next logical thing to do would be to call Michael Landau. Probably she should have done that in the first place, but there's no harm done.

THE TOWER

BY JOHN C. SYLVESTER

IMPORTING THE STONE WOULD cost billions, the newspapers cautioned. If the project were to hit a roadblock or fall behind schedule the company would be bankrupted, the career of its monomaniacal director would lie in ruins. Archie Aspen was not discouraged, because he knew the risks. He understood from the outset that his competitors would denounce him as a fantasist and possibly a madman. Jealousy, Aspen told himself, pure malice, doubly so in the case of Arianna Fulci, his one-time associate and now chair of his most prosperous rival, Arcadia Holdings. If Aspen succeeded in building the tower, as he fully intended to, the achievement would not only secure his fortune, it would render him immortal.

The Conquest Tower as designed – no, envisioned – by Archimbaud Aspen and realised by his company Century Architects would be the most famous man-made structure in the world. A war memorial on an unprecedented scale, the tightly knit complex of buildings with the tower at its centre would effectively become a city within the city, an exclusive gated community that would function as a magnet for trade and an advertisement for its creator's planet-sized ambition. It had been widely rumoured, that is to say leaked even before the ground was broken, that Aspen was planning to run his entire multinational operation from the Conquest Tower, from one of its two-dozen luxury penthouse apartments to be precise, a personal vote of confidence that sent the advance reservation deposits – even a small studio apartment towards the rear of the complex would cost more than the average middle manager could hope to earn in a lifetime – soaring into the stratosphere.

Archimbaud Aspen had remained single all his life. His commitment to his vocation, or so he insisted in the rare interviews he gave, made the possibility of a permanent relationship not only unrealistic but unfair. In truth he simply preferred a life unencumbered by unnecessary attachments, though the women and, less frequently, men who found themselves however briefly in his orbit were amply rewarded. Paid off, more like, grumbled Sidney Kruger, who had been friends with Archie since college and who now worked as his secretary, personal assistant and general factotum. From the moment it was announced that Century had won the contract for the Conquest Tower, Sid found himself battling a tidal wave of invitations to red-carpet premieres, world-class sporting events and black-tie dinners. His advice to Archie – that he should attend at least some of them, for the sake of the company – went largely unheeded, although there had been exceptions.

'Just because he's a genius doesn't mean he isn't a prick,' Sid complained to his girlfriend Lex on a daily basis. Alexis Laverick, a commercial lawyer, maintained that the qualities were often insepa-rable, not to say interchangeable, and that Sid should make the effort not to bring his work home with him, or at least not every night.

'You can talk,' said Sidney. He poured himself a double measure of single malt, the authentic kind distilled on Speyside as opposed to within a factory complex on the outskirts of Tokyo. Even the whisky snobs swore you couldn't tell the difference these days but for Sid it was a matter of aesthetics – those soft-focus advertising shots of mist-wreathed mountains and seasoned oak barrels – and what was his salary for if not to indulge his pretensions? Lex was always carping about work, not so much the cases – on matters sub judice her silence was scrupulous – as the other partners in her firm, though Sid was silently forced to admit that her talent for honing expletives was entertaining.

His was simply bitching, and mostly performative. 'You wouldn't leave Archie even for double the salary,' Lex insisted. 'If it came to a choice between him and me I know which way you'd jump.'

'Don't be ridiculous,' Sid grumbled, though he could not have sworn in his heart that Lex was wrong.

The rock was called masonite, and its discovery had been an accident. In the slow, dark years following the protracted calamitous endgame of the war with Gliese, returning prisoners-of-war had spoken of a rock they used to warm themselves whilst being held captive in the thousand-mile cave system beneath Gliese City. They referred to the rock as cold-coal, or blanket stone, or any one of a dozen other appellations depending on the speaker's native language and cultural background. The fact they all agreed on was that the rock had saved their lives.

Initially cool to the touch, the stone's inherent properties of heat absorption and conductivity – no one really knew yet, the boffins were still working on it – allowed it to store heat for a seemingly unlimited period, whilst providing a source of radiant energy at the same time. The rock acted like a radiator, in other words – a radiator with its own internal thermostat. Prisoners discovered they could place fragments of the rock inside their clothing as they slept and that the rock would never burn them, never overheat.

Once set aside, the stone would revert to the ambient temperature of its surrounding environment.

In the caves and galleries beneath Gliese City, the rock was easy to spot even by candlelight because of its blackness. The city's bedrock was greyish, not unlike granite. Masonite – named for Ahmed Mason, the geologist who first described the mineral in a peer-reviewed paper – occurred in tight bands within the bedrock, and was so dark in colour that when viewed face on it appeared as an absence, a sliver of nothingness between the layers of grey. When viewed at an angle there was a slight sheen to it, a dim reflectivity similar to that of coal, though the mineral was not carbonic, nothing like.

Masonite was heavy – heavier than coal and with a density similar to that of magnetite, though it contained no iron. When ground on a carbide wheel, its surface could be polished to a dense, mirror-like shine, the stone's blackness seeming lit from within, dancing with silvery, glittering specks of material that looked like mica but was something other. If the polished piece of rock was tilted on its side, the silver dust appeared to slide, to float, to pour itself from the higher portion to the lower, as if its particles were travelling through a particularly dense liquid.

Even the most adventurous of the scientists were inclined to admit there was something unsettling, uncanny almost in the rock's apparent liquidity, although they were the first to remind the tabloid scaremongers and keyboard warriors, the part-time commentators and full-time conspiracy theorists that glass – common-or-garden, Earth-bound silica – was itself a liquid, the windows of every ordinary dwelling-place a waterfall in ultra-slow motion. Or had they forgotten that?

Archimbaud Aspen learned about masonite the same way as his junior architects, telemarketers and kitchen porters: he read about it in one of the many thousands of personal interest stories that were the lifeblood of the media in the early months and years following the war. The conflict had bitten deep; humanity's resources were badly depleted, with many of the ancient nation states ceasing to exist as political entities. Later studies estimated that more than twenty million people worldwide died from starvation alone, not to mention the fifty million who perished in the wave of pandemics that overwhelmed the healthcare systems of every surviving country in the world. At least one of these diseases, it was rumoured, had been Gliesian in origin. There was a hunger for good news as much as good rations, for stories that held out hope that a future was possible. The memoirs of returning prisoners – tales of survival against the odds – became a source not only of optimism but of shared community.

Archie was not immune to emotion, but he was no slave to it, either.

While recognising the social value of the prisoners' testimonies, he experienced a stirring of feelings – optimism, empathy, opportunity – that had lain dormant in him since his college days. As a student, Archimbaud Aspen had been ambitious. To the point of megalomania, said his detractors, though Archie being Archie such slights did not bother him. At the age of twenty-five he had already won two important industry awards. He used the prize money to set up Century Architects, landing his first significant contract – the Megalopolis shopping mall in Lagos, Nigeria – less than five years later.

Then came the war with Gliese and everything changed. While those on the right of the political spectrum claimed the conflict as a struggle for freedom, those on the left railed against the final, desperate flourish of the colonial mindset. In Archie's eyes, the war was pure folly, an act of hubris, an economic fiasco, the wilful dismantling of a social order that if not perfect was at least functional. Through the years of the conflict and long after victory was declared he continued to think of it as political vandalism, the laying waste not only of lives and of property but of the creative impulse.

Archie was never short of work, but the projects that came his way – hospitals, barracks, munitions depots and spaceports – were briefed to be as functional and economical as possible, commissions whereby speed was of the essence and hardly the kind to set the pulse racing. Since the cessation of hostilities, Century Architects' entire capacity and expertise had been poured into the rapid and cost-effective construction of social housing. Archie did not doubt the need for such schemes. He was even proud of his firm's achievements, to an extent. But at some point amidst the tedium an inner voice had begun speaking to him, small and quiet at first but increasingly insistent: where was Archimbaud Aspen in all of this, his passion and his artistry, his flair?

He barely recognised the voice at first, it had been silent so long. It's your time now, Archie, the voice insisted. Time to get off your backside and build something they'll remember you by.

The stories about masonite in particular flicked a switch in his brain. Archie began to dream of buildings – buildings that would be self-insulating, self-heating. Buildings that would have zero energy costs and zero carbon emissions. Buildings that would offer a tangible benefit to offset the catastrophic losses suffered by almost everyone on the planet. Buildings that might persuade humanity their so-called victory was something more than a howling void.

If masonite could be sold to consumers as the cornerstone of Earth's fightback, it could change society. If Century Architects were to become the effective delivery system for that change, then so much the better.

Archie made contact with a friend of his – a fellow architecture student who had diverted into the frozen foods business and latterly made a fortune shipping supplies to the military waystations en route to Gliese – offering him a substantial sum of money to procure a quantity of cold-coal. At the time he made his offer, masonite was still a protected substance and under government audit. Archie reckoned he had a year – eighteen months at the most – to realise the commercial potential of the stone as a building material before the pack followed.

Landing the contract to build the Conquest was only the beginning – the beginning of another war, this time with the planners. It was not the design the city's bureaucrats objected to – everyone agreed the design was a work of genius – so much as Archie's insistence that the tower and its surrounding complex should be constructed from masonite. A rival package was put together – ostensibly by the city authorities, though Archie always swore the brain behind it was Arianna Fulci's – demonstrating how the Conquest could be built to the same design specifications for less than half the cost if the lunacy of building with cold-coal was abandoned.

The logistics of shipping would be bad enough, the planners argued – five light years on full warping power. Add to that the construction of mine workings, the hiring of sufficient personnel willing to undergo the hardships of an off-planet posting, the nightmarish security protocols and astronomical insurance costs.

The idea alone was madness, never mind the reality.

The upshot was that the city authorities utilised their veto, at which point Archie threatened to withdraw the design brief unless every single one of his stipulations was agreed to. If he had known from the outset that his war with the planners would rumble on for most of a decade, he might have hesitated to engage. On the other hand, he might not. Archie recognised his fate, as surely as staring into a mirror and seeing his own reflection. The Conquest Tower would be his life's work, and he was ready to fight for it.

For the majority of those weary ten years, the general public showed little interest in the Battle of Conquest. They were more concerned with the returning prisoners, the loosening of travel restrictions, the reappearance of rationed commodities in ordinary retail outlets. The reappearance of ordinary retail outlets, full stop. At worst, Archimbaud Aspen's battle with the state legislature was seen as an irresponsible waste of government money and everyone's time; at best it was an entertainment, a rather dull soap opera you could dip in and out of depending on other leisure commitments and your boredom threshold.

Around five years in, a documentary film maker from Texas named Norrie Maguire contacted Archie and requested permission to embed herself with his planning team.

'I view your project as the definitive example of post-war revivalism,' she told him when they spoke together on the telephone a week later. 'It's a statement about endurance, of mind over matter. The seeming foolhardiness of the thing is a part of that. An essential part, I'd say.'

She wanted a face-to-face meeting as soon as Archie could fit one into his schedule. Sidney Kruger advised him against. He seemed convinced that Norrie Maguire was out to double-cross them. 'What if she's working for the other side?' he said, meaning Arcadia Holdings and Arianna Fulci. But unbeknownst to Sid and flying directly in the face of his own misgivings, Archie had already agreed to see Norrie Maguire for the simple (simple-minded, in Sid's view) reason that he felt drawn to her. Something about her voice, no, not her voice per se but the way she spoke about the project, the way she seemed to grasp not only its spirit of innovation but its potential for change.

'It's just a meeting,' he said to Sid. 'A meeting is not an agreement unless we say it is.' He was doing his best to sound impatient and vaguely bored, as if the business of Norrie Maguire was a trifling side-issue of little consequence in either direction.

'Your funeral,' Sid shrugged. He'd never known Archimbaud Aspen give a damn about a woman before. Trust him to fall for some cowgirl with horseshit under her fingernails.

Norrie Maguire was a small wiry Texan who wore her greying hair in pigtails under a Stetson. She was older than him, probably, a fact Archie verified through her archived biography as soon as their meeting was concluded.

She had shipped out to Gliese, Archie noted, as one of a small number of film makers and journalists granted access to Gliese City in the first two years after quarantine restrictions were lifted. Maguire's film *Aftermath* followed three doctors drafted in to assist in the repatriation of prisoners-of-war. One of the doctors became romantically involved with a patient, an army chaplain. Another – a specialist in the pathological effects of extreme isolation – was sent home three weeks into the assignment after suffering extreme panic attacks. The third doctor opted to remain behind on Gliese for a prolonged secondment in order to help with the rebuilding of medical care facilities in the city.

'How did you find it there, yourself?' Archie asked Norrie Maguire at their second meeting, at an Italian restaurant just around the corner from the Century offices where Archie's presence was so much the norm they could talk undisturbed. When Norrie asked him if she could film the lunch on her phone, Archie found himself agreeing even though the answer on his lips was an emphatic no.

You're falling in love with her, he told himself, in the same deadpan tone of voice he had learned from company lawyers, both his own and those of his competitors, a mode of attack in which the reporting of facts – unadorned and unmitigated – was the deadliest weapon. You're falling in love with her and that's all right, unexpected but not a problem unless you let it become one. He found himself watching her closely as he asked his question, genuinely curious about her reply. Archie preferred to think of Gliese as little as possible. Even reading about Gliese – its hostile terrain and complex ecosystems, its advanced use of digital technology, the vast and still mostly unmapped cave systems that formed two-thirds of the inhabited ground area of Gliese City – induced in him a kind of low-level terror response, a desire to turn inward, to isolate himself from the networks he had built. To walk and read – novels and memoirs and prizewinning journalism from the time before Gliese had initiated contact. To retire to a hunting shack in the backwoods of Maine and do his best to forget that Gliese even existed.

Bake potatoes in the woodstove for supper, eke out his whisky supply, listen for the cries of screech owls in the gathering dusk.

No more Century Architects, no more Gliese. Fair exchange is no robbery, as the proverb said.

Archie had never discussed these feelings with anyone, yet the alienness of the place, so far away, so close, terrified him. The being watched, the war, the diminished state of the returning prisoners and especially those who had not come back in any sense except the purely physical. The image of one commander in particular he could not forget, seated in a wheelchair, shaking hand to the touchscreen controls, a once-robust forty-year-old in the body of his great-grandfather.

We were lucky, the man said in his first broadcast interview. We got out alive. He said other things too, praised the bravery of his fallen comrades, looked to the future. But to Archie it seemed obvious he was faking it, repeating words he had rehearsed like lines from a play.

Was it for this man specifically, this shattered commander, that Archie had dreamed his dream of the Conquest Tower? He supposed he could spin it that way, if such a narrative ever proved useful. But what mattered most was to speak of victory, to pretend the worst of the horror and hardship was in the past.

And it was true that in this instance the Earth had been lucky, if you could call it that. But Archie could not push the thought from his mind that the planet was on their radar now, that the war had been just a precursor of what was to come. He found it impossible to hear the cry of a screech owl without imagining, however fleetingly, a world in which all screech owls had been destroyed.

'It was a tough assignment,' Norrie said, in a voice that suggested she too was used to dealing with company lawyers. 'We were shielded from the worst of things I'm sure, but it was tough. There was a guy they brought out of the red zone. I think that was when Desmond decided to bail, actually. Well, if you watch the film you'll see.'

Archie, who had watched the film twice, remembered the man she was talking about, a civil engineer who had been brought in to help stabilise what the Earth forces called the Tungsten Bridge, a three-hundred-foot span over an apparently bottomless ravine that linked the spaceport with the army depot. For reasons no one was able to properly ascertain, the bridge had become weakened through something like metal fatigue. There had been an accident. Archie had gone to the refrigerator to refresh his drink at that point but he had seen the engineer, Torvald someone, the skin of his left arm hanging in ragged red shreds like torn-open Christmas paper.

Norrie had filmed this, had focused on his tear-slicked, ravaged face as he was hoisted aboard the *Marianne* for repatriation. 'Thing is, you could see what a place it was. Before the war, I mean. The vast scale of the building projects. The concept of a social architecture based around shared resources. Same with the technology, which really was incredible. I didn't get to travel outside of Gliese City but I wish I had. There's no way you can get to know a planet from its built environment alone. You have to get your hands in the soil. That's what my daddy would have said, and you couldn't keep him away from the desert, not even when he was ninety and walking on crutches. One thing,' she said. She propped her face between her hands. 'I've always felt grateful Daddy died before the war came. I'm glad he never had to know about any of it.'

Why her? Archie was thinking. Norrie Maguire with her greying hair swept up in a chignon for their lunch date but still somehow unkempt, her knotty hands with the nails filed short, the swipe of russet lipstick and no other makeup. She was hardly his type, but then what was his type? The women he'd dated in the past were all chance acquaintances, women who worked for him or who he'd met through his business dealings. There was no type to speak of or to quantify, no narrative through-line. He'd met Norrie Maguire through his work also, in a sense at least, though this time it had been she, Archie reminded himself, who had come to him.

Why her? he asked himself again and all he could come up with was their likeness to one another, a likeness he sensed rather than knew or could definitively prove. A likeness that had to do with the way they lived – for their work – and how they saw the world – as a house of cards. One of the reasons Archie loved buildings was for their resilience, their defiance of his fears. Here lies Ozymandias, sure, but the base of the statue remained, the poem confirmed it. The base remained.

And Norrie Maguire would film the base of the statue, standing in the desert, to prove the point. That wiry Texan woman would carry on filming and editing until someone took her out with a rifle shot or clapped her in jail.

That's why her, Archie concluded, realising at the same time how strange it was, how unaccustomed, that he did not want to sleep with her, or not immediately, not beyond the usual background hum of male desire. What he wanted was to be with her, to know he could call her on the phone and she would always pick up.

I must be getting old, he thought. He was surprised by how little he cared. So long as he lived long enough to pass the plans for the Conquest, that was. And Norrie Maguire was going to be filming the whole fucking thing.

'Why are you giving them oxygen?' Archie was fuming, although as usual he was doing his utmost not to show it. 'You do know they're our enemies?'

He used the first-person plural instinctively, embracing Norrie automatically within his sphere of influence because to imagine her outside – away from him – was too destabilising to contemplate. She's naive, he reassured himself, although he knew she was not. Norrie was astute – more astute than he was. Maybe that was the trouble.

'They're not our enemies,' Norrie said slowly. Amused or irritated? Archie couldn't decide. 'Or if they are it doesn't matter. Enemies are only a problem if they're likely to win. The fact is, Archie, you are going to win because the city wants this project. City Hall has wanted it from the beginning and this furore – this shit that's going on now – is simply haggling over the price. Reena Drayton is just local colour, so relax. So long as you keep your mouth shut and don't have her murdered she'll be doing you a favour.'

'You think I'd do that? Have her killed?' Archie laughed, an awkward, half-assed chuckle, not knowing if he was offended or amused.

Norrie blinked at him and sighed. 'Actually I doubt it. But I know guys who would take her out for sure, or have someone else do it, plenty of them, so I'm just saying don't be tempted, ride this one out.'

Reena Drayton was a nurse, one of the thousands who had volunteered to help with the relief effort. She was softly spoken, largely self-educated and with the kind of family background – mother in the military, father employed part-time by a local feed merchant – that lent her protest the stamp of authenticity. Not your typical bleeding-heart liberal but a commonsense working woman who had somehow conspired to become the nexus for the Conquest opposition movement. Norrie had filmed Reena as she went about her daily tasks, visiting elderly and disabled veterans in their homes, delivering medicines, checking in for a chat with her son who was in Chicago, studying law.

'He wants to specialise eventually, after he graduates,' Reena said. 'Environmental law. Corey's always been passionate about justice for ordinary people.'

The high-achieving son, achieving escape velocity from his disadvantaged background yet still hell bent on taking the Drayton campaigning spirit to the next level. If Corey Drayton had not existed, Archie reflected, it would have been necessary to invent him.

What Reena Drayton and her cronies insisted was that the Conquest should not be built because the war the tower was intended to memorialise should not have been fought. The waste of life, the flatlining of the world economy, the destitution and poverty and disease that had followed in its wake. What authority did the city have, to squander financial resources and manpower in such a cavalier manner, when the homeless shelters were overflowing and the food banks empty? What message did this send, not just about the planners but about the city as a body politic, if it could allow itself to tolerate such blatant opportunism?

The final ten minutes of Norrie's film was just Reena talking, Reena breaking the fourth wall, her bird's-nest hair, her shapeless, careworn face levelled straight at the camera.

'And what no one cares to remember,' she said near the end, 'is the other side of the story, the millions we killed. We might not have understood their way of living but that didn't give us the right to bomb their cities or slaughter their children. I heard from one of the guys they brought out of the caves that if the final bombing campaign hadn't worked there was a plan to poison the groundwater. That's not just a city, that's a planet. Which is exactly what this tower is about, when you get right down to it – an almighty great "well done" sign set up to congratulate people who were fixed on killing a planet if things didn't go their way. That's not something I can feel proud of, not as an American citizen and not as a human being, and I'm saying that as the daughter of a decorated soldier.'

Archie watched the footage on repeat. He marvelled at Norrie's skill in rendering this woman, with her work-reddened hands and earnest, unimaginative demeanour simultaneously as everyone's next-door neighbour and the global icon she was fast becoming. Reena Drayton was boring, and what she had to say was boring, if only because the arguments she trotted out were the same arguments that had been brought against every war since the dawn of time. And Archie agreed with those arguments – only a madman would stand against them, or maybe a president, and everyone knew how dangerous life suddenly became when the boundaries of those two provinces overlapped.

Looking at Reena Drayton, Archie experienced a kind of sad guilt, because she was right, about everything, and yet the fact of her being right didn't matter a damn. The Conquest Tower would be built because it could be built, and because the city needed it. Not just the jobs the project would provide and the cash it would generate, but the sense of forward progress. And Norrie was right, too – even the temporary diversions, the running battles between Century Architects and the likes of Reena Drayton and her mob were useful in the end, because they gave the public the illusory sense that they were having their say. Because they provided a tangible proof that the news cycle was finally shifting from the war towards what came afterwards.

The Conquest, with its sleek finishes and buzzing cafés and elegantly designed piazzas, its twenty-four-hour shopping, entertainment and conference facilities was in essence nothing less than a neon-lit permissions slip for the entire planet: get out there and buy things, for heaven's sake. We can finally move on.

Norrie Maguire had understood this from the first, which was why she was backing Archie instead of Reena.

In the end a deal was brokered and the impasse was breached. Century Architects agreed to the city's proposal that only the Conquest Tower itself – the cornerstone of the development, the de facto memorial – should be constructed from masonite. The surrounding complex would be built from conventional materials: Indiana limestone, Blue Mountain granite, Sierra Rose. Archie was not one hundred per cent satisfied but he allowed himself to be persuaded by his board of directors. In other words, he had made up his mind to be convinced before the crisis meeting started.

It was impossible not to recognise that such a concession would slash the cost of the project by sixty-five per cent. Such a saving was tempting, even for a perfectionist like Archie. More tempting still was the thought of the time they would recoup. The current uptick in the economy was tentative, but it was there; good business sense dictated they should press their advantage. Continue the fight and they risked putting the build on ice indefinitely.

'Delay any longer and there's a risk the great American public will begin to wonder what was so important about this building in the first place,' Norrie warned him. 'You don't want it getting reclassified as a great white whale.'

Her words stirred in Archie feelings of panic that were in themselves an indication that it was time to act. He signed the final contract three weeks later. There was a party, a big one, during which footage was beamed live from Gliese of the first blocks of masonite being loaded into the matter transmat. The transportation of the stone by the Allied superfreighter *Von Bismarck* from the transmat hub to Earth would take around two years, and Archie began to see the compromise he had made over materials not so much as a failure of nerve as a masterstroke of planning. The prep work for the tower's vast foundations could begin full throttle, and meanwhile some of the larger outlying buildings – the sports stadium, the Century concert hall – could be overseen as separate projects while the masonite for the tower was still in transit. Shrewd move. Archie was glad he'd thought of it.

Six months after the party, the project broke ground.

The Century Theatre and Concert Hall, the Aspen Stadium (Archie couldn't resist – he had been house champion at 10,000 metres in his graduation year after all, even if the past decade had seen his personal best slip away to a distant memory), the Kudos shopping mall, the conference centre and exhibition space, the food quarter (the size of a small village and catering to more than fifty world cuisines in every price band from 3-star Michelin to kiosk and street food), the indoor sports centre, the outdoor sports centre, the exclusive 5-star Palace Hotel with its marginally more affordable annex The Gatehouse (sited in five acres of parkland with fountains, a Victorian bandstand and a small colony of luxury self-catering weekend cabins), Parkside Drive (a gated community of one hundred luxury townhouses for long lease or purchase), Copenhagen Heights (a complex of mid-rise apartment blocks, again with gated access), The Studio (a complex of one hundred and fifty self-heating studio apartments constructed from the final, what turned out to be surplus, shipment of masonite, an overestimate that immediately paid for itself twice over in advance deposits) and then the Conquest Tower itself, the jewel in the crown, the apple of its architect's eye, the silver needle in the blue granite haystack, the pillar of gold at the end of the rainbow.

How should he describe it? Archie counted the ways. He had taken his inspiration from the old, conflagrated Chrysler building, because the skyscraper had been so beloved, so much a symbol of pre-war New York that it was still talked about as the English princess Naomi was still talked about, murdered by anti-war protestors in the second year of the conflict, or the first, hair's-breadth-from-disaster Mars mission as iconic, era-defining, unrepeatable – except here was Archimbaud Aspen daring to repeat it. Not quite twenty years after the war spluttered to its close, he was giving back to the American people a portion at least of what many had come to believe was vanished forever.

The Chrysler building in black glass, only of course it was not glass, and in spite of its shimmering surface felt neither cold nor shiny to the touch. A densely textured warmth, like blue granite or sandstone on a hot day, some said, only it was not like that either, not exactly, because the sensation you experienced from stroking its surface was entirely alien. Although Archie had not forbidden the use of the word – repressing free speech was not how business was conducted at Century Architects – he had asked everyone, those working in the press office especially, to think carefully before they made use of it, to consider what the term might mean for the project as it moved forward into the future.

Those employed on the construction team – a crew whose normal vocabulary, or so it seemed to Archie, consisted mainly of curse words – spoke in uncharacteristically effusive terms of the beauty of the material, not just from an aesthetic standpoint (who gave a damn about aesthetics when your knuckles were bleeding and the backs of your knees were rubbed raw from your polytech overalls after a twelve-hour shift?) but from the ease of handling. The world-class stonemasons tasked with the shaping, cutting and faceting of the building's facade spoke of the malleability of the stone, of the stone 'knowing what it was doing', of the affinity they felt for it even, this strange mineral that was like nothing they'd ever worked with before and beside which even Ellerton granite seemed, as one of the younger, less taciturn masons put it, 'pig ignorant'.

Could a rock be pig ignorant? Could a stone be knowing? Much of what was said about masonite by those in daily contact with the material made little sense to Archie either factually or in terms of semantics but it made good copy. The endorsements danced in his head like fireflies, like the billion specks of silver luminescence that sparked and cascaded and glimmered within the precision-cut, polished slabwork of the Conquest Tower. From the moment ground was broken, Archie found himself in an altered state in which time and ordinary space became concepts shorn of meaning. What had meaning was the project and the daily press bulletins, the site briefing meetings he wasn't supposed to sit in on – he made the crew nervous, Sid Kruger complained – but gatecrashed anyway because he couldn't bear to be out of the loop for a single second.

The vast building sites at dusk, the scaffolding looming massively like the petrified trees of a forest so sunk in prehistory it was almost mythical. The sun setting, sinking gradually from sight in a sky as pale and pearlescent as the precious, nacreous interior of an abalone shell.

The sense that what he was creating was not simply a building, but history itself.

The dawn of a new era? blazed the media headlines on the morning the Conquest Tower was finally handed over to Fixtures and Fittings. A new era, period, Archie averred, drop the question mark. He wondered if the pharaohs had enjoyed a similar sense of completion on beholding the pyramids, chiding himself for his hubris but wondering anyway. When he first caught sight of himself in Norrie's film, silhouetted against the skyline, the expression on his face so blissfully enraptured, it was like coming upon a stranger unawares.

The king always stands alone, Archie mused. He wondered if that was a quote from somewhere, made a mental note to look it up later then promptly forgot.

It was Sid who called him with the news that Reena Drayton was dead.

'Traffic accident,' he said. It was eight o'clock in the morning. 'On her way to work. The cops are looking into it.'

He hesitated, then added that Archie would be well advised to keep himself out of the spotlight for a day or two.

'Out of the spotlight? What's that supposed to mean? I have wall-to-wall interviews all week.'

'I'm just saying. Steer away from politics.'

'You're not trying to insinuate I had something to do with this?' Archie barked out a laugh. Don't have her murdered, Norrie had said. Hell, that was aeons ago. He felt curiously depressed by the nurse's death. Reena Drayton had been his opponent but she had lost. In the years since, Archie had developed a feeling of magnanimity towards her, the way a heavyweight boxer might feel about an ignominiously defeated former sparring partner. Reena Drayton had been in the game with him from the beginning. David had fought Goliath and Goliath had won. Reena had never stood a chance, but she had at least fought like the devil and Archie admired that. He had once sent the Drayton family an enormous, vastly-beyond-their-means food hamper on Thanksgiving. His gift had been anonymous, of course – not even Norrie knew about that one. If she had, she would have wanted to film the fucker arriving. What his motives had been he could not have explained, nor did he care to examine them too closely. He had experienced an impulse and acted upon it. Now the woman was dead and Archie felt sad.

'Of course not,' Sid said. 'You didn't, did you?'

For a second, Archie flirted with the idea of simply hanging up, slamming down the receiver without a word the way they did in the gangster movies.

'Don't be ridiculous, Sid,' he said instead. 'I forgot she even existed. See you at ten.'

He waited all of five seconds then put in a call to Norrie. 'Did you hear about Reena?' he said.

Norrie sounded wide awake already. 'I've been trying to reach Corey,' she said. 'There'll be a story in this.'

Corey Drayton was now an upstart attorney somewhere in New Jersey. It crossed Archie's mind that Reena was lucky, that she had escaped.

Escaped what? he asked himself. He realised he could feel his own heartbeat, which seemed faster than normal, like a dog straining at the leash, insisting on its freedom.

What wild thoughts were these? He reached for the cube of masonite he kept on his desk, its reassuring smoothness and velvety sheen, the flecks of silver that glimmered in its depths the way the stars still glimmered in reckless profusion above the war-blasted, rain-soaked ruins of Gliese City.

There's a rebuilding programme, he reminded himself. Resettlement for the displaced. Frictionless trade.

The rock seemed to pulse in his hand, its warmth spreading from palm to wrist to crook of elbow, an act of seduction that, Archie reminded himself, was simply a part of its chemistry, nothing more. Any idea that he and the rock were psychically linked was an illusion, a scare story dreamed up by adherents of the more outlandish conspiracy cadres.

He recalled a photograph he had seen on one of their sites, Corey Drayton's daughter Ellie sitting on her grandmother's knee. Our world is adrift, Archie thought distractedly, our world is not ours. He felt his stomach flip softly over, as if he were speeding on a fairground whirligig and could not get off. He wondered why he felt afraid suddenly, what this feeling of disjuncture could possibly mean.

From Archie's penthouse apartment you could see for miles. In the hour after dawn, before the clatter and hum of the city had properly started, the translucent, roseate glow of the dew misting off the parks and buildings and sidewalks at the base of the tower was like the cloud of sweet gas that fizzed up from the shivering surface of a glass of champagne.

Sweet as roses, tart as wine. The full-height windows that wrapped themselves around two sides of the apartment gave Archie the sensation of walking on air. Some visitors to the penthouse claimed the effect was disconcerting. Archie, who secretly agreed with them, made a show of amusement at their discomfort.

'The glass is almost literally unbreakable,' he would assure them. 'Reinforced with titanium. An embedded latticework of micro-wires, a kind of spiderweb effect developed specifically with buildings like this in mind.'

Only there were no buildings like the tower, not anywhere in the world, and his guests all knew it. For the interior of the apartment, Archie had settled on a palette of blue slate together with a neutral shade called gypsum, enlivened at strategic intervals with accents of fuchsia. He had been unsure about the fuchsia, but Norrie had assured him the colour would work, that it would strengthen the overall impression – restrained yet energised – and of course she was right; the bold, saturated pink incorporated exactly the element of risk he had been hoping for. His lack of confidence when it came to colour had always perplexed him. He had developed a habit of seeing everything in black and white.

'Because you're used to visualising a project in terms of architectural blueprints,' Norrie said. 'It's only natural, when you think about how much time you spend at the drawing board. You shouldn't let it worry you.'

'I don't,' Archie said, although he did, a little, as he worried about any area of his life where his control of the situation did not feel absolute. Norrie herself was such an area, though he worried about her less since they had begun sleeping together. The first time had been shortly after he moved into the new apartment. They had been attending a champagne reception on one of the lower floors, Norrie in a grey silk shift dress and with her hair down. Archie was not used to seeing her that way – conscious of herself, her reactions heightened – and the effect was unsettling. When after the party they rode up together in the elevator he had placed his hand on her hip, his eyes on their joint reflection in the mirrored walls. He half-expected to be rebuffed – rebuked or even ridiculed. Her response to his overture – head tilted back, lips parted – appeared to him at first like a gesture from a movie although when he placed his mouth over hers there was an instant ignition that reassured him of its sincerity. He heard rather than saw the heavy, paste-encrusted bangle she was wearing – the zircons ironic, he assumed, though their raffish glamour, he was forced to admit, was Norrie all over – slide from her wrist to her elbow and he was hard as nails.

'Is this a good idea?' he heard himself asking as they stumbled through the doorway of his apartment. They were still clinging to one another fiercely and Archie thanked the god he had never believed in that he had already memorised the six-digit combination for the security alarm. He had never felt anything like this. Not a cliché but the truth, he realised, and the sensation of being undone was as bewildering as his uncertainty in choosing colour. He could not credit it, hence his hesitation, though Norrie brushed off his question with a shake of her head, raising her eyebrows in a sardonic gesture that reminded Archie

– the memory bright and brief and intense as a flash of lightning – of his eighth-grade chemistry teacher Ava Kennedy.

'For Pete's sake,' Norrie said. 'Let's just fuck already.'

And so they had fucked, the topaz-coloured sheets, Archie noted with relief, had been put on fresh by the housemaid only that morning, and he was surprised all over again by Norrie's willingness, her eagerness, or so it seemed to him, to lose herself in the moment, to not think of the aftermath. What was better almost than the sex was the way things reverted to what he thought of as normal the following morning. Norrie made coffee and they sent down for bagels, sat side by side at the breakfast bar catching up with the overnight news and watching the city far below stir gradually to life.

They both relished the early mornings, Archie had discovered. He liked the way Norrie did not rush to arrange herself, the way she seemed more interested in CNN than how she might appear to him.

He let out his breath and sipped his coffee (so hot you almost can't drink it, he had laid down the law to Sidney Kruger the first morning of his employment, think of it as the eleventh commandment) and allowed himself to believe that what had happened the night before might have been a miracle as opposed to a mistake that would ruin his life.

The Friends of Reena Drayton refused to go away. If anything, the death of their figurehead had made them more vociferous, more doggedly persistent. They seemed undaunted by the fact that the tower was a fait accompli, that Century City, as the complex was known, was already exceeding its forecast profit several times over. Tourists flocked to the lower level bars and cafés, stood in line to have their photograph taken in front of the already legendary Conquest Tower. There was a waiting list of more than a thousand for the Centurion health club, while the twice-weekly tours of the complex's commercial plazas were booked a year in advance. Century Real Estate, which handled Century City's rental and leasehold portfolio, had been forced to suspend its enquiry line due to excess demand.

Century City was booming. Within a year of its official opening, the complex was already contributing to the restitution not only of city finances but of national morale. Archimbaud Aspen was now a rich man. Not rich in the ordinary way but at a level that required a different metric for analysis. Archie felt satisfied, not so much by the money itself – when you achieved that level of wealth the concept ceased to have meaning – but by the cold hard fact of his bank balance, which stood as vindication of the risks he had taken to earn it.

People had said he was crazy and he had proved them wrong.

The Friends of Reena Drayton were a thorn in his side, a mosquito-whine of dissent, irritating and incurable as tinnitus; you could make yourself get used to it but it was always there. Archie had raised the subject of the protestors at a board meeting once and Anders Thorrinsen, Century's chief legal spokesman, had stared at him with the gimlet-eyed precision of an eagle homing in on its unsuspecting prey.

'They're leftovers,' he said. 'They have no case to argue. Let them have their room party. It's just a barrel of noise.'

In the legal sense of course Thorrinsen was right. His words should have set Archie's mind at rest, which they did – in the legal sense – though there were times when he found himself unable to ignore the underhum, the buzzing in his brain that felt more like a warning than a threat.

What did these people want, exactly, what did they *think*? Archie was used to people plotting against him, people believing they hated him, the usual kind of class envy, dog-in-the-manger outrage that was really just an admission of their own failure, their frustration that he, Archie Aspen, had managed to get his hands on stuff they wanted for themselves. He was used to filtering out the hurt, the urge to self-justify, the desire to explain because if his decades in business had taught him anything it was that such urges consumed valuable energy and accomplished nothing.

The majority of the Reena Drayton people could be dismissed, filed away under their various headings: tub-thumpers, point-makers, haters of the moneyed classes, moral evangelists. Not all of them, though – not the ones who wrote pamphlets and stood earnestly disseminating their views at conference lecterns all across the country and internationally. Their dedication to the cause was more than a part-time hobby. They seemed to believe there was something larger at stake, something bigger than money, something existential. Something Archie felt he should know about, even if it did turn out to be just a barrel of noise.

Tower of Babel, the extended essay published by Corey Drayton as a chapbook at his own expense, spoke of Century City and the tower in particular as being not merely a squandering of public funds but morally objectionable. The Conquest was a physical embodiment of triumphalism, a stark assertion of power that purported to memorialise the dead whilst actually erasing them. The looting (Drayton's word, not Archie's) of Gliese's natural mineral reserves for the construction of a brutalist folly, a Neuschwanstein Castle for the post-war age, was not only grossly offensive but potentially harmful. In this epoch of détente, Drayton wrote, we should surely consider the repercussions of speaking in a language the war itself should have rendered unworkable.

Was the tower offensive? Archie wondered. He did his best to consider the question objectively, though he was objective enough to understand this was impossible. Everything he thought and felt came filtered through his own assumptions and biases, his private lexicon of belief. His impressions and obsessions, the prejudices, experiences and delusions of almost six decades of living inside the mind and body of Archimbaud Aspen.

Corey Drayton believed the Conquest Tower to be an almighty phallic symbol, code for the revival of colonial ambition, a giant V-for-victory sign in the midst of a political landscape where the very concept of victory had been rendered obscene. Archie Aspen knew his tower to be an architectural marvel, a down-payment on the future, a realised legend that would fill the purses and fire the imagination of the city's exhausted citizenry for generations to come. The war with Gliese was a part of their history. The conflict had defined not only Archie's life, but that of his entire generation. The internalised trauma, the perpetual shadow of planetary annihilation had ravaged his soul in ways Archie refused to articulate and would die resenting. But the war had happened. Part of his job, not only as an architect but as a citizen, was to do what little he could to help clear up the mess.

The Conquest was Archie's masterpiece, his contribution. Drayton and his so-called ethics could go take a bike ride.

*

Archie kept a file on Corey Drayton without knowing why. Depending on what mood she was in, Norrie found his obsession with the man either amusing or borderline sociopathic.

'What is he to you?' she asked him once. They had been together on a permanent basis now for more than three years. Norrie lived mostly at the Conquest apartment, though she still kept her walk-up for when she was working at night or just needed space. Their relationship was stormy at times, though the flare-ups were shallow and brief, minor oil slicks set alight by some transitory disagreement. Beneath the burning oil lay the depths: unfathomable, mute and immutable, the salt, enduring acceptance of one another that was the sea they swam in.

In their ongoing argument over Corey Drayton, the bulk of the problem lay in the fact that Archie could not explain himself. 'He's nothing to me,' he said, knowing this could not be true or they wouldn't be having the conversation. 'He's in my business,' he added reluctantly. 'If someone's in my business I need to know why.'

Archie was aware that Norrie had approached Drayton about making a follow-up film, a sequel to the documentary about his mother. If he were Drayton he wouldn't touch her with a bargepole, Archie reflected, not now she was sleeping with the enemy. But Archie wasn't Drayton, and who else had Norrie's resources or her talent? He would lay money that Drayton was tempted and so what if he was?

Know thine enemy, he mused, mouthing the words to himself as he tried to remember who had spoken them originally. Someone in the Bible, possibly. Nor was Drayton the only irritant. Archie's files contained intelligence on literally hundreds of conspiracy theories concerning himself or the Conquest and usually both. Claptrap about how he, Archie Aspen, was laundering millions of dollars' worth of foreign currency through Century City's casinos, how the entire complex had been built using slave labour, how the Republican Party (or the Democratic Party, depending on who you happened to be reading) had underwritten the project in exchange for a network of surveillance-proof bunkers directly accessible from one of the tower's vast basement areas.

Pure invention, flights of fancy, a barrel of noise. Archie had asked Sidney Kruger to keep his eye on the most vociferous of the nutjobs, those who looked like they could turn violent or get lawyered up. For the record, he insisted, just a precaution, forewarned is forearmed. Sid shrugged in that way he had when he thought Archie was wasting his time – Sid's time or his own, which amounted to the same thing in the long run, although he must have taken Archie's wishes on board because it was Sid who alerted him to the article in *The Western Wind*, the investigative essay by Miranda Calvi that Archie himself had missed, because you don't expect to find crap like that in the pages of a respectable high-end weekly like *The Western Wind*.

Calvi's piece was couched as memoir, bucolic recollections of truffle-hunting in the mountains of Umbria with her grandfather Giorgio.

My grandfather was a chef, Calvi wrote. *He began his working life as a kitchen boy in a hotel in Perugia. The head chef noticed his talent and took him under his wing. By the age of twenty-nine, Giorgio had opened his own restaurant, an establishment still in operation today under the management of one of my cousins, Luisa Costello. Granpapa Giorgio was not just a brilliant chef; his love of food and hospitality was enlivened and enhanced by his fascination with food science. Giorgio Calvi made it his business to know about soil composition, pollination ratios, genetic modification. His chief passion was for fungi. Even as a child of nine, I recognised Granpapa's enthusiasm as something rare and infectious.*

Archie read on, half interested because he'd always had a hankering to visit Italy, but mostly puzzled because he couldn't figure out why Sid had bookmarked the piece as one he should take a look at. That was before Calvi's meanderings took a sharp left into more familiar territory: a masonite sculpture she had happened to see at an art gallery in Portland, Oregon, the curator's offhand comment concerning a theory she had heard, that masonite was not in fact a mineral but an organic substance.

She reminded me that amber and jet, both commonly described as semi-precious stones, were actually derived from organic matter, petrified wood in the case of jet and solidified tree resin in the case of amber. 'Of course,' the curator added, 'no one really knows anything about masonite yet, do they? It's a brand new alien material. It could be anything.'

It could be anything. Archie found the words were stuck on repeat inside his brain. They came to him as a revelation – the expression of an idea he had not previously entertained. Miranda Calvi had been sufficiently intrigued by what the Portland art curator had said to her that she immediately began to wonder if there might be a story in it. She had set out to interview specialists – a geologist at the Smithsonian, a journalist who won a Pulitzer for a series of investigative articles on the grey market gem trade, a palaeontologist with a thirty-year career researching amber inclusions.

Calvi had also spoken at length with a mycologist, Dr Beverley Watanabe, who had made an extensive study of the matsutake mushroom. The matsutake, or pine mushroom, was an expensive delicacy in Japan. It was also considered a mycological marvel, owing to the fact that it grew and flourished in post-industrial landscapes. Watanabe described such sites as edgeland habitats, discouraging to all but the hardiest of species. *The matsutake presents a conundrum,* Calvi explained. *In its particular resilience and solitary burgeoning, the pine mushroom might almost be described as an alien species, an invader uniquely placed to take advantage of our inattention.*

Such a realisation forced me also to become aware of why the masonite sculpture I had seen in Portland left me feeling so uneasy, Calvi went on. *Even more so than the matsutake, the alien 'mineral' masonite as a commodity is the product of exploitation. Like the sought-after mushroom, masonite is harvested from a devastated local environment in order to satisfy a luxury market on the other side of the world, or in this case the galaxy. The decade-long furore over the construction of New York's exclusive business and leisure enclave Century City was focused primarily on the vast expense of the project, as well as the practical and moral dilemmas inherent in promoting such an investment at a time when many were arguing the money would be better spent elsewhere. These were worthy questions — questions that still resonate even while the Conquest Tower has since become an inalienable component of the city's skyline. What seems still more disturbing with hindsight is how little attention was paid to the unknowable and unproven nature of masonite itself, an alien material smuggled into our environment and native ecosystems, a bio-contaminant Trojan Horse. In the words of that curator in Portland, it could be anything. When we consider that we ourselves as ordinary citizens were never consulted, this breach in trust and security becomes more disturbing still.*

In the manner of most exclusive or novelty products, masonite is rapidly becoming mainstream. Its extraordinary properties have created whole new markets for its exploitation, distribution and consumption. The eco-mining sector has entered a boom-time that has been compared with the first gold rush. Moreover, the value of masonite as a seemingly inexhaustible supply of clean energy makes it difficult to mount an argument against future imports. Whether we have saved our planet, or gambled away its future is now a question that will only be answered in the fullness of time.

Alien fungus ate our planet, ran the tagline of a think-piece on Calvi's essay, one of the dozens that proliferated in the days immediately following the publication of Calvi's original in *The Western Wind*. The writer had taken Calvi's existential comparison between the matsutake mushroom and Gliesian masonite entirely at face value, suggesting that even now — *even as you read these words* — a vast mycelium (the scribbler seemed particularly proud of this word), a hyphal net (ditto) of gargantuan proportions, was burrowing its way through the foundations of the Conquest Tower in its deadly alien quest to contaminate the fragile ecological environment of New York City.

How long before the alien organism poisons our water table? the writer shrieked, rhetorically. *Your grandmothers will remember the 'alien panic' of the 2090s, which many historians insist was an indirect facilitator of the open, armed conflict that followed. As it turns out the Gliesians need not have gone to the trouble of mounting an invasion force. Why bother, when your host hands you a first-class ticket and celebrates your arrival with a ticker-tape parade?*

'What are you reading?' Norrie asked him. Archie turned to face her, momentarily disorientated. He had become so absorbed in the Calvi commentary that Norrie's return to the apartment had barely registered. How dark they were, these courts of conspiracy, he thought, how narrow, one overheated theory opening upon another like trap-doors descending gradually into hell.

'What is it?' Norrie asked him, again. She eased off her boots and tossed them aside. Her feet were long and narrow and they always smelled. They smelled now because she had been traipsing about most of the day trying to track down some loser to his Brooklyn chess club or wherever he'd hacked off to and Archie loved her for it. He loved her smelly feet because of the way she tore off her boots and didn't give a damn. Norrie had recently started work on a new series of films, following up on some of the soldiers who had featured in *Aftermath*, which had transcended its controversial status – the film had been banned in some countries – to become a classic. Norrie was successful – as successful in her own field as Archie was in his, though she seemed not to notice. Her passion for the work itself – her hunger to investigate, to illuminate, to record – remained undiminished, and it was her hard-headed pragmatism Archie fixed upon now: the sight of her boots, toppled together against the skirting board, which seemed to symbolise the reality that had existed before he read Calvi.

He could feel his heart racing, and out of nowhere came the thought that those most at risk of dying from heart attacks were men over fifty.

'Nothing much,' he said. 'Just some articles Sid looked out for me. You know I've been tracking the conspiracy stuff?'

'I could do something with that,' she said absently. 'I'm going to take a shower.'

What Archie most wanted was to ask her to read Calvi's essay so they could discuss it together, so she could frown and then smile and then tell him what garbage it was, how Calvi most likely knew someone at *The Western Wind* or she would never have got it published. He listened for the sound of the shower being switched on, the initiating thud, the water bursting from the eight high-pressure faucets with an indigent hiss. He knew already that he wouldn't tell her, that he would let her forget she had even asked, because he was too afraid.

In the weeks and months that followed, that fear abated. He instructed Sidney to keep tracking the crazies – for legal reasons, he insisted, though what he actually wanted was to find out if Calvi's theories about masonite were gaining traction. So far as he was able to tell, the brief upsurge of interest and speculation – *alien fungus ate our planet* – tapered off pretty rapidly and did not recur. In that respect at least, the Air Pacific jumbo crash over North Carolina worked like a magic trick, redirecting public attention like the brief, hot, brilliant flash of an orange silk handkerchief in a conjuror's hand. There were always a million and one conspiracy theories around air crashes, especially civilian air crashes. Something about the violence, like a bomb going off inside a crowded theatre, the instant dissolution of one reality into another. Stood next to a real-life jumbo crash, some wacko theory about living stone seemed not only hokey but dull.

Nor did it hurt, that the actor Denise Santander had been aboard that plane; Hollywood royalty, and a vocal critic of the NRA. Conspiracy dynamite. The Conquest Tower was where out-of-towners went to get themselves photographed. Who cared?

No one seemed to give a monkey's about alien fungus, and aside from one relatively small-scale protest in Century Square (the ex-president of Denmark, a notorious fascist, was rumoured to be holed up in the Palace hotel, hosting lavish parties for his one-time acolytes) the Conquest was simply the Conquest, beacon of post-war enlightenment, a paean to progress. A symphony, as one noted architectural critic had described it, in black and silver. As a news story, the Conquest was about as interesting as warmed-over hash. The ship had sailed.

'As an architect and a businessman, how do you keep yourself motivated when you have arguably already achieved your greatest ambition?'

Archie was asked this question so often he had stopped giving interviews. Journalists, he found increasingly, were no longer interested in documenting his success story because its details were so familiar they had ceased to be interesting. What they hankered after now was its inverse, the disastrous excess and tragic fall of success's aftermath: substance abuse, financial mismanagement, relationship drama. If they failed to unearth a scandal they would settle instead for a mental breakdown, the creeping ennui and creative decline that was surely inevitable, they prodded and hinted, now the battle for Century City was fought and won.

In fact, five years on from the gala opening, Archie's mental health and strength of ambition were as vigorous as ever. He had no time to dwell on what kept him motivated because there was so much to do, and – his passion for single malt aside – he had never had much of an appetite for drink or drugs. At the present moment, he told the young reporter from the *New York Post* who had somehow wormed her way through his defences, he was high enough on expectation as he waited for news of Century Architects' next big commission. The Red Tower would in fact be a black tower, a stone-for-stone reproduction of the Conquest, built entirely from Gliesian masonite. The building was to be erected on the foundations of the bombed-out Saint Basil's Cathedral on Moscow's Red Square.

The Russian president, Ludmilla Belayeva, had stayed at the Conquest as a personal guest of President Rogerson. Not long after her visit, Century Architects received an official approach from the Russian government. The months following the pitch meeting seemed to inch by as Archie waited for confirmation that the project was to go ahead. His source in the Kremlin assured him there was nothing to worry about, that factional infighting was part of the process, that all the pieces would fall into place by the end of the year.

The source turned out to be correct, though that did little to relieve Archie's anxiety at the time. The first of his dreams – a phantasmagorical nightmare in which Ludmilla Belayeva skated across Red Square in a blizzard before transforming into a giant glass replica of herself – came in October. The month was unseasonably cold; a story about an abandoned baby found frozen solid at the Washington bus depot dominated the headlines for most of a week. Seen within that general context of freak happenings and general disquiet, Archie's nightmare made perfect sense, only two or three nights later he had another that made no sense at all.

In the dream, Archie found himself running through a landscape of soot and ash and partially destroyed buildings. The sky was a glaring red, and he was dragging a child by the hand, a child he called by its name as he tried to encourage it, to entreat it to run faster, a child he loved with all the gut-churning, terrified strength of a father in peril.

Archie had no child, he had no siblings even and yet this boy, this boy whose hand he held, meant the world to him and more.

The boy was crying for his mother, which was useless, utterly pointless because his mother was dead. Archie knew he would have to tell the boy the truth eventually, that he would have to bring his son's world to an end a second time. The knowledge seared his soul like fire and for an instant he wished – desired it fervently – that he had died in the bombardment. Better still, that the boy had died too, for how could any child survive in this hell without its father?

The alien soldiers were smoking out the survivors. Forcing them from the caves with their flamethrowers, their poison gas and vacuum pumps, gunning them down like rats amidst the tumbled, shattered remnants of their own city. To the alien soldiers they were no more than vermin to be destroyed. Archie knew he and the child could not hold out much longer in any case, with or without the shooting and the bombs. Not unless they found water and shelter at least. Not unless they could discover a way to leave the city.

The war, the bloody war, Archie thought, the words thudding in his brain like drumbeats as he struggled out of sleep. As if his waking life was nothing, a thoughtless joke. In a terrified part of his dream-self he found he even believed this, that his dream was not a dream but a feverish, sordid glimpse of the life he was living. That his brain, worn out from the horror, had constructed another reality for him to escape to. A world where the alien invasion had never happened. A reality where he sat in expensive restaurants sparring with friends. An existence in which his lover was a famous film maker, in which his press agent called him at all hours, seeking his opinion on the final, decorative touches to their latest propaganda.

A world in which his secretary and personal assistant was a competent, tolerant saint named Sidney Kruger. Where he himself, Archimbaud Aspen, was the monarch of all he surveyed.

Waking was not so much waking as a recovery of self. He lay on his back with his eyes shut, a swimmer half-dead from fatigue, hauling himself on to the rocks from the waters below, the scene so clear in his mind he could taste the salt. In the moments before he opened his eyes, Archie felt sure that when he did open them, he would not be looking out upon his bedroom in the Conquest – its floorboards reclaimed from an antique Dutch barge, its silken curtains of a blue so magnetic that opening them had the feeling of pulling back the sky – but the raw rock ceiling of the cave in which he was sheltering with his son, their one piece of luck the stripe of cold-coal, shimmering black as velvet in the cavern's back wall.

They would not freeze this night at least, they might recover some strength. And all at once he was not the man and not the father nonot-atall but the slumbering warmth of rock beneath the boy's bird-breath body. The almost-spent son, the boy with his fingers upon me, his palms outstretched. Cheek and body pressed so tight upon my breast, glimmer of tears against glimmer of stone, silver in the rock like crystal in the boy and yea I will comfort ye, comfort me my people for ye are of this place and of this planet and we shall go forth from it together and we shall purify we shall be free . . .

Archie jerked awake. His pulse was racing, his armpits brimming in sweat. The first thing he saw as he opened his eyes was the bedside alarm clock: 9:40. Beside it stood the glass of green tea he remembered Norrie bringing him before she left the apartment. She was filming today, Archie knew that, she was spending the night at her own apartment as she did occasionally because it was closer to where she needed to be for the rest of the day.

The tea was stone cold. His thinking still seemed sluggish and distorted. Archie Aspen never slept past 7:30, it just didn't happen. He must have woken briefly then fallen back into his dream, and of course he had dreamed of Gliese because Norrie was filming today, she was filming her soldiers.

Archie felt himself relax, his heartbeat gradually slowing. He showered and shaved in a hurry – Sid Kruger would be calling at ten as usual with the overnight report. With any luck there would be news from Russia and they could all get off their asses, book the necessary flights. He put on a suit – cream linen – and switched on the coffee machine. He was just pouring his first cup of the day when Sid's call came through. From the moment Sid's face appeared on the screen Archie knew his hunch had been correct: the Russians had sluiced their shit from the pipes and finally Hallelujah they were in business.

There was a plant called lithops, a variety of succulent that thrived in the arid grasslands of southern Africa. The common name for the plant was living stone. Archie knew what lithops looked like – his maternal aunt had grown cacti and succulents in a glass-roofed lean-to at the back of her apartment. Small, squat, pebble-like, they barely looked like plants at all and yet, his aunt had told him, the succulents were growing, they were alive.

In the autumn, Archie read, *the lithops put out flowers, which require cross-pollination from another plant to form a fruiting body. The lithops' seed sac opens in response to rainfall. For the remainder of the year, the plant's naturally speckled surface helps it blend invisibly with its environment.*

A Dutch postgraduate student had plagiarised and collated a number of previously published papers on lithops succulents, weaponising them in support of his crackpot theory, that masonite was not a rock at all, but a species of plant. His so-called essay, published in a subscribers-only magazine for UFO enthusiasts (*this gets better and better,* Sid Kruger had scribbled on another of his yellow Post-Its) had attracted a long and entertaining stream of letters and comments, many of them making reference to obscure works of science fiction from the twentieth century, though a significant number appeared to take the piece at face value. One of them even mentioned the Miranda Calvi piece in *The Western Wind.*

They know all about it, but no one's talking, the respondent insisted. *There are plenty saying the Conquest should be demolished, even from within the government, but the legal guys won't have it. They say the building's insurers wouldn't pay out, so all you paranoid alien-watchers can go screw yourselves.*

In the mainstream press, Century City had by this time carved out a niche for itself as the byword for financial impropriety, political intrigue and celebrity scandal, none of which was bad for business, quite the opposite. In its claims and counter-claims, its exclusives and libellous exposés, the media was a ready and constant provider of free advertising. There was even a soap opera called *The Tower*, set in a shiny new high-rise in which three rival business dynasties vied to gain a controlling stake in the domestic economy, all played out against the backdrop of their cross-party love affairs, family secrets and political betrayals. The series had become so addictive, so ubiquitous a reference within popular culture, that residents of the real-life tower were constantly angling for cameo roles in it, even those who normally steered well clear of the media spotlight.

Archie himself was rarely a focus. He had never been one for the party circuit and aside from occasional outside meetings with important clients he spent most of his business hours yo-yoing boringly back and forth between the penthouse apartment and the Century offices. The Conquest Tower was home to a good number of individuals who were not only richer than Archie but who had few scruples about demonstrating the fact. Ostentatious consumption guaranteed publicity, as did dubious taste. The escalating feud between a telecoms tycoon and his former lover had the rumour mills spinning out of control on a twenty-four-hour cycle. The first high-profile murder at the Conquest – a political assassination disguised as a drugs killing – made headlines around the world. The city governors spent most of their first, hurriedly arranged meeting following the murder arguing and speculating over what effect the crime might have on real estate prices. Would tourists become suddenly anxious about security? Would there be an upswing in disadvantageous gossip about the prevalence of drug use?

Of course they did, and of course there was. But the effect of the murder overall was to send sales skyrocketing. The tourists were eager to see for themselves where the crime had taken place, and for those who could afford it, a Century City address now flaunted the gleaming patina of risk on top of the durable glow of respectability.

'I'm getting worried about you working there,' said Lex. 'You should tell him you won't do overnights. Not until the court case is settled and those guys are locked up.'

'No one gives a damn about me. Seriously,' said Sidney Kruger. 'I'm of less interest than the cleaning staff. The cleaning staff get to know stuff. I heard about a guy who works the elevator who made a tidy ten thousand the other week, just from telling some hack where she could find the refuse sacks from Apartment 2340. I'm Mr B for boring. Everyone knows who I am and no fucker cares.'

Apartment 2340 was the city residence of Irena Pagwame, the actor who had shot to fame in *The Tower* playing the lover of murdered Russian oligarch Oleg Kaminsky, and who it was rumoured was the real-life lover of real-life Russian oligarch Svetlana Nemirova. These relationships were complicated, Sid thought. It was difficult sometimes to remember who was real and who was a TV character, especially when you were up to your eyes trying to keep the lid on your boss's paranoia as well as everyone else's.

Sid felt surprised and touched by Lex's intervention. The word 'worried' did not often feature in her vocabulary and he had rarely heard her express her concern for him so openly. They both worked tough jobs – jobs in which a certain amount of in-house craziness was an occupational hazard. Lex's job was the riskier, a fact Sid preferred not to think about because what would be the point? Start obsessing about who might pull a gun on you and you'd lose your mind or go broke or both, probably in that order. Which was why there was also no point in telling Lex that so far as his own situation was concerned, things had been off recently, more so even than usual, not so much with the nutjobs as with the boss.

Archie Aspen was good to work for and always had been. The hours were crippling and the demands were high but the rewards were commensurate with that and – Sid didn't lie to himself – he enjoyed the buzz of being at the centre of things almost as much as he enjoyed the salary. He and Archie went back a long way. They were used to each other, which was why Sid was able to notice things others in Archie's orbit wouldn't pick up on. Like how Archie's legendary powers of concentration seemed somewhat lacking recently, an increasing propensity for small mistakes. Lapses of focus that were nothing in themselves – they were easily caught and covered for – but were worrying to Sid precisely because they wouldn't normally have happened.

Sid wondered if Archie was sick, or simply tired. Most likely the latter – yes, probably that was it, though Archie's exhaustion could hardly account for the accumulating strangeness of the tower itself. The feeling Sid sometimes had, that the building was listening to him, following his thoughts along the tracks of his veins, spreading through the meat of his brain like a goddamned nerve agent, that stuff they'd poisoned the Russian with, or maybe some kind of nano-weapon.

Was there such a thing as a nano-weapon, or were they just in the movies? Sid made a note to himself, to do some more research, because although they'd ordered that military-grade deep-clean in the wake of the murder, what with the shit that was out there these days there was always going to be a risk of contamination. Sid could never forget those scenes in *Aftermath*, that film Maguire had made about the soldiers after the war.

He shuddered, hoped Lex hadn't noticed. Sid always thought of the boss's girlfriend as Maguire – Maguire and never Norrie, Maguire as in the mob boss from the 2020s. He wondered if Stoner Maguire and Norrie Maguire were in any way related. Sid wouldn't be surprised if they were. Maguire was smart as a whip, still a good-looking woman too, and her pushing sixty. The boss had struck gold with that one, though Sid remembered he hadn't thought so at the time.

'I'm not talking about the job,' Lex was saying. 'I'm talking about the building.'

'The building? What do you mean, the building?' Sid was acting, he realised, playing himself in a movie, the dippy guy who's so wrapped up in his own shit he hasn't a clue what his wife is on about. He wondered why he didn't tell Lex the truth, admit to her that he was scared – because scared was what he was. That feeling of queasiness when he walked through the lobby, the moments of panic that threatened to overwhelm him at times – especially those times he'd queried something with Archie, some minor point of correspondence, or even what he wanted adding to the weekly food order, and Archie didn't seem to register. The time he'd caught sight of his own face in the elevator mirror and failed to recognise himself. Just for a second – a micro-second even – yet still it had happened.

The worst incident had been when he'd decided to take the back stairs, the eerily concealed fire escape stairs. Sid could not remember now why he had done this – something about not wanting to speak with the elevator guy – only that once he'd taken the decision it seemed impossible to go back on. In theory he could have keyed open the service door, stepped back into the building proper at any point, but he kept not doing it. One hundred and twenty floors he had climbed down and not one single other person had crossed his path. As if he was no longer inside the tower at all but in some other, secret realm.

Why had the service shaft seemed so dark when every fucking light was on? And the walls, those goddamned silver dots jumping and blurring like sparks of moonlight in a waterfall, rippling like scales, like the million diamond scales of a monster serpent.

Peristalsis – that was the word. Sid had come upon it recently, in one of those crackpot articles he'd clipped for Archie. Involuntary muscular contractions inside the body. Like when you swallowed, like in your intestines. *Not so much the action of glaciers, as peristalsis.*

The building's fucked, was how Sid would put it. Instead he raised his eyebrows as if to suggest his girlfriend was crazy.

They'd lasted more than a decade now, him and Lex. Sid experienced a sudden, bursting epiphany: his life was raked-over coal and she was a diamond.

Lex gave him a look. An appraising look, Sid reckoned, as in *are you for real?* 'The building's fucked,' she said. 'I can't say what it is that's wrong with it, but that building is fucked.'

'Well,' Sid said. He hesitated. 'I can tell him I need to cut back on the overnights. I'll say you need me around more. Because of the baby.'

'You didn't tell him yet, did you?' Lex had that look on her, the look he loved. The look that said you're a dick Sidney Kruger but you're my dick and I guess I'm stuck with you.

'He's been distracted lately. The Russia contract, you know. Now we've got the go-ahead things should start easing up.'

There would be a month in Moscow at least once they'd finalised the paperwork, then Sid would tell him, he'd give it to him straight. No more overnights.

Archie awoke in semi-darkness, the grey dawn light hazy about the cave's entrance, like the inverse of a shadow. The boy slept. When he awoke he would be hungry, Archie realised, and suddenly this was all he could think about – the boy's need, which he would try to conceal, his own burning awareness of what he knew the boy required but was powerless to give him. The ponderous question of what would be better, safer – to return to the city where they could find food or to continue walking into the scrublands, into the desert, where there was safety from the bombs but nothing to eat.

The choice tormented him because he could not decide. How could he decide, when making the wrong decision could mean the difference between life and death?

Sid had said something about a baby, Archie thought sleepily. Sid and Lex were having a baby? He turned over and woke up properly, his body responding to the change in cabin pressure that told him the pilot was preparing for their descent. They would be landing soon. The window shield was down and when Archie pressed the lever to release it, he saw Moscow spread out beneath them, the carpet of lights extending to the horizon.

The coffee machine was on, the dense, dark scent of Arabica filling the cabin. Sid had set the timer the evening before, and they had talked. Archie pondered their conversation, trying to work out if Alexis being pregnant was something real or part of his dream. He could not remember Sid mentioning a baby, exactly. Mostly they had spoken about Corey Drayton, about the class action Drayton's firm were bringing against Century Architects.

Recent scientific studies suggest . . . hazardous material . . . insufficient testing . . . far-reaching and irreversible damage to our native environment.

Drayton, who had teamed up with the fungi freaks somehow, was suing Archie on account of the wilful mishandling of an industrial biohazard. He was demanding that the Conquest be demolished.

All constituent materials to be made safe and isolated in perpetuity.

A spoiler action, Anders Thorrinsen insisted. The so-called scientific studies were nothing more than the arbitrary speculations of a bunch of cranks. Nothing peer-reviewed, nothing official, nothing MIT. Let Drayton waste his money. His efforts would come to nothing because there was no case.

Sid had seemed quiet, much quieter than usual. Because he was worried about the baby most likely, and about Lex, who was quite old to be having a baby, when you came to think about it. Corey Drayton would have to go, though. Archie saw the sense of this as he stepped into the shower, the truth of it washing over him, strafing him clean. They could not afford the bad publicity, especially not now, with the ink on the Moscow contract still wet, not even if Corey Drayton were a certified lunatic.

Archie towelled down, began to dress. He felt the crispness of his shirt against his skin, the raw silk with the integrated Paisley pattern concealed in the weft of the cloth like a lattice inside a crystal, a secret armature. Archie took pleasure in the shirt as a work of art, the satisfaction that arises from the contemplation of something well made, and wasn't the shirt in its way a symbol of everything he had worked for and made happen? Everything Corey Drayton believed he had the right to take away?

Already he found he could imagine the man's death, he could read the headlines: *OverTure defense lawyer dies tragically in motorcycle hit-and-run. Corey Drayton, son of the pioneering environmental campaigner Reena Drayton* . . . As if the accident itself had already happened. A surge of wellbeing flowed through him as the cabin's door-buzzer sounded and there was Sid, right on cue, telling him they would be landing in ten minutes.

'Collie's nagging me to get you belted in,' he said. Collie was Allison Collier, Archie's regular pilot. Cautious to a fault especially for ex-military but better safe than sorry and Collie was first-rate.

'Kiril and Martina are meeting us on the tarmac,' he added, 'so I guess we're on.'

Sid smiled, a rare gesture for Sid, and Archie smiled back. 'Thanks for remembering to put the coffee on,' he said, unnecessarily, because Sid always remembered to put the coffee on, but Archie knew he would accept the words as a cover-all thank you.

He straightened his tie, with its masonite tiepin, a single shard polished to such a high shine that whenever the sunlight struck it, it seemed to disappear. A thing of beauty is a joy forever, Archie mused. He thought of the boy, asleep in the cave, the curve of his cheek gleaming softly in the chalky dawn light. His heart fluttered for a moment in panic, then he remembered the boy wasn't real, that the boy being lost and hungry was none of his concern.

OVERTURE DEFENSE LAWYER DIES TRAGICALLY
IN MOTORCYCLE HIT-AND-RUN

Corey Drayton, son of pioneering environmental campaigner Reena Drayton, was killed on his way to work this
morning when struck by a motorcycle that briefly mounted
the pavement before speeding from the scene. Witnesses
looked on in horror as Drayton, 35, was thrown off his
feet and into the road. Police are appealing for information
about the identity of the driver, who has still not been traced.
Paramedics attending the incident pronounced Drayton,
familiar to millions through his appearances on Court TV,
dead at the scene.

There was a moment in which Sid Kruger let himself believe the lawyer's death had been an accident, a moment before he realised he had
to admit at least to himself the truth of what had happened: Archie
Aspen had ordered Drayton's murder. That is, he had ordered someone
to pay someone else to have Drayton killed. How Sid reacted to that
knowledge was up to him, but lying to himself about the fact of the
matter was not an option. Life was too weird already.

And what of the fact that Archie had decided to leave Sid out of it?
Had this been because Archie didn't trust him, or because he'd known
Sid would refuse? Having refused, he might become dangerous, and
then where would things end? Sid took a deep breath, took another.
By choosing not to involve him, had Archie been protecting him? As
an explanation for Archie's actions this had a ring of truth about it,

but that still left the question of who Archie had told, who he now trusted more than Sidney to get his business done.

Whoever this person was, would they be looking to put Sid out of the picture more permanently in the long run?

Palace schisms led to coups and thence to beheadings; it was the law of history.

Sid wondered what Lex would think. Tell him to keep well out of it probably, which was what he was doing, pretending he didn't know and hadn't guessed. Preserving the safety bubble he lived inside, where he knew what Archie was thinking and who was in control. Voice his suspicions, even to Alexis, and the bubble collapsed. The chaos and danger of what lurked outside would pour into the vacuum, sweeping him away.

'I'll be away for a while,' Norrie said. 'I've been thinking you could come with me.'

'To Arizona?'

'We've taken a ranch house and annex. The annex is a self-contained office suite. There's twenty acres. You'd have the run of the place.'

'With Moscow just getting started? You know that's not possible.'

'I know it's *possible* for you to run the Moscow operation from right here in your living room, so why not from there? You can be back in the city in less than a day in any case, if there's a problem. It would be good, you know, to have you around.'

Good for *them*, ran Norrie's subtext, he could trace the letters. Good for Archie to crawl out from under his desk and see what she got up to for a change. Good for Norrie to escape the nagging feeling of being a sideshow while he, Archie Aspen, got on with the real work. The idea that he could handle his job remotely – that he could operate out of some plank-built ranch house five miles down a gravel track out in the boondocks – well, it would be possible in an emergency, he guessed, but this wasn't an emergency. Archie in chinos and a plaid shirt, hair growing long over his collar? How was that going to be parsed by the people in Moscow?

'Sid can deal with the day-to-day stuff,' Norrie was saying, like she could read his mind, see straight into his soul, a quality of hers he'd come to depend on but that was beginning to seem more like a weapon, a piece of technology she'd stolen and utilised against him. 'You can manage a fortnight, surely?'

'Sid,' Archie said, tasting the word, testing its substance, as if he had temporarily forgotten who Sid was. Sid was Sidney Kruger of course, whom he had known for more than half his lifetime and who others in his entourage had secretly nicknamed the Phantom Limb. Archie was not supposed to know this but he did know, as he knew everything that happened around him, all the more so since the building. And wasn't the truth of it that Archie was afraid to leave the building? Of course he could *leave*, as in go to a restaurant or the opera or the city library, the new assembly hall he was designing on Fifth, the reception he was supposed to be attending for the Saudi ambassador. He could leave as in walk out the door but the thought the very idea of existing in a different time zone from the building, for a fortnight and *for no discernible reason* made the pegs inside his mind begin to loosen. As if whole aspects of himself were coming adrift, releasing themselves from their moorings and unspooling inside his brain.

At night, the walls between himself and the tower's other occupants – the captains of industry, the A-list celebrities, the failed heads of state, the bankers the shipbuilders the oilmen, the squabbling Mafiosi picking over the corpses of all the above – began to shift and bleed. They were all in this together, Archie thought, bonded, and Archie considered the many and disparate meanings of the term bonded, which encompassed truth and connection and imprisonment, the elective relinquishment of freedom for the greater gain. The gain meaning the building, which he, Archimbaud Aspen, had conceived and built. What greater bond could there be than that which existed between the architect and his building, between the creator and the world he had imagined where no one else could?

This project of Norrie's – the reason she had chosen to be in Arizona squatting in a ranch house for weeks on end – the exchange programme between post-traumatic soldiers and their counterparts on Gliese. Archie could never say so but the thought of Norrie's project – no not the project as such but *them*, the soldiers, the alien soldiers who were coming who were coming *here* – triggered involuntary convulsions (peristalsis) in the pit of his stomach.

Like he wanted to vomit, only he had to resist it, and this straining of his body against its nature was like being compelled to ingest something repulsive, forced to eat shit.

'Will they be bringing the boy with them?' Archie asked her suddenly, the words bursting from his mouth like effluent, a warm and gritty spew he found he could not keep down for another second.

'The boy? What boy? Do you mean Lex's baby?' Norrie furrowed her brow, and there was a part of him that knew he would have to destroy her just for being in the room, for bearing witness to his disgrace, for *overhearing*.

'The lad you mentioned,' he mumbled. 'The lad who's into photography. The apprentice.' He spoke the words patiently, with just a hint of irritation, half-convinced and then fully convinced that sufficient focus on the idea of such a creature as this apprentice would be enough to bring that creature into being. 'You said he was keen to join the project. For work experience.'

'Maybe,' Norrie said. She was still frowning, stalling, though the concern on her face had faded into uncertainty. Reassured, Archie's mind drifted to the woman, Arianna Fulci, who had taken the apartment on the floor below his, the apartment recently vacated by Anthony Maupassant, the chair and billionaire sponsor of the failing *New York Times*.

Maupassant had committed suicide, or at least that was the story, the version that flowed out into the world via the various sewage outlets, up to and including his own paper. Suicide while the balance of his mind was disturbed, and Arianna Fulci, chair of Arcadia Holdings and Archie's old rival, had taken the showstopper apartment, swooped in to claim it like the vulture she was, 'for an undisclosed sum'.

At the party she had thrown to celebrate her new acquisition, Fulci had worn a masonite collar, the heavily faceted tiles suspended like blocks of jet nothingness in a platinum net, cradling her neck in its glittering embrace like a protecting hand.

'I guess this means we're even,' Fulci had said to him. When she smiled he saw one of her incisors had a diamond stud. 'Let bygones be bygones?'

Archie's cock was stiff as granite at the memory. He turned away towards his desk and then sat down.

'Well, think about it at least,' Norrie said. 'The way you've been working lately I'd say you're due a break. I can't stay over tonight,' she added. 'The rest of this week, actually. There's a ton of shit to organise before I fly out.'

Archie stared at her without speaking, and as she moved towards the door he found himself noticing how her gait had changed. The confidence had gone, he realised. She was lighter on her feet now, more skittish. As if she was trying not to be noticed. As if she was afraid.

There are things people don't understand unless they live in the tower, Fulci said. Things they can't process, not properly. It's good that we understand this, that we're all in it together.

'As if we've come home,' she added. 'Can't you feel it?'

The curtains were pulled back, the sky beyond the windows ablaze with stars. The covers had slipped from the bed, lay pooled on the polished floorboards, dark and faintly glimmering as a minor oil spill. Fulci's fingers on his naked body were not fingers but light years, the distance between them bridged by the lingering touch of flesh on flesh.

The distance was endless, and yet he could cross it in less than a second when he went inside her. He was both here, and also there. The boundary between where his body resided and the place of the cave had ceased to exist.

'I feel it,' Archie whispered. He missed Norrie. More even than Norrie he missed Sidney, whom he could not remember having spoken to in several days. Strange shapes hovered in the neighbouring room, barely out of sight. My son, he thought confusedly. The boy has come home.

The walls shimmered. The stone spoke to him more clearly with each day that passed. There were times he hated Fulci, hated her web inside him, but those moments were only moments, dark spots amidst the shining silver and barely there.

He lay beside her on the rumpled sheet, the brief distance between their bodies seething with mute attraction like the charged and potent space between two magnets. As he floated towards sleep, he found himself thinking about his great-grandmother, who he had never met, though his father, the first of the Aspens to be born in America, had shown him photographs: an upright, stern-looking teacher from a town in the north of Scotland, on the Dornoch Firth. Her name was Helen Stone. She had written books on the town's history and on the local geology. Archie, who had read the books, who had been to considerable trouble to track the books down, remembered a passage in which his great-grandmother described the town as a sanctuary, where those fleeing persecution had once been offered protection by the Church of St Duthac.

Dissenters, heretics, aliens, all have been welcomed. As Scotland's oldest burgh, the town first gained its royal charter in 1066. The oldest buildings on our High Street are repositories of ancient history and sacred memory. The stone that built the town was quarried from the very hillside that overlooks the firth. An isolate place, yet a place that can boast connections with centres of higher learning throughout the British Isles and far beyond. On a winter evening, the weary traveller will be assured of a hearty welcome at the Royal Hotel, a fine, centuries-old edifice that, like all coaching inns, boasts its own fund of myths and legends, its own roster of the criminal and the sainted, the cruelly murdered and mysteriously disappeared. The light of the firth in summer has a quality of magic, a brightness one might almost imagine to be the light of another world. There are stories about the town that suggest its destiny as a seat of revolution is yet to be fulfilled.

Helen, Helen Stone, who spent her summers camping in the mountains, recording her observations of the Highland ecology. Towards the end of her life, Archie's father had told him, Helen had begun to go off the rails a bit.

'She believed there was an alien artefact buried in the forest,' he said. 'She kept wandering off, trying to look for it. She couldn't walk so far by then but she would never give up the search. That's what I call steadfast.'

He had spoken of her with affection, Archie remembered, Granny Stone and her search for the great white whale. I can see her in you, you know, he had insisted. It's as if there's always something more out there, driving you both. A light in the storm.

The light between stars leaves no blackness, Archie mused. The sooner the world comes to know this the sooner we will be one.

'I haven't been able to reach him,' Norrie said. 'Not since last week.'

'Right,' Sid replied. He wasn't sure what he should say to her, how much she knew.

'Should I fly home, do you think?'

'No,' Sid said quickly. 'I think it's best you stay where you are.' Safer, was what he meant, although safety was relative, becoming more relative by the day, a fact many sensed in their bones but were loath to admit.

'Well, OK, if you say so.' Her voice wavered, uncertain, and Sid dreaded she might ask him something else, something about Archie, the kind of question he had decided in advance he would not answer. But when she spoke again it was about the lawyer's widow.

'I did hear from Marie,' she said. 'Marie Drayton.'

'Yeah?' Sid waited for her to go on, wishing he'd thought to disable the video link. He wondered how he looked to her, whether the freshly pressed shirt and neatly trimmed beard were an adequate disguise.

Things are bad here, he had said to Lex, just before he insisted she and Caleb get out of the city. They'd had a row and she had called him a blowhard but in the end she had agreed. Not because she was ready to start taking orders, from him or from any man, but because she was afraid.

Shit, Sid was afraid. There were moments – a fucking avalanche of them, if he were being honest – when he wondered what in the name of hell he was still doing here.

'Marie said – she said she might fly down, have a talk.'

'That sounds like a plan,' Sid replied. 'What did you tell her?'

'I told her she should come.'

'Good,' Sid said. 'That's good. Will you keep me updated?'

'I'll do that,' Norrie answered. She fell silent, her image flickering on the poor connection. The sight of her was both reassuring and sad, Sid thought, like sifting through last year's news, celebrations and disasters and scandals that happened so long ago they no longer mattered. Norrie Maguire was brave – brave like Marie Drayton, brave like Alexis.

Sid wondered what next year's news would look like, assuming there was any.

He found himself strangely reluctant to end the call.

CHACONNE

YEHUDI MENUHIN DESCRIBED THE Bach Chaconne as the greatest work for solo violin that has ever been written. His own account is rock solid, lush with elements of the fantastic that lift it way above the average – this is Yehudi Menuhin we are talking about – though personally Robin prefers Nathan Milstein's reading, the one he put down in 1973 for Deutsche Grammophon. Milstein shares Menuhin's rigorous approach to structure but combined with a grittiness, a harder edge Robin likes better, those iron-clad downstrokes, like scaffolding poles, like the rusted cast-iron bars around a mausoleum.

Of the modern recordings the one Robin returns to most often is Gidon Kremer's for ECM (2005). She has seen Kremer's playing described as cold, his technique so icily sure of itself as to preclude emotion, though what comes through for Robin is his sense of adventure, his disregard for convention and even propriety. His performance of the Bach Chaconne is a controlled demolition, a taking apart and then putting together, a practical demonstration of the art of construction. Kremer meditates and then revises, staking out the original dance steps before dismantling them, showing how the simplest, most quotidian thesis might through a process of rigorous enhancement become profound.

At around the ten-minute mark he appears to lose interest in his own argument, spiralling off into another universe, conversing privately with his instrument as if he has forgotten he is being recorded or even listened to. The final quarter of the ciacona – Robin has read that Bach preferred the Italian form of the term – is like an improvised fantasia, with the same heretical relationship to the original dance rhythm as Chopin's transfiguration of the polonaise in his Opus 61.

Robin closes her eyes, the music insinuating itself into her thought processes like a silver fish hook as she imagines Miles Shipley following Frank Landau following Edmund de Groote. Like the blind leading the blind, all chasing some crazy baseless theory about an interstellar war.

The war and again the war, Robin keeps coming back to it, the idea moving in circles, infinitely repeating like a painted wooden stallion on a fairground carousel. Since returning from Scarborough she has found herself unable to decide if Miles Shipley's involvement in Frank's case is relevant or a blind alley. She telephones Rachel and tells her Shipley would probably have called her if he hadn't died first. He had your phone number, she says, Michael must have given it to him.

Michael?

Yes, Robin says. I spoke with one of the room attendants. She said she saw Shipley talking to Michael in the bar. Which means I'll need to speak to Michael. Shipley might have told him something.

Wouldn't Michael have said, if he had?

He might not realise. People don't always realise which information is important. Also, Michael is likely to have been one of the last people to speak to Shipley. He might have picked up on something.

Talking to Michael is also essential for another reason. Everything Robin knows about Frank so far has been filtered through Rachel. She needs an alternative viewpoint, another snapshot. She asks Rachel if she has Michael's number handy and Rachel reads it out, hesitating several times as if she is unhappy at the idea of passing it over.

I haven't told him, she says in the end. That I've spoken to you, I mean. That I've asked you to look into Frank's case.

You think he would be against it?

I don't think so. I like Michael. We always got on. Rachel hesitates. It's just we don't often speak now. We were in touch a lot in the beginning, after Frank went missing, but not any more.

Because there is nothing left to say, Robin thinks, just the same things over and over, the endless reiteration of final impressions and last words, the sharing of memories that feels constructive in the early days but comes to seem pointless, an empty mockery, almost a lie, as if the moments being described never actually happened. Robin has seen the scenario play out a hundred times, the corrosive effect of a person's absence on those who remain.

Would you like to meet up later in the week? Robin says. I could give you an update.

Her teeth are chattering, as if this has been the point of the call all along, not to get hold of Michael's number but to ask out Rachel, an act that feels beyond the pale even as Robin asks herself what's so bad about meeting up with a client, how wrong can it be?

I'd like that, Rachel is saying. The waiting feels easier if you tell me stuff. Even if there's nothing to tell I like hearing you explain how you work. Does that make sense?

Rachel laughs, and Robin imagines her hands, the way they are, she has such small hands Rachel does, beautifully manicured, gold varnish on her fingernails.

Not everyone can take gold nail varnish but Rachel can, like the Caspar David Friedrich in its worn gilt frame, a masterpiece of European mysticism in a shoddy gilt frame, abstruse and unique.

I didn't see him before he went, Michael says. I never said goodbye. That's what gets to me. I was out with Rafik – that's my boyfriend – and I stayed over at his place. I'd forgotten Frank would be leaving first thing in the morning. I wasn't thinking about Frank at all. I know it's stupid to blame myself but I can't help it. I feel I should have looked out for him more. Frank had his head so far up in the clouds sometimes he never saw the trouble that was right in front of him.

No one really got Frank, the doctors especially. I met Dr Browne and he's a good guy but straight, you know? He does everything by the book. Michael laughs. Frank was many things but by the book wasn't one of them. Frank lived through his imagination, and I mean literally. There's this idea about mental illness, that people like Frank must be dangerous because they can't always tell what's real and what's just in their head. But mostly it's the opposite – people like Frank aren't dangerous, they are in danger. Frank believed some weird stuff but that is the point – he believed. He always spoke the truth, so he didn't always understand when people were lying to him. I hate to think what he might have walked into, who he got mixed up with.

Frank drove me nuts sometimes but he's my brother and I love him. He never stood still, Frank. His mind was always working overtime, trying to figure things out.

Michael Landau is slim in build, denim jacket – most likely the same denim jacket he'd been wearing when he was in Scarborough talking with Shipley – skinny wrists sticking out like poles from the buttoned-up sleeves. He is seated opposite Robin at the café table, a funny little place called Reuben's, half greasy spoon, half bagel bar not far from where Michael lives with his boyfriend off Lewisham Way. He moved out not long after Frank went missing, Michael has told her. He and Rafik had been planning on getting their own place for a while. For ages, really.

It seemed like the right time, Michael says. I know this might sound strange, but losing Frank made it seem more urgent, not less – you never know, do you, how much time you're going to get. Faith's still living at home so it's not like Mum's on her own or anything and Raf and I are only down the road. God, Michael says. He wipes his mouth with the back of his hand. I hate the way I've started talking about him as if he's not coming back.

Robin has never seen Frank in the flesh of course but going by the photographs she is startled by how alike the brothers are: the rangi-ness, the slope of the shoulders, the wheat-coloured hair. The vibe they give off is different, though. Michael seems more present, more solidly grounded, more coloured-in. Frank in the photos looks nervous and pale, adrift somehow. Robin realises suddenly who Frank Landau reminds her of – the homeless man, the guy Alec Dunbar sent her to interview about the Sidcup railway murder, not long before everything went pear-shaped and Robin resigned. Dunbar was convinced the homeless guy knew something, had seen something. Thought a woman cop might get him to talk where his usual strong-arm tactics had hit a brick wall.

The Sidcup case had been horrible, the grimmest, and Robin still prefers not to think about it especially in the light of everything that followed.

The homeless man, though. There had been something about him, something that nagged at her. A fortnight later she'd been back to check on him but he had vanished. None of the other homeless on that patch knew where he'd disappeared to — either that or they weren't saying, and given the treatment they'd received from Dunbar, who could blame them.

Is that how you think of Frank, she says to Michael, in the past tense? Brutal but Michael can take it. He has learned to be resilient, Robin can tell. She guesses he has had to.

No, Michael says. He shakes his head. It's a habit you get into, a way of speaking. But if Frank was dead I'd know. He's my brother.

Would you say you were close as children?

We've always been close. Frank looked out for me when we were kids, on the estate and that. Then when Frank got ill, we kind of swapped places. Frank's five years older than me but it came to seem like the opposite, like I was the older brother.

Did he confide in you?

About what?

His beliefs? His worries, his state of mind?

Frank lived in his own world, mainly. Michael looks uncertain and vaguely uncomfortable. Most of the times we were together we'd chat about normal stuff. Films or games or books we were into, what we were doing at the weekend, work maybe. Frank was always telling funny stories about the people he did jobs for. He'd come out with Raf and me now and again – Raf and Frank got on great so no worries there. You know what it's like in families – there are certain subjects you know to steer clear of. Frank was OK a lot of the time but he was easily upset. There was always the thought at the back of your mind, the fear he'd get sick again.

I tried not to think about it, if I'm honest, all the weird shit Frank was into. I could never get my head round it, the way he could be perfectly normal, sitting there having a pint and laughing about some show he'd seen on TV and yet all the time he'd be having these thoughts, these beliefs that stood completely outside the way most people see the world. As if I didn't really know him – not just me, all of us. Maybe Rachel knew him better, but Rachel and I didn't talk about any of that stuff, either. We both loved Frank, that was all that mattered to us. Now you see why I can't stop blaming myself. I should have taken more notice, but I didn't want to face up to the fact that my brother had real problems – problems that needed sorting. Too much of a coward, I guess. It was the same with that journalist – Miles. He asked me a whole load of questions and I could barely answer any of them.

Tell me about Miles Shipley, Robin says. She is fascinated by him, she realises, not Michael himself so much as his likeness to Frank – his form, his mannerisms, as if Frank were speaking through him as through a two-way mirror. How did he first get in touch with you?

He contacted Mum, by email. About three months after Frank

went missing. He said he was looking into Frank's case for an article he was writing about online grooming. Mum was upset. Because it was so out of the blue, I think. She wanted to know how come this guy had our contact details, how he knew about Frank. I told her it was most likely through the forums and that I'd deal with it, tell him to back off if necessary. I was expecting Miles Shipley to be a sleazy tabloid reporter but he wasn't like that at all. As soon as I spoke to him I realised he was serious about wanting to find out what happened to Frank, to look into his story, which is why I agreed to an interview. He said he'd be in Scarborough that weekend for the UFO conference and could we meet up there. I didn't say anything to Mum because I didn't want to get her hopes up but I felt elated. Finally someone was interested. Finally someone seemed to believe what we'd been saying all along – that Frank had been lured away against his will, that he was genuinely missing.

So you went up to Scarborough as agreed?

Michael nodded. Raf wanted to come with me but I told him no, it would be better if I went by myself, less complicated. I promised to call him immediately if anything seemed dodgy but then that depends on what you call dodgy, doesn't it? I went to some of the talks while I was up there. I'd never been to an event like that and I was curious, plus I thought it might help me understand – where Frank was coming from I mean – but if anything it was the opposite. The thing that got to me most was the way the speakers seemed to take it for granted that everyone in the audience thought the same way they did, that they all knew the truth and anyone who didn't agree with them was either an idiot sheep or part of the conspiracy. And they all looked so normal – dull. See any of them on the street and you wouldn't look twice. And of course I couldn't help wondering what Frank would make of it all – if this was his world or what.

I went down to the dealers' room at one point. You wouldn't believe the number of books, DVDs, all pushing some theory about how we're living in a dream world, about how we're all puppets. I asked Miles Shipley if he thought people had always believed stuff like this or was it the internet and he told me once you started researching the subject you found there was no end to it. Conspiracy theories are as old as time, he said. What the internet mostly does is help the people who believe in them find one another more quickly.

How much time did you spend with him? Shipley?

Two hours maybe? We met in the bar around midday on the Saturday and then we had lunch together in a pub around the corner. He said it would be easier for us to talk away from the hotel. He wanted to know about the people in Paris, the people Frank met through that forum. Where they lived, what they did, which of them Frank was supposed to be staying with when he went over. I got the idea he might have been afraid of them – Shipley. Afraid they'd find out he'd been investigating them and come after him.

What made you think that?

I don't know. Just a feeling. Maybe the way he insisted on going to the pub rather than staying in the hotel. He needn't have worried anyway because I had nothing to tell him. It's like I said before – there was a side of my brother I knew nothing about. It never occurred to me to ask Frank where he'd be staying – not when he had a mobile. I remember Mum reminding him to pack his phone charger.

And did he?

Mum says he did, that the charger was gone from his room, anyway. She says she first tried calling him on the Friday – that was two days after he left and she hadn't heard from him. She thought he'd at least text, let her know he'd arrived safely. The phone went straight to voicemail. She left a message asking him to call but she says she wasn't too concerned at that point because Frank could be like that, he'd get wrapped up in something and it wouldn't occur to him that people might be worried. But then Rachel turned up at our place on the Saturday, asking if we'd heard from him because she'd been trying to reach him, she'd left loads of messages but hadn't heard a word since he boarded the Eurostar. She was trying to hold it together but I could tell she'd been crying. This was when we started to panic. And the cops couldn't care less, not once they realised Frank was over eighteen. They made us feel like time-wasters.

He glances at her sharply and Robin has no trouble guessing what Michael is thinking: you used to be a cop so you should know. She understands his distress yet there is a part of her – the part that used to be a cop, no doubt – that feels frustrated by how little she has learned. Everything Michael has told her she knows already. Did Shipley tell you what he was working on, she asks, why he became interested in Frank in the first place?

He said he was researching a book. I asked him if he meant the grooming thing, what he'd said in his email, and he said that was part of it, but his main focus was conspiracy theories, why people and especially young people get drawn into them. He said conspiracy theories were the new religion. I asked him how come he knew about Frank going missing and he clammed right up. He said that as a journalist he had to protect his sources. I wondered then if he knew someone in the police. I didn't push it, couldn't see the point. I'd been hoping he might have something to tell me – information about Frank – but he seemed as much in the dark about everything as I was.

Did he happen to mention the name de Groote? Edmund de Groote?

Eddie, the guy from the forum? Not that I remember.

Did you know de Groote was at the conference?

He was in Scarborough? You're joking. Michael falls silent, stares down at his hands. Do you think Shipley spoke to him?

I'm sure he did. I think de Groote was probably the reason Shipley was even there.

But then Shipley turns up dead.

It's best not to read too much into that. Shipley died of a heart attack.

It's hard not to read something into it. From where I'm sitting.

They meet each other's eyes and Robin thinks how if this were a spy movie this is the moment they would choose to join forces, the missing man's brother and the disgraced cop. Former cop. She lets out her breath.

Do you think he could be dangerous, this Eddie? Michael is saying.

I can't see it, somehow. He's a lecturer in film studies. Until we know for certain that Frank actually met with de Groote in Paris there's no proof he was involved.

What does Rachel think?

You'll have to ask her.

Is she doing OK? Rachel?

She's managing. She says she's thinking about enrolling on a teacher training programme.

That's great. Michael smiles, for the first time really since they sat down together, and Robin finds herself thinking again how much like Frank he looks. Frank in the photo Doris Akele found in Miles Shipley's wardrobe, Frank happy and shy and smiling and in love.

In an article he wrote for Unsolved magazine, Miles Shipley describes how from the Enlightenment onwards, philosophers and political scientists began to argue against religion as a founding principle of the progressive society. Belief in a god stopped you thinking for yourself, while fear of god enabled those in power to oppress the toiling multitudes – not for nothing does Karl Marx denigrate religion as the opium of the people. The more religious faith declined, so went their theory, the more you would begin to see a new, equitable, universal system of values based around justice and scientific evidence and established facts.

In fact, Shipley maintains, the opposite has happened. The decline of religion and the rise of the secular society has led to the fragmentation of established belief systems into a multitude of micro-faiths: spontaneous amalgamations of pseudoscience, cod philosophy and conspiracy theory that appear to tap into the same reservoirs of popular extremism, moral rectitude and abnegation of intellect as any of the more established religions and with a similar proliferation of factions and hierarchies. Conspiracy theories are the new religion, Miles Shipley argues, a set of postmodern belief systems founded upon arcane mysticism.

Robin spends hours reading through Miles Shipley's archive, more than a hundred online articles on everything from illegal pesticides to cargo cults, searching for hints about where his research might have been leading him. She is looking for a pattern, something that will link the slew of features and profiles and interviews with the photographs of refuse sites and abandoned power stations that were found in Shipley's hotel room after he died.

She scans the articles repeatedly for any mention of Edmund de Groote. She wonders if the name meant anything to Shipley other than the tentative link with Frank Landau, whether he was aware of its associations with organised crime. To anyone with an interest in London's ganglands, the name de Groote is as notorious and as fascinating as Richardson or Kray.

Robin is worried there is a chance her own knowledge of the de Grootes is pulling her off track. De Groote is just a name after all, with the same moral freight or lack of it as any other: Maxwell, Murdoch, Churchill, Brady, Kennedy, Cameron, Thatcher. She types de Groote into her search bar, clicks on the first dozen or so links, enough to tell her what she knows already, that de Grootes are everywhere: Julia, Michael, Olivier, Paul, Isabelle, dancer, cellist, solicitor, lecturer, beauty therapist, all of them de Grootes, all of them nothing to do with anything. Should she go on? According to Wikipedia, de Groote is a common Dutch surname meaning 'the great'; common alternative spellings include Degroote or Degroot as well as the shorter form Groot. The name occurs most abundantly in Flanders but as would be obvious from the most cursory examination of the search results, there are de Grootes to be found in profusion all over the world.

What if Frank's disappearance has nothing to do with de Groote or with any of the Paris people? Frank Landau is a vulnerable individual. He has generalised anxiety disorder, with several lengthy residential stays in mental health institutions. He was travelling alone in a foreign country and might easily have become upset or disorientated. What if Frank collapsed and ended up in hospital or even in a police station with no memory of who he was or where he came from? Unlikely perhaps, but possible – at least as possible as him being abducted by a UFO cult.

Robin wonders if the police ever thought to ring around the hospitals, liaise with their counterparts in Paris on the off-chance they had an unidentified British male in custody on a drunk and disorderly, the simplest, most obvious checks, although the idea of Frank disturbing the peace seems pretty far-fetched. She experiences that strange, self-defeating impulse she has occasionally, to call up Alec Dunbar and ask his opinion. Dunbar's a bastard but he's a fine detective, the kind that gets away with murder. Gets away with anything he damn well chooses because his team will stand by him whatever, because the suits are so in love with his solve rate they'll look the other way.

Types like Dunbar always fall in the end but never soon enough. She nips the impulse in the bud, calls Dianne instead, asks if she can come round for supper. Dianne does them scrambled eggs with bacon and her own home-made latkes. One of the fluorescent bulbs is flickering slightly, that familiar low-key humming sound, and the normality of the scene, of being back in Dianne's kitchen, makes Robin feel pissed off with herself all over again for having caused them so much grief when there is plenty of grief to choose from as it is. Just because the world's a toilet disnae mean ye have tae shit in it, as Dunbar would say.

There's this case I'm working on, she says. She wipes up the last of her egg with a forkful of latkes. She has not discussed cases with Dianne before, not really, it was always Ash she turned to first, the two of them sitting up till all hours raking over the possibilities even though Robin knew it was out of order to take work home with her and if the habit ever came to light most likely actionable. Seriously though, who gave a shit? She told Ash stuff anyway because her dislike of being told what to do has always outstripped her respect for the letter of the law. Yet one more reason she is an ex-cop and not standing in line for her sergeant's stripes even as she turns over the memory in her mind.

She feels a weariness tug at her chest, though whether this has to do with Ashley or Dunbar or Rachel she cannot say. She tells Dianne about Frank, about Rachel hiring her to look for Frank, filling in the background, paring back the detail, careful not to mention Eddie de Groote or at least not by name. In this sanitised version of events he is the college lecturer. There is a pleasure and a satisfaction in giving them all Cluedo names: the college lecturer, the missing person, the girlfriend, the room attendant, the journalist. The case seems tidier that way, more open to solutions, who did what to whom. Means, motive, opportunity, those old-school lecture notes.

I'd look on the forums if I were you, Dianne says. She is stacking the plates. If Frank is still in Paris someone on the forum will know about it. And people talk.

Robin remembers something Milan Harwicz said about how most detective work could now be done without putting your shoes on. If she'd told him more about the case he would have made the same suggestion as Dianne probably, asked Robin what she was doing haring off to Scarborough after Miles Shipley when she would have made more progress following Frank's digital back-trail. She wonders why she has neglected the forums until now.

Did you talk over cases like this with Dad? she asks Dianne.

Sometimes, Dianne says. When we were younger, before we had you. A lot of the cases I handled for social services ended up in the courts. Me and your dad, we'd often find ourselves having to deal with the same people, members of the same family anyway. Cases like that don't always make it into the newspapers but when they do it's usually the social workers who get the blame. I was pleased to give it up. I wouldn't admit that to myself at the time but I know it's true. These UFO people you've been looking into, she adds, they're not dangerous, are they?

Robin shakes her head. The more I go over the facts, the more I feel convinced Frank's disappearance is random. That he's had another breakdown. The stuff about supersoldiers is a red herring. So is Miles Shipley.

What about that note Shipley made, though, about Frank being spotted in Inverness?

False sightings are an occupational hazard. They used to drive us mad when I was on the squad because every single one of them had to be investigated, no matter how unlikely they sounded. She pauses. Would you ever have told me what happened to Marianne? If I hadn't found out, I mean.

I've thought about that question non-stop, Bobbie, and the only answer I can give you is that I don't know. I realise that's not a helpful answer, but it is an honest one. I know I said it was all about timing, but that's not the whole truth. Mostly I was scared of losing you. I didn't want your mother's tragedy to come between us. Stories like that have a habit of changing things, and I couldn't bear the thought of our relationship being spoiled by something that happened so long in the past. I was stupid not to see that it was me who was spoiling it, right here in the present. I always thought of Marianne as a catastrophe that was better kept secret. I had no right to do that and I'm sorry.

I'm sorry too, Robin says. I shouldn't have gone off at you like that. Mostly it was the shock. Like I was suddenly living in a different world, she thinks, and the directness of their exchange, the steady back-and-forth of it comes as a different shock, a recognition that the difficulty between them – Dianne's grief, Robin's anger – has reformed into something different, a deepening of trust. The subject of her birth mother has been a wall between them, an obstacle previously submerged dragged into the light. Hauled up to the surface like the shopping trolleys and twisted bicycle wheels, the fridge-freezers, the crumpled Ford Fiesta pictured in the photographs of illegal fly-tipping in Shipley's files. Sordid detritus that can kill you without you having realised it is even there.

Robin feels sure of Dianne now as she always has, swept into clear water, though she cannot yet bring herself to admit her hurt, not now, maybe not ever. Best to offer something else instead and hope it will do. You know the best thing? she says to Dianne. Discovering Marianne was a musician, I mean knowing it for real. That cancels out some of the more awful things. It's almost like she's back with us. Back in the world.

Dianne reaches across the table, squeezes her hand. I'm glad you see it that way, Bobbie. I feel like that, too.

There's a cousin of mine, Rachel says. Abel. He is obsessed with space exploration, always has been. I remember when we were kids he wrote off to NASA, asking how he could be enrolled in the space program.

Did he hear back from them?

They sent some publicity booklets, I think – Abel would read anything with a rocket on the cover. He's an engineer now, he works for BMW. Don't you think that's sad?

Sad how?

Having such big dreams, then ending up in a car factory.

I don't know. BMW sounds like a decent enough place to work.

Decent isn't what Abel had in mind though, not back then. He was always so passionate.

Sounds like you're close, you and him.

Uncle Jeb lives just down the road from us, so we were bound to be. Our dads are brothers. I think they were worried for a while, that Abel and I might get together but it was never like that for us. Abel's married now, he has three boys. One of them is as obsessed with outer space as Abel was. He is so totally into Star Wars it does my head in.

They are in the same Turkish restaurant where Robin had lunch the day she first called on Rachel to discuss Frank's case. Rachel seems relaxed and the way she is dressed – ankle-length tapered skirt, burgundy silk blouse – makes Robin wonder what's going on here exactly, whether this is a date. Robin is wearing jeans and a jacket the same as always, and that pendant Ashley gave her, 007 in silver with a gold plug in the second o. It is meant to be a joke but does it just look naff?

It's good to be out, Rachel says. I haven't been anywhere, not in ages. Thanks for suggesting it.

Her hair is down, caught back on one side in a gold clip. She looks better in general, more present, as if sharing the story about her cousin has helped her to regain a sense of connection with the outside world.

I've been monitoring the forums, Robin says. I'm hoping to iden-tify some of the other people Frank was in contact with. Discover their whereabouts if possible, see if any of them also know Eddie, or might have been in Paris at the same time as Frank. She is unsure how much she should tell her, how surprised she has been by the amount of online speculation around Frank's disappearance. If the cops and the mainstream media have largely ignored the story, their lack of interest, Robin has discovered, is far from typical. On LAvventura and across a plethora of other sites there has been a sustained, months' long enquiry into Frank's possible whereabouts, his true identity, his background in surveillance tech, his relationship with his father and likely connection with the supersoldier program.

On one of her searches, Robin has even stumbled upon a photograph of Rachel, standing with Frank on a beach promenade, Folkestone maybe or Margate, one of those places. Rachel is wearing denim shorts and gold slingback sandals, a baggy white T-shirt cinched in at the waist with a plaited gold belt. She is holding Frank's hand. Frank is in jeans and what looks like a school aertex sports shirt. He seems anxious, dishevelled, a million miles away. The photograph was posted together with the information that it was taken just weeks before Frank's disappearance.

How the poster knew this or whether it is true Robin has no idea. Her instinct says not – Frank looks much younger in the photograph, though there is no way of telling for sure and she feels wary of asking Rachel about it, not unless the photograph proves to be significant. Meanwhile, the online theories about what happened to Frank seem to sub-divide and proliferate by the day. Like mould, Robin muses, or cancerous cells:

Frank has been extracted, abducted or terminated by his original spymasters.

Frank has escaped from a secure mental facility where he has been subjected to advanced mind-transfer techniques and the almost-total destruction of his cognitive pathways.

Frank has escaped from protective custody after having witnessed the assassination of an investigative journalist with a Russian nerve agent.

Frank is currently being held at an undisclosed location in preparation for dissection, a hostage swap or undercover placement.

Frank has been deployed to an off-world location by the same deep-state organisation that augmented his father.

Frank is actually a super-advanced experimental AI captured by the Russians, the Chinese, the Israelis, the United States for the purposes of replicating his illegal surveillance devices.

Frank doesn't actually exist – he is a construct, a lure, a shell identity created to divert attention from a parallel disappearance or to identify and isolate fringe groups that might pose a challenge to the acceptance of consensus reality.

Frank is a rogue agent who managed to transport himself into our time-stream from a future where Earth is teetering on the brink of an interstellar war.

On one site, someone has posted a twenty-second video clip purporting to show Frank outside a scruffy-looking apartment block in the Saint-Denis area to the north of Paris. The camera tracks a figure in a dark anorak walking along the pavement for a couple of seconds before panning round to reveal a white van parked at the kerb, a garbage truck surrounded by four operatives in hi-viz overalls, a vacant lot strewn with car tyres, a dented metal filing cabinet with all its drawers pulled out and a large quantity of broken glass. The shot of the rubbish-strewn lot reminds Robin of the photographs taken from Miles Shipley's hotel room. The guy in the anorak outside the flats has his back to the camera. He is of a similar height and build to Frank but it is impossible to tell if it is Frank or not.

Robin watches and re-watches the clip obsessively. She finds it mesmerising. She lets herself imagine that the next time she plays it, the figure will turn around and stare straight at the camera.

I was checking the forums all the time in the beginning, Rachel says. I had to stop in the end though, because it started to get to me. All that crap about Frank from people who had never met him. I began to wonder if it does something to your brain after a while, seeing stuff about yourself you know isn't true but gets read by strangers as if it is true and any attempt you make to set the record straight, people say you're lying. As if the truth about yourself is debatable, up for grabs, and if their voice is louder than yours you lose the fight. It's so ridiculous it's terrifying. I don't go online much at all now. Sometimes when

I'm walking to work I find myself staring at the trees, the pavement, the shop fronts and wondering if they're real, or if I'm just a figure on someone's screen somewhere and they can close the window any time they want.

Like the fake Frank, in that video, Robin thinks. Me watching someone watching him.

You're sensible, she says to Rachel. It's best to stay away from all that. Let me go crazy for you, that's what I'm here for.

They smile.

How did you become a detective? Rachel says.

That's a long story. Robin feels flustered and faintly discomfited. How does anyone become anything?

That's not a proper answer though, is it? You don't wake up one morning and find you're a cop.

My dad was in the police. It didn't seem unusual to me.

Like joining the family firm?

Maybe.

I'm curious, that's all. I'm interested.

There's your answer then. I'm curious, I'm interested. Being a police detective is about keeping your eyes open, trusting your senses. Ignoring what people want you to think and working out what you really do think. Being a private detective is the same thing only double, because you're on your own. Every day you're on a case, that's the thing you're most aware of – that you're on your own. When you're used to being part of a squad it's like being stripped naked.

So why did you leave?

That's an even longer story. Robin tries to smile again, misses the mark. I don't like filling in forms. I don't work well with other people. Take your pick. She cannot imagine what she will say if Rachel presses for more details. She quickly asks if she thinks Emily Landau might be willing to let her search Frank's room.

I'll call her, Rachel says quietly. She doesn't know about you yet, or at least she didn't. I suppose Michael might have told her.

Thanks. Robin puts down her glass. She feels dislocated from her surroundings, overcome by vertigo. Six weeks or so ago she had no idea Rachel Gabon existed. Now all she can see is gold: the gold chain around Rachel's neck, Rachel's gold nail polish, Friedrich's Winter Landscape in its shitty gold frame.

Are you OK, Robin? Rachel is saying.

Fine, Robin says. I've not been sleeping.

Me neither.

The world from before has ceased to exist. Or maybe it's rattling along just fine without Robin in it.

A VACANT LOT

IT IS MICHAEL IN the end who meets her at the house. Emily Landau has given her permission for Robin to search Frank's room on condition that she doesn't have to be there or answer questions. Emily finds the subject of Frank too difficult and too upsetting. She has already told the police everything she knows.

She doesn't mean to be rude, Michael explains to Robin over the phone. She's kind of numb with it all.

Robin tells him that's fine, though it is difficult for her to hide her disappointment. She had been hoping Emily would agree to meet with her. As things now stand, Emily Landau is a hole in the argument, a vacant lot, a space that cannot be quantified, or filled. Robin cannot do anything about that, not for the moment anyway. Michael has hinted that if any new information comes to light, Emily might be willing to talk, though it would be foolish to count on it.

The house stands on a large corner plot, the front lawn neatly mown behind a low brick wall. Many of the houses on the estate have had their front gardens paved over to provide extra parking but the

Landau house looks the same as it would have looked in the 1950s, when it was new. A red Nissan— Faith's – stands parked on the drive in front of the garage, one of the only garages left on the estate with its original wooden doors.

The place seems too quiet. Empty of feeling. As if the house has become aware it is no longer whole.

Hey, Michael says as he opens the door. I'll stay downstairs if you don't mind? Mum said she'll be back around four so if you can be through by then that would be good. Frank's room is at the back. You can't miss it.

He offers her a cup of tea, which Robin declines. It sounds weird I know, she says, but I don't want to take anything into the room that doesn't belong there. This might be a sensitive question, she adds, but do you happen to know how much Frank's room has been disturbed since he left? How many people have been in and out?

All of us, in the beginning. Mum thought she might find something – an address, maybe, for where Frank had been staying. If it's there she never found it. She hardly goes in Frank's room at all now. Does it matter?

Robin shakes her head. Though it does matter, as with Emily's refusal to meet with her there is nothing she can do about it. There is still plenty to be gained, in any case, from witnessing the house in its present state, the house sitting in a silence that is not peace so much as stasis, a condition that has for now, for the foreseeable future, become what passes for normal. The people who inhabit this space – Emily, Faith and intermittently Michael – have learned to step around the hole in that normality that Frank has left behind. They are careful with one

173

another, careful with what is said and how their words are received. Sometimes they laugh, eat Indian takeaway, watch TV. Yet the eerie silence from the words not spoken eats into everything.

Robin's entry into that silence feels like a forced entry, and yet, she reminds herself, Emily Landau has invited her to come here. In granting her permission to violate Frank's privacy she seems to be offering Robin a trust she has not yet earned. Robin feels grateful, moved, though Dunbar at least would insist she should use her compassion to drive her and not be softened by it.

Compassion is like jam, lassie, like treacle toffee, it gums up the works. Robin closes her mind to his voice, that practised grittiness: two parts Clydebank, three parts performance. There is no place for it here.

The curtains in Frank's room are open, the bed made, the dark blue duvet cover smooth over the pillows, the black-and-silver coverlet folded neatly, a pair of red Adidas trainers placed squarely side-by-side at the end of the bed. Mute, west-facing autumn light trickles in. Outside the windows, the long back garden and beyond that the copse, once a patch of wasteland where kids played at soldiers and now a new estate, its scrubby meadows overwritten with concrete, with squared-off back gardens and tarmacked cul-de-sacs.

How long has the copse been gone? Robin writes in her notebook. She begins making a list of the things inside the snow globes that crowd Frank's windowsill, twenty of them, arranged in neat and sparkling rows like alien eggs: London bus (old-style Routemaster), cash register (old-style manual), typewriter (Olivetti), the Taj Mahal, St Basil's Cathedral (Moscow), Buckingham Palace, the house from Psycho, Norman Rockwell's American Gothic, Chitty-Chitty Bang-Bang,

church in winter (Winter Landscape??) Scottish castle (Dunrobin?)
Neuschwanstein, cemetery in winter, fairground carousel, ballerina,
Indiana Jones, a lone wolf in a pine forest, Japanese pagoda. Outmoded
objects and lonely places, symbols of abandonment. Some of the snow
globes appear to be antique and are possibly valuable. All have been
recently dusted, presumably by Emily.

Robin picks up the Routemaster snow globe and shakes it. White
flakes rise up in a maelstrom, drift gently down. She imagines Emily,
tenderly folding, cleaning, obscuring, placing the trainers neatly upright
by the side of the bed. Frank's desk runs the length of one wall, a shelf
of white MDF. Lined up along the back are Frank's coding manuals,
thick red-and-white volumes, soft covers, a uniform edition. On the
desk in front of the manuals there is a laptop computer. Robin stares
at it dumbly, like an off-world explorer stumbling by chance upon alien
life. She wonders why no one has thought to mention that Frank's
computer is still in his room.

It must be a backup, she realises. She remembers Milan Harwicz
once telling her that until you took a hammer to the hard drive a computer was like an archive of past misdemeanours; information could
still be recovered, even when the owner believed that everything of
interest had been deleted.

Even when they'd wiped their digital arse, as Dunbar might have
said.

If Robin can obtain Frank's logins and forum IDs, she might be
able to discover more about who he was talking to.

Robin turns to the wardrobe: two pairs of blue jeans, both Wran-
gler, two grey sweatshirts, one printed with an @ sign, the other plain,

one burgundy Gap hoodie, three black short-sleeved T-shirts, precision-folded, two white T-shirts (ditto), two dark-grey button-down shirts on plastic hangers. There is something about the wardrobe's contents that makes her want to weep. The frugality, the rigidity, the lack of deviation from what such clothes suggest, uniformity made to seem casual, made to look *normal*. Cool-adjacent, Frank dressing himself as Frank, becoming an expert in what Frank would wear, learning himself by heart, making what amounted to hours and years of practice seem second nature.

The clothes are all that is left, an emblem of loss. Robin wonders how Emily feels about this room now, if she can still find comfort here, or only emptiness. She turns to the bookshelves above Frank's bed, working systematically left to right, noting down each title, flipping through each volume searching for underlinings and for inclusions – bus tickets, phone numbers, other rogue slips of paper – that might be hidden between the pages. There are books on environmental pollution, pesticides, big pharma, big data, the moon landings, moon landings conspiracy theories, a slim hardback called Scottish Lichens: a beginner's guide, more than two dozen books on asteroids, UFOs, alien abduction, Area 51, The Furthest Migration: panspermia and the next alien invasion.

Fringe-theorists, university professors, world-class experts rubbing shoulders and comparing notes. Scholarly tomes versus self-published pamphlets, investigative research versus half-baked doom-mongering, the kind that lures the preachers and the preppers like wasps to jam but that would never pass the threshold for creditable journalism. There is nothing here about the war specifically, though there is a volume entitled Extremophiles: life in the borderlands, together with a badly dog-eared copy of a monograph on film and magic by – yes – Edmund de Groote. As Robin flips back the cover to take a closer look, some pages slip free: a printout of an essay on modernist music and alien conspiracy theories. The author byline on the article is Jeanne-Marie Vanderlien.

Robin is holding her breath. There is a sound in her ears like the sea and then, so clear it's like he's in the room with her, the voice of Alec Dunbar: get you on Mastermind lassie, specialist subject the bleeding obvious. If ye smell shit that's cause youse standing in shit – first rule of decent detective work. Then that great raucous belly laugh of his, hilarious when you were in on the joke, not nearly as funny when you were a part of it.

Twere a long time ago lass, ancient history. No need to unbury the bodies, eh? So to speak.

Alec Dunbar, a brilliant mind in a semi-ruined body. A heavyweight bully, though Robin doubts many have dared confront him with that fact, not since he was in school anyway, most likely not even then. Especially not then. She remembers the rush she felt, spitting the words *fuck you* in Dunbar's face. Vindication like the backdraft of an explosion, the redness flaming in Dunbar's stubbled cheeks like the flare of a torch.

Her hands are shaking and her heart is hammering. And she is cold, cold in spite of the central heating, a sure sign of shock. She sits down on the carpet next to Frank's CD player and almost without thinking she presses the eject button. The disc in the tray is a recording of Bach cantatas, Herz und Mund und Tat und Leben, Ton Koopman and the Amsterdam Baroque. Koopman's recordings are always admirable, all the intellect of Gardiner without the dryness, though Robin realises she has never heard this one. She returns the disc to the tray and presses play. There is a burr and then a hum then the burnished joyous clangour of the opening chorus, steeping the room in sound as a thistle's roots are steeped in moisture after rain, and Robin finds herself thinking how her own appreciation of this music, no matter how ardent, no matter how profound can never approach the wonder of those who heard it first. Those who heard it as Bach composed it, not as a work of art but as an act of worship.

> *Jesus my joy abides*
> *My heart's nectar, consolation*
> *Defends me from hell's blight*
> *He is my life's strength*
> *My eye's sunshine and desire*
> *My soul's treasure and rejoicing*
> *And so I shall never let Jesus*
> *Leave my heart or fade from sight*

Belief in this age of steel, in this age of space flight, in this age of nuclear fission is a pallid thing, even for the faithful, clinging on like the last leaves of autumn, the holding out of hope over experience. The concertante violin etching its line in silver against the tapestried, warm-toned congruence of the neat little chamber choir; the song of the oboe sweet but with a lingering tartness, forgiving if only of those who can truly repent.

Even in a major key Bach feels autumnal, the drawing down of blinds.

Jesu joy of man's desiring, holy wisdom love most bright. The pity of war, Robin murmurs. A man has vanished, an unknown soldier. How many more?

She glances at her watch: three thirty. Fifteen useful minutes, twenty if she pushes it. She leaves Frank's door standing ajar the way she found it and crosses the landing. Emily's bedroom is filled with the saffron light of the late afternoon, a late afternoon in southeast London as the world turns its way towards a point of irrevocable transition everybody is busy pretending does not exist.

Robin glances briefly at her face reflected in the dressing-table mirror, then at the panoply of objects laid out like sacrificial offerings on the polished glass: a Wedgwood bowl, a crystal perfume flask, an oval Bakelite hairbrush with its matching comb. Olay moisturising fluid, 'Oyster' nude nail varnish, a tube of mascara. Gentle things, ordinary things, not how she has imagined Emily at all. Robin has pictured her angrier and more dishevelled, a woman at war.

Why should she be though, why the hell should any woman be anything that is not her own self?

She slides open the dressing-table drawer. A Liberty-print address book, a pair of leather gloves, mustard-yellow and buttoned at the wrist. A small bundle of letters, secured with an elastic band, and face down on top of the letters a silver photo frame. Robin picks it up carefully, turns it over. In the photograph she sees a young couple, she in a summer dress – yellow halter-neck, large black polka dots – he in camo pants and a khaki T-shirt. They are holding hands across a café table. The Eiffel Tower is plainly visible in the background. The man's hair is clipped short, army-style, but even so the likeness is obvious, loud as a thunderclap: the rangy limbs, slight hunch of the shoulders, the likeness there in the smile especially, the way he tilts his head.

Robin photographs the photograph quickly with her phone then puts it back in the drawer. Michael is calling to her from the foot of the stairs.

We should go, he says.

I need to borrow Frank's computer. Would that be OK?

I'm not sure. It's just his old one, he hadn't used it for ages, so far as I know. I should ask Mum really.

Look, you have my number, you know how to reach me. This is important, or at least it might be, she corrects herself. Do you happen to know if the police examined it at any stage?

I don't think so. They weren't interested. How long will you need it for?

I should think maybe a week? I need to get a friend of mine to look at it – he's in digital forensics. There could be valuable leads.

Michael looks unsure but at least he is nodding. Did you find anything else? In Frank's room?

Several things. It's been useful background. Please say thank you to Emily for me. She asks Michael if Frank ever mentioned someone called Jeanne-Marie Vanderlien, if the name sounds familiar to him at all, but Michael says no, so far as he is aware he has never heard it before.

The guy this thing belonged to, Milan says. Did you say he was murdered? Milan lives in a tiny mews flat round the back of Baker

Street, squeezed in between an office block and a chain hotel. There is computer shit everywhere except in the kitchen area, which is surprisingly pristine.

I don't know yet, Robin says. He disappeared last April. I'm trying to find out where to.

There's not a massive amount on here. Could it have been his backup machine?

Robin nods. His brother said he hadn't used it in a while.

There is a photo cache – a lot of weird shit but nothing illegal, nothing nasty. Same with his internet history. He wasn't on social media so far as I can tell. None of the usual platforms, anyway. Mostly he's a lurker. I've compiled a list of the sites he visited most frequently. Elementary level paranoia, mainly.

Did you manage to get his forum logins?

Everything's there. The file on the desktop marked users.

This is fantastic. Thanks for making the time.

No worries. Milan shrugs. What do you think happened to him?

I think he's in trouble but I'm not sure what kind. She takes a breath, a moment in which she is still trying to decide how much she should tell him, especially when there's nothing to tell yet, just her stupid theory, but then that moment is past and she is telling Milan Harwicz there is a chance Frank Landau's disappearance may be gang-related.

The guy he was supposed to be meeting in Paris, the film lecturer. His name is de Groote.

Milan gives her a look. Isn't that like saying his name is Smith? In Amsterdam it would be, anyway.

That's what I've been trying to tell myself. But then the other day when I was going through his stuff I found something else.

Robin tells him about the article she found in Frank's bedroom, the essay on music and counterculture, watches his face as she tells him who wrote it, sees his eyes narrow and then widen, sees his surprise.

The article mentions Ulrike Meinhof, she adds.

Ulrike Meinhof as in the German terrorist?

Robin nods. Jeanne-Marie Vanderlien is a freelance journalist. She writes mainly for music magazines, articles on John Martyn and Malcolm Mooney, a piece on Nico, an interview with Jim Morrison that's been reprinted a lot. She had a book deal at one point, for a novel about the Moors Murderers, but it never came out. Too controversial, apparently. She once did a photo shoot for a German magazine that makes it look as if she's being shoved out of an aeroplane. Her online bio says she lives in Berlin but it's ten years out of date.

They don't exactly sound like gangsters though, the two of them.

I realise that. On the face of it, the whole idea is ridiculous. These people hide in peculiar places though. I'm sure there's something here.

The thing that happened with Dunbar, Milan says. He studies her carefully, as if she is a bomb that might go off. Are you thinking this might be connected?

That's something else I don't know yet. Listen, she says, I don't want Dunbar knowing about this.

He won't. Not from me, anyway. The man is a liability.

Thanks, Robin says. She nods. Have you spoken to Ash at all recently?

I've seen her about. In the office. She's good, I think. Everyone is on overtime with this hotel fire case so I've not really—

It's fine, I get it.

Let me know how this thing pans out, OK? We should meet for a drink or something.

That would be good. Robin smiles. Thanks, Milan. The thought of holing up with him in a pub somewhere and just letting rip, spilling the whole sack of beans – why she left, what really happened – is so tempting she can smell the beer, so tempting it is dangerous, but she knows she won't do it. Once information is out in the world it is there for good, which is why such decisions should never be taken in anger or with malice aforethought. If you can smell shit it's because you're standing in shit, Dunbar was right about that as he was right about so much else. How was it possible to hate someone and still admire them?

Milan hesitates, and Robin can sense he is thinking of asking her if she wants to stay over. She makes an excuse and exits before that can happen. Way too complicated, and she likes him, values his friendship as well as his expertise too much to risk losing him, to risk their relationship coming unravelled as it so easily could. It is late by the time she gets home but she still feels restless. She logs on to Frank's computer, reminding herself of what Milan said to her as she was leaving, that if Frank is alive the tiniest trace of activity may alert him to her presence. Anyone watching Frank, or watching the watchers, may be alerted also.

Data is testimony, and digital traces are immortal, radioactive. Be careful where you tread.

She opens the photo cache, an action that should remain undetectable unless the laptop itself is under remote surveillance. Unlikely, given the machine's months-long inactivity and she has to start somewhere. She knows the guilt she feels at her act of trespass is misplaced, a sign that her investigation is in danger of becoming compromised by personal feeling. That she is too close to her subject or more likely her client. This is something she will have to live with, a breach in her defences she must learn to navigate, take care to step around.

Nothing nasty, Milan said, nothing illegal, though in Milan's line of work both nasty and illegal are relative terms. She is half-expecting to see photos of Rachel – nude photos, intimate images, because that's what people store on their hard drives and why should meek mild-mannered Frank Landau be any exception? Robin has promised herself that if there are any photos like that she will skip over them, not even itemise them, there would be no point. What she is not expecting is for the contents of the cache to be familiar to her. She wonders why Milan didn't think to mention that they are the same images – many of them, anyway – the police retrieved from the folder in Miles Shipley's hotel room. He didn't notice, most likely, because why would he? Milan is not obsessed.

Robin scrolls through the images, unnerved not so much by the photos themselves as by the fact that she is seeing them again. The jpeg files are all labelled:

N#1/disused airfield sainton lincs

N#2/old soapworks sale manchester

N#3/decommissioned reactor site environs tallinn estonia

More than fifty images in total, waste dumps and old chemical works, overgrown brownfield sites, disused quarries full of fly-tipped sofas and big-box monitors. Once again, there is no obvious means of telling where the images are sourced from, though at that moment their provenance seems less significant than the fact that both Miles Shipley (dead) and Frank Landau (missing) had them on file. This must count as a definitive link between the two of them, although according to Michael, Shipley had denied either communicating with Frank directly or meeting him in person.

Robin logs on to LAvventura using Frank's idents, an action that carries the risk of immediate detection but that will give her access not only to Frank's comment cache but also to any direct messages he has sent or received. She quickly ascertains that there are hundreds of each, none of them posted later than the date immediately preceding the day of Frank's departure for Paris. This sudden cessation of online activity is evidence – evidence of a significant break in routine, even if by itself it cannot count as proof that Frank has come to harm. Robin finds herself astonished all over again at the fallibility, the possible culpability of the police, at their stubborn lack of interest in a man who was ostensibly missing and clearly vulnerable. She prints out the comment cache, a document that runs to several dozen pages, then logs out of the site. Her total onscreen time as Frank clocks in at seventeen minutes. Not long, though more than enough time to attract attention if the site is being monitored.

Frank's involvement with LAvventura dates back five years. For the first year or so he is mainly a lurker, as Milan said. The pieces he does occasionally comment on are longer, more articulate essays on topics such as 9/11, something called the Rendlesham incident, Area 51 and an ongoing series of posts on a physicist named Fred Hoyle.

Frank's contributions are engaged and knowledgeable and in time he becomes one of the forum's most regular posters.

By tracking back through the comment threads, Robin is able to pin-point what is most likely Frank's first online interaction with Edmund de Groote, a comment he placed on an article by de Groote about a film released in 2013 called Upstream Color. De Groote's essay is long, almost six thousand words, and written to combine elements of both film criticism and memoir, a technique Robin recognises immediately from other pieces by de Groote she has read online.

This film scared me a lot, Frank commented.

Because you understand the difference between fantasy as a vehicle for the imagination and the imagination as a tool for investigating evidence of what is real, de Groote posted back. Frank and de Groote appear to strike up an instant rapport, exchanging several more comments on the Upstream Color piece and then dozens of others subsequently. In the fifteen months before Frank's disappearance, he and de Groote exchange more than two hundred direct messages. These cease abruptly around three months before Frank's trip to Paris. Robin can only assume they moved their conversation either to another forum or to a private app.

Robin has not seen Upstream Color, has never heard of it even. She ends up watching it twice, mainly because she can barely make sense of what is going on the first time, although the narrative does become clearer on a second viewing. The film is about a group of people whose bodies are deliberately infected with a parasitic worm. The worm has some kind of psychological effect, causing those who have become infected to develop a telepathic, almost symbiotic relationship with one another. In his essay, de Groote argues that the parasitic insects are of alien origin, although the script, by the film's director, Shane Carruth, does not say so specifically.

It's fiction, Frank, Robin mutters, the word fiction rattling inside her head like a nascent headache, like twigs going tap-tap-tap against a pane of glass. She scrolls back and forth through Frank's comments, trying to work out why it is that most people are able to watch a film or read a book no matter how disturbing and never question the fact that it is simply a story, when there are others – often sensitive, vulnerable or imaginative individuals like Frank – who seem compelled to treat such stories as instalments in a secret narrative only they and their fellow initiates recognise the truth of.

Robin can see how the film must have worked on Frank – the maggots, the pigs, the memory loss, the secret doctors – how he must have become convinced that the movie was based around events that were really happening. Truths that were being hushed up by the authorities – just like Roswell and 9/11 and the deliberate weaponisation of COVID-19.

In real life, Edmund de Groote is thirty-nine years old, a lecturer in film and media studies at a further education college near the Porte de Clignancourt in the eighteenth arrondissement of Paris. As well as the monograph on film and magic, he has written numerous articles, essays and reviews, both popular and academic, across a variety of platforms and publications in both Europe and the United States. Judging by the interactions on his social media accounts, he has a good career and interesting friends.

His twitter handle is EdmundofGloucester, which is the name he uses on LAvventura and several other forums. Robin wonders about the significance of the name. She has a vague memory of Edmund of Gloucester as a character from Shakespeare and when she looks him up she discovers she is right; Edmund of Gloucester is in King Lear, the bastard son of the Earl of Gloucester, older half-brother to Gloucester's self-righteous and overwhelmingly boring legitimate heir Edgar. Edmund is often seen as the villain of the piece, argues one online crib sheet, though such analysis could be construed as overly simplistic. Edmund is more complex than that, a canny political operator and a natural rebel, a deeply resentful outsider who has been stigmatised all his life for his bastard status and who has finally, as the play opens, had enough.

Robin logs back on to LAvventura from her own computer and creates a personal account using the screen name joker. As a handle it is hardly original but she has no wish to attract attention, she wants to blend in. Just one more UFO nerd, and if she comes across as a bit of a dick then so much the better. She adds a comment to the Upstream Color piece.

Late to this party I know but I think this is excellent. Have been watching the movie again and enjoying your analysis. You should write a book ☺

When LAvventura asks if she would like to switch on notifications, Robin ticks yes. De Groote's post is a couple of years old. There is no guarantee that he will respond but it is something to try at least, something relatively harmless, and her gamble pays off – EdmundofGloucester comments back in less than an hour.

I have written a book. You can find details here. He provides the link to the publications page at his website that Robin has already visited numerous times.

Cool, Robin types. *I'll check it out.* She resists the urge to communicate further, to ask questions. She has made contact. She has established that de Groote still posts on LAvventura, which is useful information to have, even if she does not know yet what to do with it. She scrolls back through Frank's DMs, noting the screen name of everyone he had direct contact with. There are surprisingly few. Aside from his voluminous correspondence with EdmundofGloucester, Frank seems to have conducted most of his interactions on the open forum. A couple of other names do recur though, and the one that crops up most frequently is JeanneDark. JeanneDark begins corresponding with Frank about his work as a coder, a factual line of enquiry that seems at odds with LAvventura's predilection for the esoteric until Robin works out that what they are actually talking about is the likeness of mathematical sequencing to alien linguistics.

JeanneDark as in Jeanne d'Arc as in Joan of Arc. St Joan the warrior, the rebel, the heretic, a handle that signifies much, like Edmund-ofGloucester. Robin performs a search for JeanneDark on the open forum. She does not post as frequently as EdmundofGloucester, or as frequently as Frank, come to that, but her comments are lengthy and detailed and rather didactic. She has uploaded two long essays, one on the paradox of intellectual martyrdom ('the problem of making a radical discovery is that no one will believe you') and another on the demonisation of the female revolutionary.

The second essay links back to another site, a left-leaning political forum called Red Word, where the essay was originally published under the byline Jeanne-Marie Vanderlien.

TAINTED GROUND:
JOHN SYLVESTER,
SHANE CARRUTH AND THE
INTIMACY OF CONTAGION
BY EDMUND DE GROOTE

I̶N MY FIRST YEAR of college, a biology student I knew slightly attempted suicide by swallowing a large quantity of prescription painkillers then chasing them down with own-brand supermarket vodka. It was a Saturday night in December, and the student accommodation where he was living was uncommonly quiet. Had it not been for his roommate, who returned unexpectedly to their apartment to change his shirt, the young man, whose name was Robert Ferrier, would not have been found until the following morning and would probably have died.

This is a small story, almost a commonplace. The first few months of a university career are a period of profound change and acute vulnerability. Robert Ferrier would not have been the first to find himself adrift and sinking and lonely, unable to make the necessary social adjustment.

It sounds callous to say so, but I did not pay particular attention to the incident at the time. It was simply something that happened: mildly shocking and tragic yes, but I had my own problems and anxieties to deal with and the young man had lived in any case, so there wasn't much of a story there to tell.

I would undoubtedly have forgotten the entire episode, had not a student in my tutor group, a woman named Marine, told me more of the detail behind Ferrier's desperate actions.

A girlfriend of Marine's had heard from someone in his department that Robert Ferrier had been suffering from panic attacks since becoming lost on a field trip to the Brière marshes earlier in the term. His group had used the village of Crossac as a base from which to explore the surrounding area, a famous nature reserve and region of historic significance. Ferrier's disappearance took place on the third day of the trip. Others in the group had not realised at first that Robert was missing. When finally his absence was noticed the rest of the party spent three hours searching for him, eventually discovering him shivering beneath a pile of sacking in a partially derelict outbuilding.

Although he appeared to be unharmed, and tried to make a joke of his lousy sense of direction, in the weeks that followed his friends became increasingly concerned about Ferrier's state of mind. For a long time, Robert refused to say anything about what had so disturbed him while he was missing in the marshland around Crossac, and when he did finally begin to speak of it, his explanation for his anxiety seemed fantastical to the point of delusion. The university counsellor who spoke to Robert the week before his suicide attempt seemed convinced that the strange beliefs he had acquired in the aftermath of the Crossac incident were of far less importance than Ferrier's depression.

As one of Robert's seminar group put it: people have all kinds of ways of losing it in the first term. Usually it's drugs or alcohol. You could even say it's normal.

When I asked Marine, who was by this time my girlfriend, what it was exactly that Robert Ferrier believed had happened to him she seemed reluctant to discuss the matter. I felt angry with her for being secretive. I even suspected for a time that she had been involved with Ferrier romantically and did not want to tell me. In the end, she admitted the reason she didn't want to talk about it was that it was sad, and frightening, and the whole episode had upset her. Robert Ferrier believed he had ingested a substance of alien origin and that this substance – whatever it was – had altered his biology.

Robert's a nice guy, Marine said. I find it scary that something like this could happen to him. According to Marine's friend, Ferrier had been quiet, gentle, a conscientious student. He was eager to get involved with conservation work. His breakdown had been shocking to everyone in their little group, especially as Robert still showed no significant signs of recovery. He's a real mess, Marine said. If this could happen to him, it could happen to anyone.

*

I remember when I was a kid, say eight or nine, sitting in the back of my parents' car while we were stuck in a traffic jam. The inside of the car was hot and humid. The backs of my legs kept sticking to the seat covers. I forget where we were headed, but I remember leaning my head against the car window, staring out at whatever was outside and thinking how filthy the glass was, coated with a film of dirt and dust and the remains of smashed insects, the typical debris of a hot summer. I remember suddenly sticking out my tongue and licking the window glass. I cannot say what made me do this – most likely it was a peculiar side-effect of boredom. The taste was horrible, a sharp and bitter rankness I had not been expecting. I remember feeling disturbed by what I had done, then all of a sudden terrified that I would fall ill as a result, that the reason the glass tasted so frightful was that it was poisonous. I had an obsession with poisons as a child, and as the sourness bit into my tongue I felt the creeping sense of destiny. It was hours before my fear began to abate.

I remember walking in a public garden with my parents, another parched, hot summer's day, the sky like a cracked blue plate, the river sluggish and green. I had been running about on the grass, and felt desperately thirsty. My father pointed out a water fountain, which I greedily approached. After I had drunk my fill, my father idly speculated about whether the water in the fountain might have come straight from the river, about whether that would be healthy, especially in this heat. I remember I burst into tears. My father tried to make a joke of it, asking me if I might perhaps enjoy another glass of river tea, and I cried all the harder. The fear of contagion, it seems, was hardwired into my psychology like my instinctive fear of spiders.

There was a clip of film Robert kept watching, Marine said, about the ichneumon wasp, which lays its eggs inside the larvae of other insects. For a while the caterpillars carry on as if nothing has happened, but at some point they burst open, releasing the living larvae of the ichneumon wasp, which have eaten it alive from the inside. Robert would not let up watching this film. I didn't see it myself but his friend Anders told me about it. He said it had creeped him out. He said it was like Bobby's mind had jumped the train tracks. Don't you think that's horrible?

I had originally enrolled to study philosophy, but at the beginning of my second year I switched to major in film studies, with philosophy as an ancillary subject. In the summer vacation I had travelled to Crossac in the Brière marshes with a notebook and digital camera and no real idea of what I was looking for except that I needed an explanation for what had happened to Robert Ferrier. I was not expecting to find one, to be honest; what I wanted most of all was simply to be in the place where it had befallen him, whatever 'it' was, to test my logic against the forces of the irrational that had assailed poor Ferrier. In my own mind, I was conducting an experiment in philosophy. What it was in fact was a game of chicken.

Marshlands are strange, still places, portal worlds between the land and the ocean, a psychic sink. We came from water, though this is a fact we choose to forget. The attraction we feel for marshlands – for the aching splendour of their skies, the potential for treachery, the literal disintegration of the ground beneath our feet – is I believe a tacit acknowledgement of our alien origins in the oceans of space, a living metaphor for the discomfort we feel in being restricted and grounded in our earthly milieu. I had no such thoughts at the time. I was simply curious. I wanted to find the barn Robert Ferrier had crawled inside and see if it scared me.

Of course it proved impossible for me to locate the exact spot. But I spent three days poking my head into dilapidated outbuildings, photographing windblown clapboard storage sheds with their piles of rotting tarpaulins. The project engaged me, and it was at this time I began to intuit the singular power of framing, of deliberately choosing an object, landscape or person to be fascinated by. Such focus, I quickly discovered, begets enchantment, and it was in this state of mind I began consciously to seek out the work of writers, philosophers and most especially film makers whose goal is to explore what I have previously referred to as states of uncertainty; that is, states of mind or physical locations where the actuality of what is experienced would appear to fly in the face of empirical fact.

On the final evening of my stay in Crossac I felt the earth move. The sun was very low in the sky. There was a sound, a kind of low booming that did not appear to emanate from any clear source. My body reacted to this sound instantaneously – muscles tautening, skin prickling – as a dog might react to a stimulus operating above the radar of human senses. After the boom came a hushing susurrus and I distinctly heard movement, or a close cluster of tiny independent movements, on or close to the surface of water nearby. What light remained in the sky appeared to change colour, shifting from the leached-out blue of a summer's evening to a ghostly grey-green. The feeling of claustrophobia, of being confined beneath a glass dome, seemed vastly out of proportion to this subtle colour-change. I could feel my heart racing, and the urge to run and hide was all but overwhelming.

I had learned the phrase 'existential terror' without ever having experienced anything remotely approaching such a mythical state. Although there was nothing on the horizon, no person, no beast, no shadow excepting that of the low stone barn I had recently been photographing, no overt cause for my fear at all, I felt it now. I could hear the muted sounds of curlews, fidgeting in the long grasses, and for a second it was as if everything hung in the balance, as if we stood at a fork in the road, those curlews and I, and any momentary wrong decision would lead us into a world so unlike the present we would cease to be ourselves.

Then just as suddenly the feeling receded. The tainted green light seemed to dissipate, the violet twilight of a summer's eve resumed. The marshes vibrated with bird calls and the peeping of frogs. I stood in the foreground, clutching my camera. I thought of trying to capture the moment but I knew there was no point, because I would not succeed.

*

You can choose to believe all this happened, or not. You can imagine these scenes as the climax of a strange, forgotten movie, or not. The objective truth of these events is unimportant. What matters is their imaginative truth, their accuracy and potency in revealing my troubled state of mind. For reasons I found difficult to articulate, I had become obsessed with the case of Robert Ferrier. Something of his fate bore resonance for me. I do not know what happened to Ferrier after he left college, whether he recovered, or not. Following my visit to Crossac I found I had no desire to recover. Recovery, I felt, would be an abdication. What I wanted was to pursue the truth – or otherwise – of what I had experienced.

I have written extensively on films that are the cinematic equivalent of autofiction: Guy Maddin's My Winnipeg, Jonathan Caouette's Tarnation, James Marsh's Wisconsin Death Trip, Andrew Jarecki's Capturing the Friedmans, films that make extensive use of photomontage, reportage and internal monologue, films that appear to arise out of personal experience even though this perceived use of biography or autobiography may be a fictional construct. What appeals to me about such films is the sense they convey, in spite of their openness, their lack of authorial restraint, that the whole truth is not being told, is being evaded even, that something darker and stranger lies just beyond the frame.

Of equal fascination are those instances where the dynamic between fact and fiction occurs in reverse. Shane Carruth's second full-length feature Upstream Color (2013) has acquired a new dramatic resonance through revelations made in 2020 around Carruth's personal relationship with the film's leading actor Amy Seimetz, though I became interested in this movie for other reasons, and long before the allegations about the director's private life became public knowledge.

Not much is known about the life of the writer John C. Sylvester. We cannot be sure he would have described himself as a writer even, if he perceived himself as anything other than an accountant who liked to make up stories in his spare time. His oeuvre is small: the set of eight stories based around his experiences as a serving soldier in WW2 – these were published in a local newspaper in the early 1950s – a handful of science-fiction stories printed in now-obscure genre magazines, and the novella The Tower, which appeared in 1958 and counts as Sylvester's only book-length publication. The Tower did not sell well. Reviewers at the time seemed baffled, both by the subject matter and by the author, who had the temerity to arrive from nowhere and to present the public with what one critic called 'an obscure and outlandish tale teeming with lascivious Americans and grotesque ideas'.

The book was eventually remaindered. John Sylvester died twenty years later in 1978 with no further publications to his name. Whether he was put off by the harsh criticism, the poor revenues, or whether it was simply that he had said everything he wished to say, we can never know.

On the surface, Sylvester's works – the war stories, the science-fiction stories, the novella – would seem to have little in common with one another, yet the most striking aspect of Sylvester's output is how cohesive it is. The WW2 stories are told from the point of view of an officer named Stewart Fergus, who finds himself stranded with his unit in an isolated French town in the uncertain, precarious weeks that follow the D-Day invasions. One of his men experiences a traumatic breakdown. Another goes AWOL and is captured by the Germans. Fergus himself becomes obsessed with the wife of a local policeman, whom he suspects of being a collaborator. The stories have a meandering, uneasy quality, each of them ending without any clear resolution or moral message. Fergus's unhealthy obsession with Madeleine is frequently compared with the pain he suffers from a wound that refuses to heal.

Sylvester's science fiction carries a similar quality of existential unease, with constant intimations of looming disaster. The best of these stories is The Waystation, published in Aeon magazine in 1955. The narrative concerns a starship captain placed in quarantine aboard the space station St Helena. Captain Michaels has become infected with an alien pathogen. As the contagion begins to spread throughout his body, he becomes increasingly preoccupied with the life and fate of the Emperor Napoleon, exiled to the remote Atlantic island of Saint Helena some four centuries earlier.

The themes of alienation and corruption, both literal and metaphorical, are explored with still greater intensity in The Tower, which might also be characterised as science fiction. The novella's events take place in an alternate future, in the aftermath of a military conflict with the planet Gliese. Earth is understood to have won the war, but at considerable cost. When the visionary American architect Achimbaud Aspen wins a lucrative commission to design a national war memorial, he imagines a building that will not only commemorate the dead, but also bring a sense of renewed hope and economic recovery to the living. The Conquest Tower is a triumph, both for the city of New York and for Aspen himself. What neither party realise is that the alien rock used in its construction is organic in nature, a fact that is not understood until after the material has begun to infiltrate Earth's native ecosystems. The story ends, in typical Sylvester fashion, with the disaster still unfolding and unresolved.

John Charles Sylvester was born in Tain, a Scottish mining town situated in the northeast Highlands and Scotland's oldest burgh. He grew up the only son of a schoolmaster and studied mathematics at the University of Aberdeen before being called up into the army in 1941. After the war, he settled permanently in London, completing his Articles and working for a number of City firms before becoming employed by Selfridges department store, where he worked as a company accountant until his retirement.

He was married to Mavis Oxley Bennett, who worked in the patient records office of the Maudsley Hospital, where Sylvester underwent a course of psychiatric counselling in the aftermath of his war service. Though I have been unable to gather any detailed information about Sylvester's treatment at the Maudsley it is possible, even probable, that he began writing on the advice of his doctor, as a form of therapy.

*

The Tower is an authentically strange work. Strangest of all is how prescient it feels. The cityscapes, the technology, the relentless drive for profit and growth that form the backdrop to the story all speak of a future that feels uncannily similar to our own late-capitalist present. I first came across Sylvester's novella through a film blog I occasionally contributed to as a postgraduate, when it was mentioned as part of a discussion of his story The Waystation, optioned for film in the early 2000s and trapped in development hell ever since. The student who recommended The Tower also mentioned that Sylvester had read the work of the maverick physicist Fred Hoyle. Hoyle was a proponent of the theory of panspermia, which contends that life on Earth was seeded by extraterrestrial microbes brought in on comets. I had not previously heard of Hoyle, who was an Englishman, from Yorkshire, and who, like John Sylvester, wrote a number of science-fiction stories. Hoyle worked on radar technology during WW2 and afterwards became discredited for rejecting the Big Bang theory of cosmic evolution in favour of the steady state theory, which maintains that the universe has always existed and cannot be destroyed.

Hoyle's ideas on panspermia are less well known, though there is uneasy agreement among biologists and physicists that they are harder to disprove.

What has drawn me to film, most of all, is its innate and unique capacity for conveying strangeness. This is not simply a matter of film being the best medium through which to disseminate curious or unusual or shocking images; more importantly, it is the way such images might be presented, juxtaposed, intercut with speech or music or silence in an attempt to replicate not only physical places or situations but states of mind. Take for example the sequence of images that form the opening act of Andrei Tarkovsky's 1972 film Solaris: the teacups overflowing with rain, the water weed moving slowly back and forward beneath the river's surface, the mist rising off the meadow, the nervous galloping of horses as a storm approaches all act as metaphors for the troubled mindset of the film's protagonist, the psychologist and cosmonaut Kris Kelvin as he prepares to embark upon his mission to the planet Solaris.

Such specific snapshots might be light years from the childhood or youth experiences of the audience, yet for anyone who encounters them they inspire an instantaneous feeling of nostalgia, of transporting the viewer back to a similar point of change, evolution or crisis in their own lives. The particular combination of sound, image and directorial intent lures the viewer into an alternative reality – a reality in which they too have experienced a longing for the past at the precise point of violently entering the future. Moments in which they too are overcome with feelings of regret and uncertainty when presented with reminders of their own indecisiveness or moral cowardice, as if through being invited to access the imaginative landscape of the director they are able to reconnect with those parts of their own past that still resonate most strongly.

The more I spend time on the forums the more my sense of what I choose to call reality has become fractured. There is the outward veneer, which I choose to imagine as a city of crystalline structures on a floating sheet of ice, and then the waters beneath, a vast, agate-coloured ocean whose depths are immeasurable. This ocean seems sentient, like the ocean of the planet Solaris in Tarkovsky's film, a commonwealth of partial memories and garbled ideas. Every now and then something surfaces that seems capable of disturbing the peace, a leviathan whose anger or potency or shimmering charisma threatens to shatter the precarious arrangement of tiny houses on the ice floe above. Ardent whale-watchers cling to its tail, ride the waves of its wake convinced, like those curious obsessives who chase tornadoes for hundreds of miles across a desert landscape, that the beast belongs to them, that it is ripe to be mastered.

I went through a phase of watching amateur film footage of storm chasers; brazen, confident individuals bounding through endless tracts of semi-industrialised farmland behind the padded steering wheels of their SUVs. Like all groups of enthusiasts, the storm-chaser community has a language and a jargon of its own, and all of its members seem to have stories of someone they knew who strayed too close to the tornado they were chasing and suffered disaster. They relate these stories with a lively relish. They do not imagine becoming the subject of such a story. None of them ever thinks it will happen to them.

Shane Carruth's film Upstream Color begins with a guy taking out the trash, two black garbage sacks filled with paper chains. The first time I saw the film I immediately assumed the action was taking place at Christmas time, a supposition reinforced by the fact that Christmas in the real world was less than three weeks away. In fact the paper chains have nothing to do with the festive season and the guy taking out the rubbish is in the process of committing a crime. This man is Thief, and he has discovered a new kind of organic hallucinogen, a bluish deposit or mould scraped from the leaves of plants whose roots are infested with the larvae of a particular species of insect. Thief has two adolescent boys working for him. Through Thief's intervention, the boys have themselves become addicted to the drug, which has psychokinetic properties.

Next we meet Kris, a young woman working as a picture editor at a film studio. Thief kidnaps Kris from outside her office and forces her to swallow one of the larvae. The drug present in the maggot renders her helpless, and highly suggestible, enabling Thief to gain control of her mind and actions. He returns with her to her home, where over a number of days he tricks her into handing over her life savings. In order to distract her from what he is doing, Thief occupies Kris in pointless tasks, such as copying out Henry David Thoreau's famous philosophical treatise Walden in its entirety, before cutting and pasting the transcribed pages into ribbons of paper chains. When she awakes from her hypnosis, Kris discovers she has been robbed of everything she owns. She has no memories of Thief, believing instead that she has suffered a catastrophic breakdown.

Adrift in the city, Kris is drawn into a relationship with one of Thief's other victims, a washed-up insurance broker named Jeff. Jeff has no memory of Thief either, and believes he embezzled money from his firm in order to support a gambling habit. Jeff and Kris are both insular, broken people, shadows of their former selves, yet they feel an instinctive connection to one another, almost a kinship. The closer they become, the more their memories interbleed. When Kris recalls an incident from her childhood, Jeff insists this is his memory, that Kris has stolen it somehow. Kris accuses Jeff of trying to make her story his own. Rather than driving them apart, this confusion of identities reinforces the bond between them. Gradually they begin to put together the missing pieces of their shared narrative.

Both of them are under the influence of the Sampler, a composer of avant-garde soundscapes compiled from ambient sounds and found music. The Sampler has a makeshift operating theatre in the back of his van, where he extracts the parasitic worms from Thief's victims and re-implants them in a drove of pigs at his upstate farm. As a result, the Sampled and the pigs become psychically linked.

The Sampler is an aloof and sinister presence. It is difficult to say if he is working together with Thief, or simply taking advantage of Thief's victims for reasons of his own. Through his contact with the pigs, he is able to psychically spy on the Sampled, vicariously experiencing their trauma. When Kris's pig becomes pregnant, the Sampler destroys her litter, a barbaric act that is experienced by Kris as an assault on her person, causing her to suffer a severe anxiety attack.

By following the psychic emanations of the pigs, Kris and Jeff are eventually able to locate the farm where they are being kept. Kris shoots the Sampler as an act of revenge for killing 'her' piglets. Afterwards, she and Jeff discover that the Sampler has been keeping extensive records of his human-pig experiments, which enable them to track down Thief's other victims. Together they renovate the farm and take care of the pigs. According to the principles enshrined in Thoreau's Walden, the Sampled reject the corporate world, choosing a simpler existence in harmony with nature.

The film has a dry, even shallow surface texture reminiscent of reportage photography or found footage and reminds me in places of the video clips of storm chasers I was once so obsessed with. The film's colour palette is muted, shading towards monochrome or sepia except in the startling blue of the plants that have been invaded by the alien parasite. The blue flowers represent the colonisation of the native environment by a corrosive other. As we gaze upon the flowers, the movie's colours become super-saturated, three-dimensional. There is a sense of transcendence. The film's greatest power lies in its ambiguity, the uncomfortable symbiosis of the human and the alien.

The film's minimalist soundtrack was composed by Shane Carruth himself. The score incorporates the ambient sounds collected by the Sampler: the scrape of a rusty saw against a wooden plank, the sonic boom that mysteriously draws Thief's victims towards the pig farm, the chiming of bells, the skittering rush of wind across a downtown intersection. Litter blowing in the gutters, the scratch and pull of paper chains, the plash of water held captive in an underground swimming pool. When Kris tries to describe the sound that plagues her at night she tells Jeff it is neither high nor low, or that it is high and low at the same time. What she is describing is called a harmonic, a note that is split in two along parallel lines.

Carruth's score has the painful purity of harmonics, the friable quality of an art installation, a work that can only exist temporarily but remains as a psychic reverberation in the memory of the viewer.

There is no overt suggestion that the parasitic worms in Upstream Color are of alien origin, but the effect they produce, both on their hosts and on their environment, is deeply alienating: the gradual, lethal overthrow of one set of systems by another.

My girlfriend Saira does not like Upstream Color. She insists that the first part of the film, in which Kris is kidnapped and loses her identity, is a toxic fantasy of abuse and control. She talks of the exploitative, objectifying way the camera moves over Kris's body, the way we are made to watch her wounding herself with a knife as she attempts to remove the maggot from beneath her skin. It is as if the camera is raping her, Saira says. It is such a typical man-film. Bloody terrifying.

Even at the time it was released, there was controversy online about the gendered portrayal of the film's two protagonists, the way Jeff is allowed to keep his clothes on both literally and metaphorically, while Kris is repeatedly shown in naked states of helplessness and terror. That Carruth cast himself and his real-life girlfriend Amy Seimetz as Jeff and Kris made the arguments more heated and more complex.

*

In July of 2020, Seimetz files a restraining order against Carruth, citing intimidating behaviour following the breakdown of their relationship in 2015. Seimetz split from Carruth after what she describes as months and years of psychological and physical abuse, accusations Carruth vehemently denies. In the August of 2020, a permanent restraining order is granted, to be kept in place until August 2025. Seimetz's petition includes many emails characterised by chilling threats and disturbing turns of phrase. Because of coronavirus restrictions, the hearing is held remotely, by telephone. Carruth interrupts the proceedings more than a dozen times.

You want to fight me? Carruth emails Seimetz in the December of 2018. Bring it. I will kill you.

The recent revelations about the couple's off-screen relationship have made some viewers and commentators see Upstream Color differently, though as a critic I cannot help thinking this is a dangerous path to tread. If we were to judge every work of art according to the moral character or actions of its creator, we would rapidly be on the way to an art-less society.

Saira says it is different when the monsters who terrorise women still walk among us. Still sit on directorial boards and prize juries. Still feel free to throw their weight about in any way they choose. You can't enjoy a work of art when you know the guy who created it is still making someone's life a misery. In the case of Shane Carruth, Saira is unforgiving.

*

He's a coercive controller, she insists. You can see it in every frame. It's the same in Primer, when you look closely. The women are erased.

I am relating to you these personal details only in the interest of objective reporting. I cannot see it myself. I view the connection forged between Kris and Jeff as deep and real, a means of wresting back control over their lives.

Notice the way Jeff looks after Kris, always acceding to her demands no matter how strange.

Notice the way Jeff asks Kris to marry him, right after she tells him she's been on anti-psychotic medication for more than a year.

In his final, posthumously published work, Brief Answers to Big Questions, the great astrophysicist and cosmologist Stephen Hawking posits the rise of a new, genetically engineered master race. Once such superhumans appear, he predicts, there will arise significant political and social problems with the unimproved humans, who won't be able to compete. Presumably they will die out, or become unimportant.

Eight years earlier, in a documentary series he made for the Discovery channel, Hawking warned us about the threat from alien invasion. If aliens visit us, Hawking argues, the outcome would be much as when Columbus landed in America, which resulted in the genocide of the Native Americans. In our search for extraterrestrial life – our eagerness to transmit radio broadcasts, to project our images, messages and music into space – we should be careful what we wish for.

When contemplated in the light of Hawking's words, is there any phrase more ominous than *keep watching the skies?*

In his WW2 stories as in his science fiction, John Sylvester is as concerned with the wars of the future as with the fallout from a conflict he has personally experienced. Similarly, Carruth's cinema of unease reflects back at us our mounting anxiety about the depredations of late-stage capitalism: climate change and environmental depletion, catastrophic die-backs, the winnowing away of species, the subjugation of independent-mindedness to corporate control, pristine wilderness scorched and levelled to an agri-business hell.

When contemplating such horrors we often forget that as a species we still have control over these outcomes, that such decisions about our planet's survival are still ours to make.

I believe that what I experienced that day in Crossac was an intimation of how much worse our situation would be if any and every decision about our future were to be removed from us. Such elimination of autonomy is what John Sylvester is talking about in The Tower, what Shane Carruth is attempting to show us in Upstream Color. This, I believe, is what Hawking meant, too. During the time of the COVID-19 pandemic there has been only a little discussion and speculation about how much worse our plight could have been, had the coronavirus inflicted the same mortality rate as ebola, for example, or as the plagues that swept through Europe in the Middle Ages. We do not like to tempt fate through such imaginings, perhaps, though personally I tend towards the assertion that forewarned is forearmed. When he speaks of Columbus and Native Americans, Hawking is asking us to imagine the utter absence of hope, the despair and chaos and grief that would be thrust upon us both as individuals and as a species were Earth's biosphere to become contaminated or compromised through alien interventions.

Even the Second Coming would not be so terrible; we have created God in our own image, after all. His works may be mighty yet we have furnished ourselves with the language to comprehend them.

Those who seek to warn us of our vulnerability are most often ridiculed, dismissed as fantasists or sociopaths or worse. Some of them may even be those things. We should make ourselves interested in what they have to say, though, if only out of curiosity at what the human imagination still has to offer.

Straws in the wind have substance, no matter how slight.

My advice to anyone still reading this? Keep watching the skies.

IN ANOTHER COUNTRY

I LOST MY TEMPER AT work, Robin says. I said some things I couldn't take back. That's why I left the police. My boss is a brilliant detective but he's not a good person. I couldn't be in the same room with him any more and so I resigned. I split up with my girlfriend because of it. Not because of losing my job but because I was such a mess afterwards. It wasn't her fault. I think I used my problems with Dunbar as an excuse to let things go under.

Don't feel you have to tell me this, Rachel says. Only if you want to.

I do want to, Robin replies, heavy emphasis on the do as if the word is a hammer-blow. She hears the harshness in her own voice, the anger, frustration, grief that followed her bust-up with Dunbar, that precipitated the inevitable irreversible failure of her relationship with Ashley.

I do, she says again, more softly this time, the sound like a distant drumbeat, a misty echo. I want you to know. Because you're impor-tant to me, she wants to add but doesn't, too important, perhaps, but I'm past the point of caring. She can feel the unspoken words caught in her throat, like splinters of bone she has tried to swallow and that refuse to go down. I need to tell you anyway, because of the case, she says instead. Because of Frank and because of the people he might be involved with. I'm not sure yet but I'm beginning to think I might know them. Know of them, anyway.

She is round at Rachel's place again, and something about the situation – about being alone with her – has made it seem impossible not to say these things. Robin tells herself she owes it to Rachel to be transparent, that Rachel is counting on her to make these connections, she is paying her to make sense of this jumble and that at least is true.

They send out for Chinese. The guy who delivers their order has a look of Frank about him, a temporary look, the same narrow wrists and shifting gaze, and Robin finds herself thinking of a boy she went out with briefly in her final year at school, remembers something he'd said to her right before he dumped her: You're so serious, Bobbie. You drive people crazy.

I'm serious? You go to fucking maths camp, Robin had thought, had wanted to scream but had not said at all. His going to maths camp was one of the things she had liked most about him. Her first memories are of Dianne's kitchen, she says to Rachel. The scent of tinned ravioli, that orange smell, the old-fashioned central heating boiler Derek used to dry his hat and gloves on when he came in from work.

Dianne told me I was adopted as soon as I was old enough to understand. Your mother loved you, Bobbie, she said, then asked if I had any questions and I said no. I didn't ask because I was scared the life that I had might turn out not to be real. After Dianne told me, I was constantly on the lookout for others who had been adopted. Even after I joined the police, if a note on a case file said that person was adopted I'd pay closer attention, as if I believed that by us both being adopted we were somehow related.

Dianne thinks I became a detective because of my dad, but it isn't true. I became a detective because I wanted to know things. Because I wanted to be sure I knew what was really going on.

The murder that begins it all looks straightforward, if you can call it that: one member of an organised crime group bumps off the foot soldier of another organised crime group. Payback for an old grudge, Dunbar insists, a revenge killing five years in the making. Back when you were still in uniform, lass, he adds, Dunbar's idea of a joke, the kind you nodded along with or ended up wishing you had. Robin has been in Dunbar's squad three years at this point, a sideways transfer from homicide to organised crime. She is sick of murder, frankly, the squalidness of individual cases, the incurable stupidity of most of the defendants, the hopeless rage she feels, more and more often, upon arriving at a crime scene. You think the murder squad is glamorous? Try working the result of the latest falling-out between one alcoholic wife-beater and another. Try sifting through thirty festering wheelie bins looking for a murder weapon. The state of the shitholes they call home, it's enough to send you screaming back to traffic until it's time to retire.

Organised crime is similarly squalid – rats ratting on rats – but at least there is a sense of satisfaction in getting the bastards banged up where they belong. More even than that, Robin relishes the opportunity for actual detective work, the painstaking teasing out of who had been ratting on whom and with what result. What Dunbar calls the legwork.

Dunbar's instincts are preternatural, the kind of skill that seems inborn, that cannot be taught. You don't achieve Dunbar's solve rate without getting your hands dirty, and Dunbar's mitts are filthy up to his elbows. Everyone on the squad knows Alec Dunbar's like a live hand grenade, but they all feel lucky to work with him, and that includes Robin. Each secretly hopes they won't be the one to cop it when – it's always a when and not an if with psychos like Dunbar – something goes badly to shit and the bill comes due.

Robin's birth mother is a musician – that's all she's been told. It is only when she starts becoming interested in music herself that Robin finally asks Dianne the questions that have started to obsess her. What kind of musician was she, what more do you know? Dianne goes quiet, looks embarrassed, says she's sorry. She doesn't have any details, no one ever said.

At twelve years old, the idea that Dianne might be hiding something from her, something important, is too upsetting for Robin even to consider. She has been off school for a month with pneumonia, lying weakly in bed in the flat with the radio on, becoming more and more convinced her mother is trying to communicate with her through the music. Even now she believes this must have been true in its way, because what is genetic inheritance if not a passageway for the smuggling of contraband, a secret code?

All murders are terrible, she says to Rachel, but anyone who's worked in homicide will tell you that once you've been on the job long enough they all blend into one. Right up until the case that does for you, that is. You never know when that day is coming, but when it does you have a duty to ask yourself if your time is up. The moment you start to give in to your feelings, you can't trust your judgement, and the moment you can't trust your judgement you're a liability.

The killing of Edgar de Groote turns out not to be as simple as it first appears. There are the de Grootes, and the Vanderliens. Milan Harwicz in digital forensics calls them the Montagues and the Capulets because their families have been feuding for generations. That's the thing with organised crime: it's never just a tit-for-tat. Every move in the game is steeped in symbolism. Edgar de Groote is or rather was the forty-eight-year-old son of Ivan de Groote, nicknamed, unimaginatively, Ivan the Terrible. Ivan's Nunhead born and bred, never set foot north of the river some say, those who know him best, both cops and robbers.

Ivan's boy Edgar was the wastrel son, the one who was never going to come to anything, who spends his time making trouble for those who were. Some of the guys on the squad are convinced Edgar's murder is a misfortune he has brought upon himself – not connected with business in other words, the next best thing to a random killing. Their reasoning is based upon the fact that if the Vanderliens were involved they'd have taken out Edgar's younger brother Graham instead. Graham (aka Golden Graham) has a Classics degree from Oxford and younger sibling or no he is known to be next in line to the de Groote throne. Why would anyone bother with Edgar when it's Graham that counts?

What the sceptics seem to have forgotten is that it was Edgar, not Golden Graham, who was responsible for the death of Mervin Van-derlien's teenaged son Tomas. Tomas snorted bad coke – coke that one of Edgar's runners had supplied. Tomas died of a heart attack under Waterloo Bridge, lay there slowly stiffening until a cop car cruising the area spotted his corpse around seven a.m. on the following day.

According to those shadowy figures known in the trade as inside sources (aka snitches) Ivan the Terrible was that pissed off with Edgar for being so careless (aka clueless) he almost put him in the hospital, but that's not good enough for Mervin Vanderlien, he can't afford to let it be. Edgar de Groote's time is up, which means that Dunbar and the squad are bound to investigate.

No one pretends to care much about Edgar's demise – the streets of Peckham will be cleaner and quieter without him, at least for a while – but his murder was elaborate and particularly vicious. The DS following his back-trail establishes that Edgar was kidnapped from outside his own nightclub, held in a cellar where he was beaten and forced to drink his own piss before being bound, gagged and chucked down a railway embankment in front of the 8:18 to Sidcup.

We cannae leave a thing like that just hanging, lads, Dunbar insists. Shit like that keeps on bobbing to the surface until we flush it away.

Dunbar puts Robin on counterintelligence (aka legwork). The whole squad knows who is responsible for the murder, but what they don't know, at least not yet, is who's the executioner, and it's Robin's job to fish around, to flush out the attack dogs. Dangerous work unless you're on the family payroll. Robin has known lads who've chosen to go that route, who'll take what crumbs they throw you in exchange for immunity. Some of them are good officers, or at least they were.

Robin backtracks Edgar's movements, starting with the club. She is trying to build up a picture of the night in question, what the general vibe was: who was drunk and who was sober, who was being an arse. In the course of doing the interviews she finds herself getting interested – interested in Edgar. The common wisdom amongst the squad is that Edgar's a waster, a lowlife, but those she speaks to, those who actually knew him tell her different: Edgar went to college, he was as golden as Golden Graham until he went bad. Some say he suffered a head injury, the result of a punch-up; others whisper he did something to tick off the Russian mob and suffered the consequences.

He were never the same afterwards, poor old Edgar, not after what they done to him . . .

There was a war on, one witness says. There was a war, and Steady Eddie was one of the casualties.

Strange stories and conflicting accounts. None of them adding up to anything you could swear an oath on. Robin mentions the Russian rumours to Dunbar and he tells her to forget it, to stop fashing hersel with ancient history and for pity's sake confine her attention to the job in hand. They're a load of useless drunks down the Tiger anyway, he says, a statement Robin cannot argue with, though she decides there's no harm taking a look at some of the older case files, not if she does it on her own time. What she does on her own time is none of Dunbar's business.

Robin has never seen a photograph of her birth mother. Dianne insists she and Derek were never given one, so when Robin first stumbles across the file on Marianne Lees she is just a name. Marianne was twenty when she died, the same year Robin was born, a detail Robin takes note of without affording it significance. Every murder has to happen sometime, and Robin has never tried to trace her birth mother, nor (beyond those tentative, embarrassed questions when she was twelve) tried to find out more about her, even though the process is easier than it used to be. A lot of kids who are adopted set the wheels in motion when they turn eighteen, but not Robin, who tells herself her reluctance stems from a fear of hurting Dianne, of making her feel inadequate, less of a mother.

Bobbie and Dianne against the world, that is how things have been since Derek died, how they must stay.

Robin wonders now if that was all bullshit, if a part of her guessed what was waiting in the wings and didn't want to know. Marianne Lees was a student at Goldsmiths. She played piano and harpsichord, though her main subjects were musicology and composition. Her dad was an army physiotherapist – he worked in the rehabilitation of soldiers who had suffered injuries on the battlefield. Her mum was a schoolteacher – history. Marianne Lees was no one, a civilian; in the eyes of the de Grootes and the Vanderliens she was invisible. Organised crime won't touch civilians, not as a rule. If they go messing in with the civs, the cops will start messing with them and then where will it end? If there's one thing the family men don't care for it's cops in their business, not unless they're their cops and no one talks about them.

Marianne's boyfriend is this guy name of Mark Denisov. Thirty years old, a junior lecturer at Goldsmiths, working on this so-called magnum opus that is going to rock the world of classical music to its foundations. Mark was something of a wunderkind, a prodigy, but had to give up performing when he lost one of his fingers in a frigging motorcycle accident. Turns out Mark Denisov – get this – is the son of Roman Denisov, in deep with the Vanderliens and with a history of violence. Was he part of the mob that did damage to Edgar all those years ago? The CIO at the time seemed to think so, enough to believe that Mark Denisov's motorbike smash had not been an accident.

Marianne Lees was never a part of what they were planning, that seems obvious, at least to Robin. Roman Denisov owes money to one of Ivan de Groote's associates – Robin knows the backstory down to the last detail, but the details aren't the point. The point is de Groote wants to give Denisov a warning, fire a shot across the bows, and de Groote knows the best way of getting to Roman is through his son. He arranges for Mark to be kidnapped from his flat in Camberwell and held in a safe-house down on the coast (Shoreham-by-sea if you're interested) until Roman coughs up. Posturing in other words, a spot of dick-measuring. The actual debt is relatively minor, there's no question Roman will pay. Everyone gets their balls back, goes home happy.

Only Mark isn't at the flat when Ivan's runners come for him. Marianne is at the flat, so they grab her instead. The runners are eighteen years old, younger than she is, which is why they panic. We heard a baby crying in one of the bedrooms, says Lenny Tyler – that's the boy who got nicked. We were scared someone might come because the kid was screaming its head off. We had to get out of there. No one meant the girl to be hurt, it was an accident. If she hadn't tried to escape, she would have been fine.

*

That was you, wasn't it, Rachel says, the crying baby?

Robin nods. The other runner – the one who got away – that was Alec Dunbar. There was this guy – a homeless man – who was a witness to the murder of Edgar de Groote. He wouldn't go to court – he didn't want to be involved and I can't say I blame him much – but I interviewed him several times, off the record. He was getting on a bit, had a terrible cough. I went to see about finding him a place in one of the hostels but he wouldn't hear of it, said those places gave him the willies, all those cameras and room checks. Like Nineteen Eighty-Four in there, he said, which made me laugh because he's not wrong is he, or not entirely. But he must have been touched that I made the effort, that I'd thought about him at least, because he suddenly changed the subject, asked me if I knew my boss used to run errands for Ivan the Terrible.

I asked him who he meant, Robin says, but I knew, I knew without having to be told. I think on some level I'd always known, but it was the same as with Dianne, I didn't want to face it.

The Scotsman, says the homeless guy, Alec Dunbar. He was a bad kid back in them days, well off the rails. I guess we all do things we end up regretting, it's part of being young, but it was Alec Dunbar who killed that piano girl. Lenny Tyler took the rap but it was Dunbar who did for her. Went on the run for a year then came back from the dead, joined the blessed boys in blue. Freaked him out I reckon, the thing with the girl. Made him see how easy things could go places you'd never dream of. Fancy suits and knocked-off watches is one thing, but going down for murder? Not what he signed up for.

We sat quietly, Robin says, watching the river. Then I asked him how come he knew all this.

Used to go out with Len Tyler's sister, didn't I? But that was in another country and besides, the wench is dead. I stare at him and he raises an eyebrow as if to say why shouldn't he be familiar with Elizabethan revenge tragedy, just because he sleeps in doorways and has a terrible cough? He knows more about revenge than the merchant bankers who trudge past his shivering body each evening on their way to the club.

Kit Marlowe, he says. He was killed just down the road from here. I think of him as one of the lads.

What about Dunbar though? says Rachel. Wasn't he worried you'd find out? When he realised who you were, I mean.

He never did realise – not when I first joined the squad, not later. Didn't have a clue and why would he, when I didn't have a clue myself? If he'd twigged – if he had any suspicion whatsoever – he'd have found a way of having me chucked off organised crime, chucked off the force too most likely. You could even say he did, in the end. I've often wondered how it feels to be him – Dunbar. Never to have a moment's doubt about the rightness of what you do. To believe in yourself absolutely, even though you know there are people and plenty of them who would gladly see you in jail, or dead.

You never thought of going after him, of bringing a case against him? He is a murderer.

He already was a murderer – that wouldn't have been news to anyone. What's one body more or less? Dunbar has powerful friends, the kind who would go out on a limb for him. Because he's good at his job and looks after his own. I might have tried anyway, if there'd been more evidence. But it's getting on for forty years now since Marianne died. There was nothing at the scene – nothing that would link the crime to Dunbar, anyway. It would have been my word against his and I felt sick at the thought of it. I felt like a coward, like I'd betrayed her. I couldn't stand it, the endless circling, the lack of sleep. I ended up having a blackout – a literal blackout. I was on stakeout at the time. A week after that I had a panic attack in a multi-storey car park and almost got run over. Someone on the squad – I never found out who – reported they'd heard me throwing up in the toilets when I was supposed to be filing paperwork. I was making mistakes, the kind that shouldn't happen, the kind that put others in danger.

Finally Dunbar calls me into his office, says I'm obviously not hacking it and he's putting me on leave. That's when I lost it. I told him to go fuck himself. He looked at me with such hatred that for a moment I thought he was going to come out from behind his desk and thump me one. Then suddenly his expression changes. I see it happen, like he's flipped channels on the TV. He speaks slowly and terribly calmly, says I should think myself lucky he has the door closed or I'd be looking at a suspension.

Suspend me then, you bastard, I say. I know what you did.

I open the door and walk out of his office and then out of the building and that's the last time I saw him. The worst thing is I can't shake the thought that if he'd admitted it – if he'd said sorry – I might have stayed. There was no chance of that though, thank fuck. Alec Dunbar would sooner take a bullet in the head than admit he made a mistake.

*

I go back there sometimes, Robin says, to the place I spoke with the homeless guy. Duncan, he said his name was. He's never there, but I like to look at the river.

She feels wrung out, as if she's just run a marathon, her shirt drenched in sweat. I spoke to Dianne, she says finally, after I resigned from the force, after I split up with Ashley. We were sitting there in her kitchen because that's where we always sit and I asked her if she'd ever heard of Marianne Lees. I was all psyched up to tell her – to tell her the whole story – but then I realise she knows it already, I can tell from her eyes. She looks down at the table and says yes, she knows who Marianne is, she's been trying to find a way to tell me but she never knew how.

What, trying for thirty years? I say, and she says yes, that's right, and I find I'm holding my breath, waiting for her to say something that will make sense of it, her silence, but the words never come. I can't look at her, can't speak, so I get up from the table and walk out. I hear her call my name but I don't look back. I ignored her calls and emails for weeks, for months. We're OK again now but I hate the fact that I made her suffer, because my anger was never about her, it was about the silence. I needed to hear the story, to hear it spoken aloud.

You never told anyone?

Robin shakes her head.

What about your birth father? What about Mark Denisov?

Mark Denisov isn't my dad. I thought at first he must be, then I found out he and Marianne only got together after I was born. I have my birth certificate now, but my father's name isn't on it. Just some kid most likely, someone Marianne knew from school maybe. I think about him sometimes. I wonder what he's doing. I've never told anyone this either, especially not Dianne, but I like thinking about him. I like wondering. He could be anyone. I sometimes look at men's faces as I pass them by in the street and wonder if it's them. There's a freedom in not knowing. It makes the world seem larger, more filled with life.

I think Frank felt like that too, Rachel says, about his own dad I mean. Frank once told me he didn't mind if they never met. What matters is that he exists, he said, that he's out there. I used to think that was so sad, but perhaps I was wrong.

The air in the room feels humid, close. Schrödinger's dad, Robin thinks. She has never equated her situation with Frank's, but now Rachel has made the comparison she cannot unthink it.

I always wished I had a brother, she says suddenly.

Rachel looks at her, eyes glinting gold in the light from the lamp, the weak yellow bulb under its ugly orange shade, and Robin realises it's pitch dark outside, they have been talking for hours, though in a sense everything she has told Rachel is simply background. The weight of confusion has been lifted, but only partially, because there is still the rest of it, the way Robin felt when she first began to realise who they are, the people on the forum, EdmundofGloucester and JeanneDark, Edmund de Groote and Jeanne-Marie Vanderlien, the people who lured Frank Landau to Paris, the people who scared Miles Shipley so badly he had a cardiac arrest.

The de Grootes and the Vanderliens, the syllables falling like coins, like copper pennies in a one-armed bandit. Like dumb stones thrown into a river, thud thud thud.

Had they known about the war, even back then?

Had they been secretly working together all along?

Surely some revelation is at hand . . .

You don't really think that, do you? Rachel is saying, that the people on the forum are part of the same family?

Families, Robin thinks, families plural. I have to speak to her about the tower, about the war, only not tonight. Robin wants to imagine a world in which none of this is real, in which Miles and Frank and the tower are just figments, phantoms she's dreamed, in which the time has finally come to close the file.

I don't know yet, she says. I'm still trying to make sense of it all. She takes Rachel's hand in hers, feels their fingers curling together, strokes her smooth gold nails.

It's mega-late, she says, you must be tired.

I am tired, Rachel says, her eyelids are drooping, her words an affirmation, an echo, or both, Robin cannot really tell.

Robin says goodnight and leaves. By the time she is back on Hainault Road it is almost one o'clock. A bus sweeps by, yellow-eyed. Robin dumps her shirt in the linen basket, showers quickly, thinks about pouring a whisky, drifts down into sleep.

At three in the morning she stumbles awake again, hideously and without warning, like tripping over a tree stump on a forest pathway. Headlight beams dapple the curtains. Small shadows creep and tremble at the margins of the room.

They will bury you, she thinks, the words rising up out of nowhere from her shattered sleep, slamming the walls of her chest like divots of ice.

ORATORIO

S HE HAS POSTED MORE comments on LAvventura under the joker handle, which she has also used to set up a dialogue with JeanneDark. Nothing too probing, just casual questions about her career in journalism, suitably admiring.

I think your stuff on John Martyn is excellent. Did you ever get to meet him?

Several times. He let me take some photos backstage once at a gig in Berlin.

Just enough to make her presence familiar and non-threatening. Vanderlien must be getting on in age now, she must be seventy at least, though in the photos online she still appears younger: shoulder-length hair, black biker jacket, sometimes with, sometimes without a cigarette, that crooked smile, as if one side of her mouth has been injured and it hurts to move it.

Robin searches for any confirmed connection between Vanderlien and de Groote outside of the LAvventura forum and cannot find one. So far as she can tell, Jeanne-Marie Vanderlien has not been directly employed by any publication online or off for more than a decade, though freelance articles by her still surface occasionally, mainly about classical music. There is one recent book-length essay on the Berlin avant-garde at the time of the Cold War, published as a chapbook by an independent press. She shows no discernible interest in aliens, supersoldiers or interstellar wars, though her attachment to conspiracy theories about the deep state, her admiration for radical activists and fringe terrorists like Ulrike Meinhof is a constant underhum. Nothing unusual about any of that though, not within the context of her Cold War background, and esoteric content aside, Robin finds herself admiring the way Vanderlien writes, the poetry of her sentences, the originality of her ideas, her passion for music. She is almost tempted to blow her cover so they can have a proper conversation but not yet, not yet, the link is still too friable. One wrong move and JeanneDark could go to ground.

The more she discovers about Vanderlien, the more she reads her writing, the more Robin becomes convinced she is in some way the key to it all, the organ grinder to Edmund de Groote's monkey. De Groote writes about himself a lot, Vanderlien, for all her incisiveness and passion, remains opaque, a spider in the works. One afternoon in early December Robin gets on a train heading east towards Wanstead, where she and Ashley lived together, where she has not ventured since she and Ash split up. There has been no need, no excuse. Robin's desire for the place, for this wintry part of London is all wrapped up in Ash, not just her physical presence but the idea of her, an idea that is coming increasingly to seem like it belongs to another life.

Disembarking from the train, the station platform, the building's

entranceway and immediate environs are as consistent with her imagining as a familiar photograph, intimately known yet at the same
time distant. She finds pleasure in walking, in the simple defiance of
inertia, yet the sight of others – a group of cyclists in identical kit, two
young women pushing baby buggies, a group of kids running about
near the ponds – fills her with both nostalgia and unease. This will
all be swept away, she thinks, the chill of winter, a solitary blackbird,
the soft susurrus of fallen leaves scattered in gouts of gold across the
concrete pathway.

Robin breathes in deeply, trying to quell the panic and only partially
succeeding. She travels the length of Overton Drive, continuing beside
the A114 until she comes to the right-hand turning into Belgrave Road.
She comes to a standstill outside No. 53, the house where she lived
with Ashley in the first-floor apartment. She stares up at the windows,
then steps jerkily backward, almost tripping over. There is someone
staring out at her, a woman. Greying hair looped back behind her ears,
high-necked woollen jumper, heavy specs. Her face is pale and dish-
like, her gaze intense. The importunate thought – that this is Jeanne
Vanderlien – flits soundlessly across Robin's mind, comes darkly to
rest. The idea is ridiculous of course but in the glare of the woman's
gaze the thought persists.

Robin wonders if this is what it feels like to be Frank Landau:
the thrum of anxiety, the unfounded suspicions, the inescapable and
constant feeling of being watched. She turns her head to check the
rest of the street and when she glances back up at the window the
woman is gone.

She returns to Wanstead station where a train has just come in.

She feels breathless, as if she has been running. Back at the flat she checks her email and then her message cache on LAvventura: nothing new. She pours herself a double Macallan, puts on the second disc of Bach's Mass in B minor, Philippe Herreweghe's recording on Harmonia Mundi with the Collegium Vocale Ghent. She lets it play through until the Benedictus, which she listens to two, three times in succession, the sparse, brittle melody seeming to her suddenly like a precious remnant, an artefact dug from the ashes, a last vestige of civilisation hailed as a miracle then sidestepped, forgotten, relinquished in the face of the present, urgent contingencies of ordinary survival.

Christoph Prégardien's unshowy tenor robust but humane, the magnanimous through-line against warm woodwind, the most per-fectly articulated flute solo in all of Western music, the righteous, impassioned singing of a little nun.

Be-e-e-ne-dic-tus, qui ve-nit in no-min-e Do-min-i.

The glory of Bach lies in the discords, the jarring mismatches and awkward intervals that Handel – grandmaster of propriety – would never have countenanced. Handel, so magisterially of then, the glorious summer of his regal cadences. Bach is of neither then nor now, Bach is of forever and of never. Easier to compare his works with Varèse's dissonant gossamer infinities than with the dutifully sewn samplers of his own tirelessly working, good-humoured sons.

The devil is in the detail. The singing of angels lies in the silences, in the thorny gaps.

Blessed is he who comes in the name of the Father. Yes, but who is it that is coming?

Robin picks up her phone and dials Dianne, but the call goes straight to voicemail and Robin remembers tonight is Labour night, the Red Rose discussion group Dianne has been in for years, meeting at Southwark College then down the pub afterwards. Dianne will not be in until after eleven. Robin terminates the call without leaving a message, then checks her LAvventura cache again.

One new message, sender JeanneDark: *are you sure you want this?*

What do you mean? Robin messages back. Her heart is thumping. *I hardly know you.*

Do we have to play these games? JeanneDark shoots back immediately, which means she has been sitting there waiting for Robin to log on so they can have this conversation. Robin wonders what has made Vanderlien break cover and why now? Some digital tripwire she has stumbled over unknowingly, or maybe it is down to de Groote — de Groote and Vanderlien comparing notes, exchanging sightings, warning each other.

I won't play games if you won't, Robin types slowly. *Was that you I saw at the house earlier, in Wanstead?*

I have been in Marseille for two weeks recording a documentary, so whoever you think you saw it was not me.

Where is Frank Landau? Is he in Marseille, too?

I have no idea where he is. He is not here so far as I know.

But you did meet him, in Paris?

I met him, yes. He came to Marco Huus's apartment, with Eddie. He stayed one night then left. Eddie never heard from him again.

Am I supposed to believe that?

I can only tell you what I know. Whether you believe me or not is up to you.

If I ask you one question will you answer it honestly?

You can ask.

Do you seriously believe in the war or is it a cover for something else, some sort of code?

The war is real. The war is also a code, also a metaphor.

That isn't a proper answer.

Because your question is not precise enough to be a proper question. If you are talking about a war with guns and bombs and bullets then no, there is no war, at least not at present. That is the kind of war that forms the tawdry midway point of millions of years of evolution. The origins of such wars though are to be found in the ceaseless struggle for dominion over matter itself: minute cellular changes, single-cell anomalies, vari- ant mutations. If left to themselves, the wars among the microbes are bound to escalate. What happens then is the same as what happens in any other war: destruction, collapse, a loss of autonomy so catastrophic it is irreversible. The evidence of this is apparent from our own recent history. We want money spent, tests carried out, inquiries launched. Does that sound like conspiracy to you? Does that sound unreasonable? Personally I would call it taking a scientific interest in the world around us. I would not claim to be an expert in such matters but I have helped to establish connections and working groups with those who are: botanists, microbiologists, climate scientists, mycologists. Are you suggesting these highly trained specialists are also lunatics?

You killed Miles Shipley. Or Edmund de Groote did.

You know already that cannot be true. I never met Miles Shipley. Miles Shipley died of a heart attack, in his hotel room.

Edmund de Groote was the last person to see Miles Shipley alive.

. . . . . .

I want to ask you another question — nothing to do with de Groote.

You can ask.

Do you recognise the name Mark Denisov? Or Marianne Lees? Are you connected with the London Vanderliens?

That is three questions.

Not really.

The Vanderliens are an old family with many connections. I have no idea who you are talking about but it doesn't matter. Whatever you believe to be important about these people is not truly important.

The only thing that matters is the war, right?

Do not be flippant with me. If you understood what is at stake you would not be flippant.

Tell me, then. Tell me what is so important you are forced to speak in riddles.

You remember all of those tower blocks that were put up in the 1960s, the ones with concrete cancer? There was a guy I knew, a guy I wrote a story on. He was famous in the sixties as a fashion photographer, then he had a motorbike accident and he couldn't work any more. He was moved into one of those blocks. He used to tell me he could hear it in the night, the sound of the slow-motion chemical reaction that was eating the concrete. He said it got right inside his head – the language of entropy. I too can hear it in the night, the sound of what is happening to the Earth. What will happen, eventually, if no steps are taken. Do you want to know a secret?

That's a question people only ask when they're going to tell you anyway.

I recognise the sound because I have heard it before. I am old. Old enough to remember other wars. And I am getting tired.

Why did you write about Ulrike Meinhof and Ian Brady?

New Writings is a novel, a thought experiment. Such experiments are still permitted, are they not? I wrote about Meinhof because I am interested in anger, a woman's anger especially. Anger is the most interesting of the emotions because it tells you what a person truly believes. Women's anger is interesting because we are conditioned to repress it all of our lives, from the moment we are born. We must struggle to own it, to reclaim it and to use it. Men never have to struggle in that way. What makes you angry, Bobbie? I do not mean annoyed, or vexed. I mean angry enough to lose your temper. Angry enough to kill. You have asked me your questions, so here is one for you. I am interested to hear your answer.

Injustice. That's the reason I joined the police.

Wrong answer. You became a police detective because you enjoy the challenge — you like finding things out. For you, being a detective is a personal mission, not a social crusade. You care about injustice, yes, but you are intelligent enough to know that injustice is part of the state of existence, like gravity, or entropy. You can mitigate its effects, but the overall tendency towards inequality cannot be altered. Marx was wrong. Human beings and the systems they create are not perfectible, which is why all attempts to eradicate inequality have resulted in despotism. The relationship between the individual and the collective will always be a compromise, because the two are incompatible. When Tolstoy spoke of family he was also speaking of society — of utopia and dystopia, which are in fact the same thing. I loathe injustice as you do but it is repression that makes me most angry.

Peace rarely does mean peace or not peace for everyone but the peddling of lies as truth is worse even than war.

You're a child of the Cold War, you should know.

Robin recalls a photograph she has seen online, Jeanne-Marie Vanderlien with Nico, singer with the Velvet Underground, icon of the counterculture, taken in West Berlin close to the site of the old SS headquarters on Prinz-Albrechtstrasse, the two of them wearing matching black biker jackets over white T-shirts emblazoned with the symbol for CND, what Vietnam-War-era Americans used to call the peace sign.

The so-called SS-Haus was destroyed by Allied bombing in 1944; instead of erecting a memorial, the East German authorities left the ruins to stand as a reprimand and as a warning, as their own museum. A null-space, so contaminated by its own history it is thought almost to be infectious.

I am not your enemy, Bobbie. We may be coming from different places, but we are on the same side.

I'm not on anyone's side. Why would I believe you, anyway? Choosing to believe in something no one else believes is an act of self-destruction.

Choosing not to believe in something you know to be true is a bigger one. Like walking out into the desert without any water, like walking through a crowded shopping mall without wearing a mask. A defiance of your own logic.

There is no logic in anything you've told me. If what you say is true then we would know. There would be studies, scientific conferences. You can't keep something like that secret, not from everyone. Facts leak out. People talk.

What would you say we're doing now, Robin?

I would say you're a conspiracy theorist and I've been doing too much overtime.

Robin waits, expecting some sort of comeback, but the message cursor remains still, blinking stubbornly at the bottom right-hand corner of her screen. After half an hour with no response, Robin screenshots the conversation and closes the window. She feels faint with hunger, and it is only when she looks at her phone that she realises she has been hunched in front of her computer for more than two hours. She grills two stale muffins, the last of a pack she bought a week ago. There is a spot of blue mould on one. She scrapes it off quickly, wondering what traces remain, what she would see if she were to examine the bread under a microscope, how much of the muffin has been undermined, infiltrated by threads of a mycelium invisible to the human eye.

She recalls an experiment they did back in science class with a slice of Mother's Pride, the way it had transformed from pristine whiteness to bastions of fungus in less than a fortnight, unrecognisable as a slice of bread, something alien and almost terrible. A defiance of its own logic.

Robin's classmate Garry Makeba had pronounced it cool.

Garry the mould monster, they christened him, laughing. Robin had run into Garry on Peckham High Street a couple of years back, cool-dude shades and jeans so tight they were like a second skin. Garry nodded almost imperceptibly then turned quickly away, called out yo to some guys sorting through a box of LPs outside a junk store on the other side of the road.

A road as wide as a river Robin could never cross. She puts cheese on top of the muffins, turns on the TV. A forest fire in Australia raging across thousands of acres of bush, a pall of smoke over Sydney a hundred miles wide. Like we'd fallen into the sun, says an Aussie firefighter, her cheeks grey with ash. Like the inside of hell.

Robin gets up to put on coffee, jumps as the entryphone buzzes. Addison Lee, says the voice through the speaker as if that were their name. Robin is not expecting a delivery. She flicks up the latch and goes downstairs. The package is small, sealed in a plastic delivery bag. Robin thanks the courier then signs the docket, the courier's face invisible beneath the black dome of his bike helmet. Inside the bag is a compact disc, Bach's D minor keyboard concerto played by Joanna MacGregor and the Britten Sinfonia coupled with Ned Rorem's song cycle The Evidence of Things Not Seen, MacGregor on piano again, performing with a group of singers Robin has not heard of before called The Four Feathers.

The Bach is inauthentic but sensational, MacGregor's performance muscular and vigorous, pure adrenaline-rush. The Rorem piece is previously unknown to her, though its calculated astringency makes it natural territory for MacGregor. The cycle opens with an arrangement of a poem by Auden, a spiky agglomeration of fits and starts. The CD's liner notes include the full text, and Robin realises with a shiver that it is familiar to her, part of an anthology of twentieth-century poetry she studied for GCSE English. The words, juddering and smoking in Rorem's barbed wire, are bleak and oddly disturbing, a premonition of doom. She remembers how she puzzled over them when she was younger – the reader, the rider, the furnaces, the grave – how she fought to make sense of their rhythms, their distant thunder like the thunder of horses' hooves, an image that came to her mainly because of the rider mentioned in the actual poem.

O Where Are You Going *is taken from The Orators, Auden's second book of poetry, written in the Scottish coastal town of Helensburgh in 1932 and seething with the tensions and unresolved conflicts of a nation still in recovery from one war whilst being dragged inexorably towards another . . .*

Robin refolds the liner notes to reveal the CD's cover image, the hazy outline of a ruined castle against a semi-abstract background of blues and greens. Winter Landscape, Tain, she reads, from an original oil painting by Catriona Macrae.

In the lower right-hand corner is a figure on horseback, the limbs of horse and rider blending together in a blur of motion. Stuck to the back of the CD case there is a yellow Post-It note with a scribbled question: *see you there?* followed by a street address in the coastal town of Tain in the county of Ross-shire, Scotland. There is no signature, no return address on the packaging but Robin does not need to see one, she knows who the package is from, why it has been sent. Half an hour before she goes to bed she receives a new message from Jeanne-Marie Vanderlien.

The house is called Crombie House, after the Scottish lichenologist, James Crombie. It is run as a study centre for scientists and artists and researchers who have an interest in the local area. Visitors pay for their own food, and make a contribution to the house's running costs while they are staying there. You would be welcome to pay a visit.

Everything bought and paid for with Vanderlien money?

Crombie House is a charitable organisation. Members of my family have donated to that charity because we believe the research being done at Crombie House is important. Tain is a pleasant town. There is a museum of local history, an institute of botany, an interesting library archive. Also there is someone you might wish to meet.

Frank? Robin types furiously, but there are no further messages, just the cursor blinking, and Robin feels angry with herself for falling into the trap, for revealing her emotions, for letting her guard slip. The idea of hurtling up to Scotland on such slim evidence is like something out of a spy movie, an old-fashioned gung-ho melodrama like The Thirty-Nine Steps, but what was it she said to Dianne about false sightings being an occupational hazard, about how each one had to be investigated, no matter how unlikely?

O where are you going? Robin mouths the words softly to herself, listening for their distant drumbeats, which are really war music, the thudding of approaching hoof-beats over rain-soaked ground.

NIGHT TERRORS:
A CONCERT REVIEW
BY JEANNE-MARIE
VANDERLIEN

Nachtstücke und Arien for soprano and large orchestra by Hans Werner Henze with text by Ingeborg Bachmann, Juliette Clieg (soprano) Karl Brabant/Concertgebouw Orch July 16th 2021

I almost did not make it to the concert, because the day had been a disaster. I arrived at the venue still brooding over the argument I'd had with my friend Hanne, a doctor who had recently returned from a two-year stint volunteering with Médecins sans Frontières in Syria and who had spent most of our lunch date raging about what she called the Western sense of entitlement. She believed vaccination against COVID-19 should be made mandatory. When I suggested this would be unacceptable, an assault on civil liberties, she laughed in my face.

Civil liberties are a matter of social conditioning, she said. You have no trouble accepting that parents have a legal requirement to send their children to school, so what's the big deal?

I said this was different, that compulsory vaccination was an assault on the body. Some people are terrified of needles, I said. Do you want to live in a country where people are herded into medical centres against their will? Remind you of anywhere? I added, which was going too far, I guess, but I was annoyed. You know what's really going on here? You're blinded to the bigger picture. Your outlook has become corrupted by all those dodgy officials you've been forced to give bribes to.

What's really going on here, Hanne said, is that you're starting to sound like a conspiracy theorist. All that deep-state shit you're always on about.

I accused her of being burned out, then we parted without hugs or kisses, without making plans to meet again. The whole episode was unfortunate and would probably never have happened if I hadn't been upset already because of Carola. Carola was my closest friend, I'd known her since school, and she had just died of cancer. I had not seen her in several years, yet the news of her death felt like the end of something, as if part of my world had died with her, as if a formative part of my existence had been erased. I did not tell Hanne about Carola – in comparison with the carnage she had been witnessing, one death seemed pitifully small – yet I made her pay for it, nonetheless. As I stood in the queue at the Concertgebouw waiting to collect my ticket, my chest felt tight with rage and tears. A soft rain had begun to fall. I wished I had never agreed to this stupid review assignment.

Nachtstück 1

I am walking in the woods, thorns poking from the underbrush, a moon the colour of dirty linen crumpled and torn to pieces on the path ahead. I am thinking about Carola, who used to talk about the forest as an autonomous entity, who believed the way to spiritual enlightenment lay in reconnecting with the German mystics, Kleist and Tieck and Eichendorff, all that spooky brouhaha, all that pining for the mountains and spiritual Wanderlust.

You think? I remember saying to her. You don't stop to wonder if that was where Germany kind of went wrong in the first place? Carola looked aghast. Then, when she saw I was joking, told me I spent too much time with British people.

Irony killed the cat, she said. I turned the phrase over and over in my mind, in love with the rightness of it, with the accidental acuity of her innocent mistake. And perhaps it is after all a killer. Irony, I mean. Like that boring guest at a party who interrupts every amusing anecdote to correct some small and unimportant point of grammar.

Aria 1

Wherever we turn in the storm of roses
    The night flickers with the lightning of thorns
    And the thunder of foliage, once so silent in the bushes
    Now runs swift in pursuit

Just listen to those steel-capped reverberations, those nineteen-thirties harmonies, those late, receding echoes of Brecht and Weill.

I tell you, I tell you, I tell you we must die . . .

Nachtstück 2

The spectres swirl and flounce in the forest clearing at the witches' Sabbath. Horn tones and klavier, heady draught of Mahler, bottoms up. Why can't we party, why can't we drown in this leaf-blackened goblin world for evermore?

At the premiere of Henze's Nachtstücke und Arien at the Darmstadt Festival, the work drew not so much 'widespread condemnation' as bored ridicule. The cool kids staged a walkout. They didn't just leave the concert hall, they made a thing of it: see, this is us leaving, look. We're not standing for this piece of old tinsel, this dusty trash. Like they left the decorations up from before the war and forgot to take them down again. What do we want with shit like that these days, huh? Nothing.

In my own time the hall is hushed. Clieg's voice, like a dagger drawn, starlight flashing off the blade. Sounds like: the twentieth century. Travail, toil, delusion. Your watch is winding down, I think. Such a pretty thing too, rose gold.

Sounds like: I miss you, Carola.

Sounds like: the war.

There is a sculpture in the Tate Gallery in London, Jacob Wrestling with the Angel, by Jacob Epstein. In Nachtstücke und Arien, we hear Hans Werner Henze wrestling with the troubled legacy of German culture. The artists who would come to define the musical aesthetic of the 1960s – composers like Stockhausen and Boulez – believed the only way to confront the collapse of European essentialism and its sordid aftermath was to wipe the slate clean, to rebuild the language of music from its basic building blocks: sound, line, volume, the classical transparency of pure noise.

Henze and Bachmann have no trust in the language of purity, they have heard it all before. Here they are, hiding in foxholes, sifting through shrapnel, tearing their skin on leftover ordnance, sheared-off metal. A flash is a flash in the pan, dark-blue night with stuck-on stars, a tipsy waltz. What do we do with all this refuse, all this old-world litter?

To say I love you is like admitting I am already dead. Henze and Bachmann were born in 1926. 'In the shadow of fascism,' their biographers repeat insistently, but this is something more personal, something still more crushing. This is growing up under the eye of a Nazi father.

I never met Ingeborg Bachmann. I was supposed to go to a reading of hers once, at a bookstore in Munich. Something came up – I cannot remember what now, it's decades ago – and I never made it. I was young then, and in the thick of things, and it seemed not to matter. What is one writer more or less, one more guilt-racked poet? Some years later, when I heard she had died, the grief hit me like a freight train, though I could not explain this or even articulate it, not to anyone and especially not to the man I was with at the time. It is wrong of me I know, such a clichéd thing to say, but it seemed like his fault, her death. Like all their faults.

Bachmann wrote about how for women the solving of a man is the work of a lifetime, an enigma that tugs at the roots of the soul, unpicking, unravelling, unmooring, stripping away the certainties, any weak sense of self. Stripping away most of all the sense of being at the centre of one's own story. Layers of self-knowledge, like the finest of tissue paper, torn away and left to flutter and swirl like pieces of litter, caught by the wind.

I remember a churchyard in London, at bluebell time, strewn with confetti: powder-blue and rose-pink, horse shoes and stars and love-hearts and the tiniest crescent moons. I remember how the confetti, trampled in mud, was made into mulch. I remember the suicides and the would-be suicides, like Bachmann. The erasures and elisions, the silences.

Above all, I remember the silences.

For a woman, a man is a lifelong source of thinking, a conundrum, wrote Ingeborg Bachmann, but the man, he never thinks of her at all.

It gets easier, I want to say to her. Dig into the climb and you will grow beyond the pain. The view from the top is worth it, you can see hundreds of miles.

Bachmann was only forty-seven when she died. I cannot accept this.

The older I become, the more I realise my most valuable connections are with women who have reached the understanding that the only path to freedom is to be alone.

Aria 2

With birds drunk from sleep
And wind-ravaged trees
The day rises, and the sea
Raises a foaming glass to him

The use of natural imagery and themes in Bachmann's poetry is astoundingly prescient. Decades before the threat of climate change entered the popular imagination, Bachmann was writing about forests on fire, landscapes inundated by floodwaters, poisoned earth. When critics talk about her writing, they tend to equate her apocalyptic landscapes with her formative years, emerging from the shadow of Nazism, growing up beneath the threat of the nuclear bomb. I too am a child of the Cold War, and the culture and language of that time continues to resonate with me, even in the midst of what has come to be termed our new world order. But when I read Bachmann I find myself looking forward rather than back.

The extreme weather events, the perilous dynamism of her disasters reveal an intimacy with the natural world that feels painful rather than consoling. An overriding sense of doom permeates her work, of decadence and decay that might almost be interpreted as a reference to the gothic family saga, that old Bildungsroman by Thomas Mann in which a sordid moral inheritance leads inevitably to destruction.

These are Bachmann's themes, and to me they seem every bit as percipient as they are reflective. Bachmann is writing in the shadow of a war still fresh in the memory; the poem Im Gewitter der Rosen, which forms the text of the first aria, was originally written for the poet Paul Celan, who lost most of his family in the Nazi holocaust. Even so, as we read her words, we cannot help but tremble at the thought of war to come.

I keep wondering what my doctor friend Hanne would make of it, if she knew how much time I spend thinking about this next war and what it will look like. Another friend of mine, a lecturer in film studies, is convinced the next war will be fought against aliens. Not the kind of aliens you see on film posters – bug-eyed monsters and little green men – but single-celled organisms and viral pathogens, biological contaminants that have been introduced into Earth's ecosystem without our realising. Whether by accident or by design it is not yet known.

This new world war will be a war for our environment, my friend insists. He is spending much of his time now engaging in dialogue with like-minded scientists, who are fighting to gain academic credibility for their work in the nascent discipline of astrobiology. When I tell him about the interview I conducted with the mother of Lucian Cherish, he asks me eagerly if he can have her contact details. He keeps referring to Stephen Hawking, how shortly before his death he warned humanity of the dangers of trying to initiate contact with alien life forms. There are plenty who believe his warning came too late, my friend adds. Plenty who believe the invasion has already started.

When he asks me if I think he is crazy I say no, not at all. It takes courage to think differently, to explore an idea that seems strange to others or not widely accepted. I remind him that my entire career has been focused upon exploring the dividing line between delusion and genius, which a lot of the time is barely a line at all.

What is the use in thinking, I say to him, if it does not sometimes lead you into places you find dangerous or uncomfortable?

When he asks me if I believe what he has been telling me I find it more difficult to answer, because my mind is divided. In the front of my brain I believe no such thing. In the back room though, there is a fire going, and it is gaining in heat.

Only time will tell, I suppose, I say in the end. I shrug my shoulders and smile, and we both laugh.

Nachtstück 3

Owls cry in the wind-snapped branches, their dark latticework jaggedly trembling against a darker sky. These are the things Bachmann spoke of constantly, the things she clung to. The fall of moonlight across tree bark, the harsh yelling of a fox. I can feel how the world is winding down, the air of finality huffs cold breath against my salt-streaked cheeks. So long as there are owls in flight, I think. So long as there are pine needles underfoot in the darkness of winter then there is a life we can feel our way towards, a life worth fighting for.

During one of my conversations with the film critic it transpires that he too is familiar with a book some of my friends and I were into when we were students, an obscure little novel called The Tower, about an architect who designs a monstrous apartment complex built from alien rock.

A guy I knew back then thought The Tower was a work of genius. Like the flip-side of Ayn Rand, he said, the ultimate critique of fascism.

He had an idea for adapting the book into a stage play but it never took off. There is a passage in The Tower that has always haunted me, where the architect dreams of abandoning the city and going to live in a cabin in the forest, pretending that the war with the aliens has never happened.

'And it was true that in this instance the Earth had been lucky, if you could call it that,' the author writes. 'But Archie could not push the thought from his mind that the planet was on their radar now, that the war had been just a precursor of what was to come. He found it impossible to hear the cry of a screech owl without imagining, however fleetingly, a world in which all screech owls had been destroyed.'

I had not read the book in years, but sitting in the auditorium at the Concertgebouw I found myself remembering this passage especially, the impact it had on me when I was younger and so full of rage. The Ayn Rand guy went out with Carola for a while, though they were not well suited. Carola told me later she believed The Tower was a kind of code, a secret warning about a real alien invasion, a war of the future.

Carola wrote letters to Ulrike Meinhof when she was in prison. I was more than a little in love with her at that time, Carola I mean, in love with her openness, her daring, and perhaps that is why thinking about that strange story again now it seems more ambiguous even than it used to. When I first read The Tower I found the character of Archie Aspen despicable and yes, fascistic. Now I find I can see him as vulnerable and prey to fear. That passage about the screech owls still haunts my imagination, and I wonder if it was this that Bachmann was seeing somehow, a world in which all screech owls had been destroyed.

*

Hans Werner Henze and Ingeborg Bachmann first met in 1952. They formed an instant sympathy with one another. Born just a couple of days apart, they both had Nazi fathers, a legacy they spent much of their lives and work attempting to reckon with. Henze and his brother were forced to join the Hitler Youth. Bachmann always spoke of the day of the Anschluss, when she saw German tanks and soldiers parading through the streets of her native Klagenfurt, as the day on which her childhood ended, her adult memories and understanding of the world began.

Henze and Bachmann lived together as friends for several years, first on the island of Ischia and later in Rome. When Henze first relocated to Italy in 1953, Ischia was still a fishing community, unspoiled by mass tourism and attractive to artists because of its mild climate and cheap rents. Henze quickly became integrated into the creative life of the island, forming friendships with the British poet W. H. Auden and his American partner Chester Kallman, who later collaborated with Henze on his 1959 opera Elegy for Young Lovers. Henze was particularly close to the British composer William Walton. Walton, who became a lifelong champion of Henze's work, had been spending half the year on Ischia since the late forties, and moved there permanently in 1956.

In one noteworthy and embarrassing episode, Walton invited his new friend to dinner with another German, the ex-leader of the Hitler Youth movement Baldur von Schirach, only recently released from his twenty-year jail term at Spandau prison. Henze was a good enough friend to realise that Walton had no idea of the gravitas of Schirach's crimes, and so did not blame him for his faux pas, but he nonetheless made his excuses and left the house immediately.

Imagine turning up at your brother's place and finding a major contributor to a fascist news site seated next to you at table. My guess is that you would leave, too. Apart from anything else, what would you find to say to such a person?

In the decades since, Ischia has suffered multiple assaults on its ecosystem, including a catastrophic oil spill and the routine discharge of raw sewage into its fragile marine habitats. Most of all there is the pressure of numbers: 60,000 people crammed on to an island just ten kilometres wide, and that's not counting the millions of tourists. Nachtstücke und Arien was composed in Naples in 1957, and received its premiere at the Darmstadt Festival in Donaueschingen a year later. Henze's use of polystylism – the free intermingling of jazz, world-folk and Romantic elements within his music – enraged the Darmstadt purists, who dismissed Henze's work as retrograde and standing contrary to the avant-garde sensibilities of the time. Karlheinz Stockhausen, Pierre Boulez and Luigi Nono, who together formed the holy trinity of the Darmstadt School, walked out of the concert hall just fifteen minutes into the performance, making no effort to hide their displeasure in a gesture that stood in effect as an act of protest.

Other Darmstadt luminaries, including the programme director, snubbed Henze for the remainder of the festival. In an interview with the composer and conductor Peter Ruzicka in 1999, Henze said: 'Throughout the whole of my life, whatever I created, these were my themes, my substance, and if this happened to collide with the themes and interests of others, well OK then, so what?'

It is this tenacity, this stalwart attitude of mind that enabled Henze to process and ultimately surmount the pain of his inheritance, both as a German and as a gay man. By contrast, from the early 1960s, and following the failure of her relationship with the German writer Max Frisch, Ingeborg Bachmann found herself in a downward spiral. Her imaginative power remained undiminished, yet her capacity to withstand her inner anguish – her sense of self-worth, both as an artist and particularly as a woman – became badly eroded. She became addicted to prescription medicines and to her own despair. She even stopped writing poetry, because she believed she had exhausted the possibilities of the form and would end up repeating herself if she persisted.

I am convinced it was this self-enforced separation of the artist from her art – like a wilful refusal to listen to music – that became the major contributing factor in her numbing addictions. This self-inflicted wound, this act of erasure is an act all but impossible to imagine in the case of a male artist, yet is one that remains disturbingly, depressingly common among female radicals, who so frequently find themselves aliens in a hostile landscape.

Still this pathetic choice we feel forced into making: love, or fame. Love, or greatness. As if a man faced with such a choice would hesitate for more than a second.

Bachmann died from burns sustained in a fire at her home, a fire that began when a dropped cigarette set her bedclothes alight, a kind of suicide. For me, thinking about her death is like watching a jet fighter tumbling, engines ablaze, from a tumultuous sky. I realised long ago that such a death is impossible to come to terms with. It is too painful, too pointless, too great a loss.

Nachtstücke und Arien comes out of the sound-world of Schoenberg's Gurrelieder or Strauss's Elektra, speaking in the musical language of chromatic dissonance, radiant with the shadow-strewn, violet-tinged light of Götterdämmerung. Yet the insistence of his detractors, that Henze was a reactionary throwback, the final, superfluous product of a played-out worldview seems itself reactionary, a salutary reminder of Darmstadt's limited mindset and aesthetic fanaticism, of attitudes that are simply a more articulate version of totalitarianism. Henze's repurposing of the musical language of his forebears is in its own way transgressive, an insistence that there not only can be music after Auschwitz, to contradict Celan, but that there has to be. If there is no music, what is the point of anything?

A week after the concert, I telephoned Hanne to ask if I might take her out to lunch. I could feel my heart racing as I waited for her to pick up, afraid in case she had been redeployed already, that she might be killed or badly injured in a faraway place, without my ever having had the chance to put things right between us. As it turned out, she was still in town. From the way she spoke to me, tired-seeming and vaguely distracted, I got the feeling she had forgotten our argument already, that she had most likely not thought about me at all since the day it happened.

I did not know if I should feel affronted, or grateful. I settled on grateful, though the emotion does not come naturally to me. We agreed to meet at the same restaurant as before, another indication of how low down in Hanne's list of priorities our disagreement had figured. I was pleased about that, not just because I like the restaurant but because it is where we usually meet and I have always shared Mann's opinion on the value of routine as a means of imposing external order on internal chaos.

In contrast with the worn jeans and sloppy pullover she had been wearing previously, Hanne had on what looked like a new linen suit, with striking enamelled cufflinks. I could not remember her ever wearing cufflinks before. I could not take my eyes off them.

My intimations about her being redeployed were not far wrong.

I have a new job, she told me. At the new teaching hospital for traumatic injuries in Wuppertal. She did not speak of the background to her decision, the reasons behind her change in direction. Instead, she focused on specifics: who had told her about the position becoming available, the crazy time she had getting to the interview. Relief – not so much at the generous salary as at the prospect of being able to live a normal life again – seemed to flow from her in waves.

You'll never guess what, she said, running off at a tangent. One of the interviewers turns out to be married to the British pathologist who did the post mortem on that guy you wrote about for Bruxelles Soir. You know, the alien guy?

The alien guy? I repeated, pretending that I needed reminding, although of course I did not. I knew at once that Hanne was talking about Lucian Cherish. I kept my eye on her while I waited for her answer, wondering if in fact she had not forgotten our argument after all, if bringing up the subject of Lucian Cherish was her not-so-subtle way of rubbing my nose in it. I even wondered if the whole story about the job interview – the new suit, those pretty cufflinks, everything – might be a ruse, an elaborate pantomime. But of course that was ridiculous.

I really am sorry for last time, Hanne said suddenly. I was tired, that's all. That's part of the reason I decided to take this job.

*

On the evening of July 16th 2016 Lucian Cherish, a thirty-nine-year-old conspiracy theorist from Ramsgate in Kent dies on a sofa at the home of Maria Rubin, a science-fiction publisher from Poland. Lucian first travelled to Poland in the April of the same year, to speak at the Earth Project conference in Warsaw, which is where he met Maria. Maria was attracted to Lucian immediately. She encouraged him to extend his trip, inviting him to stay with her at her home in a suburb east of the city, a pleasant settlement on the river Vistula, close to local nature reserves and boasting a variety of interesting buildings, both historic and modern.

At some point during the evening of July 16th, Maria realises that Lucian, asleep on the couch, is no longer breathing. She telephones the emergency services, but the paramedics who attend are unable to resuscitate Lucian and pronounce him dead at the scene. The police are informed that Lucian died of natural causes. No investigative action is taken, and at this point there is no autopsy. The room where Lucian died is left unexamined and unsecured, and those present at the time of his death are allowed to leave without being questioned.

Three days later, a video appears online, that is purported to be Lucian's final interview. The recording is audio only, though later some bizarre footage surfaces of Lucian bouncing on a trampoline. Lucian slurs his words and talks in circles, repeats himself continuously. He sounds confused and occasionally incoherent. It seems obvious, to me at least, that he has been drugged.

The tape runs for over an hour. I find it painful to listen to, as if I am being made complicit in a crime. Six days after his death, Lucian's body is flown back to Britain in a sealed casket. The coroner orders an immediate post mortem, but because of the time lag the results are inconclusive. The UK authorities launch an inquiry into the death of Lucian Cherish. Finally, on the 30th August, the Polish police belatedly announce their own investigation.

Their silence until now has only increased the flood of gossip and speculation that has poured into online spaces during the intervening weeks. Lucian's mother Vanessa has revealed that her son had been afraid he was going to be murdered. His final text to her is beginning to take on the patina of sacred scripture. Reports that Lucian spewed up black liquid just before he died are being cited as evidence that Lucian was poisoned, inhabited by an alien entity, or both.

I first learned about Lucian's case through the LAvventura forum, a well known hangout for UFO enthusiasts, alien conspiracy theorists and other alternative thinkers. From the outset, I find the facts of Lucian's story both strange and troubling. A man has died, suddenly and far from home, and I cannot understand why the police made so little effort to find out what happened. At best they have been incompetent; at worst there has been some sort of cover-up.

Most of all, it is Lucian's final days and hours that prey on my mind. He was a young man alone, isolated in a foreign country and surrounded by people who if not exactly strangers did not know him well. Did they exploit his vulnerability, or were they not aware of it? Clearly Lucian was frightened – frightened enough to believe his life was in danger. Accounts of his death seem conflicting and lacking in detail.

I make a few rough notes, jotting down what facts I have been able to verify. I begin thinking about a story in which a private detective sets out to discover the truth behind the disappearance of a man who believes that Earth stands on the brink of an interstellar war. I ask myself what might happen if the detective becomes convinced that the war is real.

Wherever the blaze of the roses is smothered
Torrents sweep us into the flood. O furthest night!
Still this leaf, gravely met, flies downstream on the waves
At our backs, to the river's mouth.

In the year 1212, a shepherd boy named Etienne began preaching in the squares and common places of towns and villages across northern France, claiming Jesus had entrusted him with a sacred message. The power of his sermons attracted large numbers of disciples, many of them young people like himself. Stephen of Cloyes is believed to be the inspiration behind the tale of the Pied Piper of Hamelin. He and his band of followers were part of what has become known as the Children's Crusade, a strange outbreak of religious fervour that rippled through Europe as the plague did, a century later.

Many of Stephen's disciples abandoned their pilgrimage early on, realising perhaps that they had allowed their emotions to run away with them, that they were better off at home. Others were not as perceptive, or as lucky. The children especially identified so strongly with Stephen they could not bring themselves to abandon him, even at the risk of their health or even their lives. Thousands died from starvation. Thousands more perished from exhaustion or illness along the way. Stephen's story has been the basis for many works of art, including the chamber opera by the English composer Benjamin Britten. Britten composed his score to a libretto by Berthold Brecht, dedicating it to his friend and colleague Hans Werner Henze in 1968.

There are many who insist that conspiracy theories and alternative facts are a poisonous by-product of the internet age, a new and virulent form of mania born out of the proliferation of social media and the indiscriminate dissemination of uninformed opinion. But if Stephen's story shows us anything, it is that our secret enthusiasm for esoteric knowledge and occult drama is as old as time. More even than that, it proves the reasons for our need of such mythologies have not altered: disgust with the status quo, the fanatical, sometimes violent conviction that a better life must be possible, that the world can be changed.

Young heretics like Stephen fascinate and compel us because they remind us deeply and painfully of ourselves. Of ourselves at a time in our youth when ideas still mattered to us, when we would willingly relinquish our safety and comfort in pursuit of an ideal. The desire to belong, the urge to resist, the search for meaning. The illusion of control in the midst of chaos, the terror of the void. The feeling of belonging, of being family, of knowing in the depths of your soul that this is the way.

In these months of restless unease, I find myself thinking constantly of Lucian Cherish and of Stephen of Cloyes. Of Ingeborg Bachmann and Shamima Begum and my dear, dead friend, Carola. Of Copernicus and Galileo. Of Christopher Columbus's racing heart as he first sighted land. I think of the power, the fire, the tears, the rage, the thumping of the drum and the winds of change. The words, the books, the songs, the scorn, the revelation and the ire and the holy fool.

The scribbling down of protest songs, of poems.

The rending of vestments, the lights in the sky and the screaming of slogans.

The whisperer in darkness, the brute cacophony, the love.

The love, the love, the love.

The greatest of all these is love.

Who would not run from a world that denies the reality of their existence? Because we cannot go on alone. Because the power of faith is sometimes greater than the power of truth.

QUARRY

I T IS ENOUGH
My aching arms have held the Saviour
The hope of the faithful
I am content
I have seen him
In truth I have filled my heart with him
Now I can leave this place with joy
Even today

Ich habe genug, Cantata BWV 82 for solo bass and oboe obligato was written in Leipzig in 1727 and first performed for the feast of Candlemas, on February 2nd. The text was written by Christoph Birkmann and based upon the Canticle of Simeon as it appears in Luke's gospel, popularly known as the Nunc Dimitis, let thy servant depart in peace . . .

Robin brings up the CD liner notes on her iPod, the old kind, already obsolete when she bought it. You can still find refurbished models fairly easily, though the algorithms do everything to discourage you, to make you go Bluetooth, a corporate tyranny Robin refuses to submit to. Like Dianne's neighbour Breda, who has a thing about tungsten-filament lightbulbs and has stockpiled enough of them, she once told Robin proudly, to light her flat until the day they carry her out of it in a wooden box.

Klaus Mertens with Sigiswald Kuijken and La Petite Bande, a recording Robin happened to hear one night on the World Service and fell for immediately. Mertens has a beautiful legato way of delivering the lines, a warmth and evenness of tone that lends the words their appropriate gravitas without becoming bogged down in it. A sense of wonderment that overcomes Simeon's exhaustion with life, his world-weariness, a fellow-feeling that reminds Robin of Thomas Quasthoff's reading and is the opposite of Hans Hotter's, which carries a depth of despair and alienation that seems unconquerable, the same as in his Winterreise.

In terms of his authority, his knowledge of the text, Hotter is unsurpassed, yet at the same time Robin finds him almost unlistenable. She prefers Lorraine Hunt, whose idiosyncratic account is inauthentic to the point of wilfulness, whose personal response does not so much sidestep tradition as negate it. What matters to Hunt is her relationship with the score, with what Bach has written down. Whenever Robin listens to her she likes to imagine Hunt is singing for her alone.

Hunt died in her fifties, of cancer, a tragedy the critics harp on relentlessly, as if it helps to explain her passionate tendency towards breaking the rules. Her recordings refute this utterly. There is only the music.

*

I rejoice in my death

    Would that death were here already

Duplicitous words, weasel words, the kind Robin can imagine being spoken by the victims of the Jonestown massacre just before they drink the Kool-Aid. The cantata's final aria is magnificent but its words are repulsive, the tension between text and music so powerfully intense Robin begins to wonder if the distance might not be intentional, a deliberate irony. The music's robustness, its vigour, its forward momentum speak not of a longing for death but of defiance of death, its minor-key, three-quarter rhythm tenacious and sinewy, determined. A dance to drive out mortality, not invite her in.

Robin finds she is angry nonetheless, irritated by the sophistry, the oppressive nature of a system of thought that defies all logic. She remembers what Jeanne Vanderlien said about anger being the most revealing of the emotions, and wonders why in fact she feels angry, what it is that is driving her. Bach wrote Ich habe genug three hundred years ago. He walked in a world where God existed and heaven was real, a world that still shone with the brightness of Renaissance art.

She thinks of Bach thinking of Simeon, an old man whose death had been denied him, who was living on borrowed time in fulfilment of a prophecy. Spine bent and sight occluded, mind exhausted. Bach imagines Simeon's rejoicing at the thought of the rest that he has been longing for, as a man who is tired from the fields might rejoice in sleep.

*

Then I shall escape the distress

That yet binds me to this world . . .

As Robin disembarks from the train at Glasgow Central, it occurs to her she need not travel further, that she could be done with this pointless quest, this case that was never a case so much as a fantasy. Find a restaurant or a burger bar close to the station, grab a quick meal, catch the next train back to Euston, be home before midnight. The vision beckons, the idea so tempting she can already see herself buying a beer from the on-board buffet as the train recrosses the border, heading south.

The image burns her with its colours, its verisimilitude, like a snapshot from a holiday two decades in the past, like the photo she still keeps in her wallet of her with her first girlfriend Kerri the summer they went interrailing. The summer before Kerri had chucked her when Robin said she was serious about becoming a cop.

My cousin Charley's best friend Darren was killed by a cop, Kerri said, the outrage scarring her face as if the memory was raw still, which it probably was. Robin had tried to argue, insisted not all cops were like that, but Kerri wouldn't listen, not even when Robin reminds her that her dad was a serving police officer for thirty years. When Kerri runs away from her down Brownhill Road Robin refuses to follow because she's still pissed off. She assumes they'll speak later – that she will call or Kerri will call and they'll patch things up somehow, that Robin will find a way to explain her decision better and Kerri will accept it, that things will work out.

She didn't, and things hadn't. Robin wonders where Kerri is now and what she is doing. She wonders what would have happened if she had run after her after all: who would have won the argument, whether she'd have changed her mind about joining the police, whether her whole life would have been different or whether she'd have ended up here regardless, right here on the concourse of Glasgow Central at this precise date and time asking herself what the holy fuck she thinks she's doing.

She has half an hour to get to Queen Street, half an hour before she misses the train to Inverness. If she misses the train she'll have a two-hour wait, which would mean she wouldn't get into Tain until nine o'clock that evening. Hardly the end of the world, but she has been sitting on a train for five hours already, and if she is going to follow through with this escapade she would prefer to arrive at her destination before nightfall.

She takes out her phone and checks her messages: nothing new. She has not heard from Jeanne Vanderlien since the day the CD arrived. There is nothing online about a Crombie House study centre or charity, no information at all except the stone facade of the house itself as it appears on Streetview: flat, grey, silent, inscrutable, just a bloody house.

But she has paid in advance for her hotel room and it is this detail, this minor idiocy, that makes up her mind for her. She begins walking towards Queen Street station, following her phone. She has wasted so much time being indecisive she will need to hurry now to make the train, and as she crosses the intersection of Gordon Street and Renfield Street she finds herself thinking about Alec Dunbar, about how she is on Dunbar's home turf finally. She feels strange about that, on dangerous ground, though as she understands it Dunbar grew up some distance from the city centre on one of the post-war housing estates. Rutherglen, Robin seems to remember, wherever that is.

She imagines a prepubescent Alec Dunbar running wild with his cronies, his team, his rapscallions, drink, drugs, knives, maybe even guns. Why Dunbar decided to leave this place behind and head to London is not hard to guess at because why does anyone? A broader stage on which to wreak havoc, a deeper hinterland to mask the darkness of his own interior.

Robin wonders if Dunbar's hardness, the lack of pity that is fundamental to his nature comes direct from his point of origin (those bleak tenements and pebble-dashed tower blocks, the unassailable fastness of the place, like a sandstone citadel) or if Dunbar is simply Dunbar, shrugging on his city's attributes, drawing them snugly about his shoulders as he puts on his coat, that black three-quarter-length jacket that has been Dunbar's sartorial trademark since forever.

Who gives a shit either way? Robin is done thinking about him. Queen Street station feels older, more ramshackle than Central, an odd byway of a place. The departures board teems with Scottish place names: Perth, Oban, Aberdeen, Montrose, Stirling, Pitlochry, Aviemore, Edinburgh, and Inverness – her train will be leaving in six minutes' time from Platform 4. Robin buys coffee and a bacon roll from one of the kiosks and dashes through the barrier with a minute to spare. She can feel her heart pounding, the ridiculousness of her predicament, the panic. So what if she misses her train, there will be another.

She is surprised by how soon after leaving Glasgow they are in the open, in the midst of a vast and expansive landscape she has barely conceived of. The train tracks flanked by granite walls swarming with buddleia and with nettles, with limitless confectionary drifts of rosebay willowherb. Past its best now, banking down now, but its tips still purpled in vigorous growth, sustained by the memory of its glory a fortnight earlier. Londoners call the plant fireweed because of the blitz, Dianne once told her, because of the way it spread like wildfire over the bomb sites after the war. The only blooming thing that would grow there or so my mother said, and isn't it strange how you grow sick of that colour after a while?

It's not a strong purple, not like foxgloves, there's something cheap about it. The oversweetened, knocked-off brightness of watered-down paint.

North of Dunkeld the Cairngorms rise as a body like a choir of stern nuns, the tops of the hills steeped in heather and rounded with time. The landscape is a kind of ghosting, a record of the movements of glaciers, the predations of wind. Through the mountains flow tea-coloured rivers, densely moving with robust awareness of their own forward motion. Robin feels the seismic thrum of the mountains, shouldering themselves free of the Earth, the train, her gaze, of everything human, a company of gods rising and waking in an alien land.

What is left is like a fossil, etched with the method, the instructions for building a planet: the skies, the burned-out galaxies, the great kaleidoscope of memory, of cleaving, of shift. A broad belt of gunmetal cloud belches up through a cleft in the mountains like a routed battalion, the train chasing it away down the glen, a warlord on the rampage, forcing the retreat.

Did Frank come this way after all? This is a question Robin must ask – it is why she is here – though the trail of breadcrumbs she is following still has the feel of an improvisation, a thin deception that may be erased from view, churned into the dirt at any moment. She falls asleep still considering, her thoughts inconclusive, awaking in a panic just to the south of Inverness. She has to change trains again, to the single-track local service that runs on to Thurso and finally to Wick, four hours further north. The modest town of Tain lies a simple hour away.

After the Cairngorms the countryside seems eerily flattened, tracts of estuary flanked by moorland, a landscape of penitence. Penitence and pestilence, Robin finds herself thinking, two words with equal weight of syllables, yet unalike. One sharp enough to cut your fingers with its barbed 'n' and 't', the other a slippery wraith with its snakelike 's' and 'c'. Plague and pestilence, the brute hard-soft of it, the bone and then the mulch. Tain station slides up to meet her from the autumn afternoon, a rest-stop on the way to somewhere bleaker. The town itself seems neat and pleasant: rows of narrow grey-stone cottages running steeply downhill, a dozen or so more ambitious buildings, the town hall, the old magistrates' court, the Royal Hotel. The main street is busy with cafés and local businesses, a supermarket and a Chinese takeaway, a DIY store. The basic shape of a town unchanged for centuries.

Robin checks into her hotel. The room is clean and fairly spacious though its position at the back of the building makes it uncomfortably dark. She sits down on the bed. She feels exhausted yet restless, the fact of where she is preys on her mind. Until the moment she stepped off the train, this place was theoretical, imagined. Now she is here in reality she feels somehow less solid.

She thinks about phoning Rachel then decides against. She has not told Rachel about her trip. She has not wanted to get her hopes up. She leans back on the bed, hooking her knees around the square of the mattress and gazing up at the ceiling. She falls asleep almost immediately, though when she wakes an hour or so later she feels convinced she only closed her eyes for a couple of seconds.

Her knees are painfully stiff from being locked in position and she is ravenously hungry. She thinks about ordering a meal in the hotel restaurant then decides to grab a burger from one of the takeaways, stretch her legs. Maybe afterwards she will pay a visit to Crombie House.

She wonders what they will be like, these acolytes, these UFO enthusiasts. She thinks about the time a girl in her class persuaded her to attend a meeting of the sixth form Christian Union, everyone nodding and smiling and not really saying anything. She finds the house easily, a grey Georgian villa set back from the road not far from the station. She wipes her hands on her jeans then presses the bell.

She half-expects to be turned away, to be told she has made a mistake, that there is no such thing as the study centre, that Crombie House is just a house, she is on a fool's errand.

What she is not expecting, has never dared hope for not even secretly, is for the door to be opened to her by Frank Landau.

She recognises him at once, skinny and scruffy in years-old Levis, so like his photos it is uncanny. Robin feels a wave of déjà vu that leaves her nauseous and she wonders if she is sickening for something. You're Frank, she says, Frank Landau. She wonders immediately if she should have waited before revealing herself, if she has blown her cover too soon, though Frank seems unfazed.

Eddie said you would be coming, he says. We were worried you'd missed the train.

Eddie? Robin says. Frank ignores the question, or does not hear it.

Come through, he says. He steps back into the hallway to let her inside. Robin can hear voices, music, the notes of a violin. Not a recording but someone playing. The idea seems outlandish, some kind of diversion. Frank is leading her along the corridor to a room at the back. This is where we eat, he says, where we do everything, really. There's food if you're hungry. You must be hungry. That's Saira playing. She was born here. Here in this house, I mean.

A woman in early middle age, her wavy, coarse fair hair hangs to her waist. She is playing a Scottish dance tune, and though she looks up as Robin enters the room the pace and verve of her playing do not alter. Aside from Saira there are six, seven other people in the room. Frank says some names – Kemal, Abigail. Someone – a guy with a reddish beard and wearing a lumberjack shirt, Robin thinks his name is Rory – pours her a whisky. Robin holds the glass to her nose, inhales the aroma. Her mouth fills instantly with saliva.

Glenmorangie, Frank says. The distillery's just down the road from here. Saira's Eddie's girlfriend, he adds. She's a botanist. Rory's a botanist too – he came up here from Edinburgh. Kemal is a soil scientist. Abigail's a lichenologist. She's documenting the project, you should see her photographs. There's a lot going on here – it's complicated. Eddie said I should show you the site. We can go up tomorrow morning, if you like.

He seems comfortable around her, more so than she would have expected, more confident, especially given that they are strangers to one another, at least in theory, though she is belatedly coming to realise the truth is hazier. She has spent months studying Frank, researching the facts of his life, digging into every space and private corner without scruple and without once stopping to ask herself how much Frank Landau might know about her. What Edmund de Groote might have told him, or Jeanne Vanderlien. How careless she has been in covering her tracks. How much they are truly strangers, if at all.

Watching the detectives. Robin hums the tune to herself, mentally smirking at the irony within the irony. She appreciates how childish it is, this silent joke at her own expense, a way of skirting around the fact that she has made a mess of her investigation or at least potentially. Dunbar would read her the riot act, either way. The life of this house and its people is different from how she has imagined it. Like Frank, they seem comfortable around her, unconcerned by her presence among them and here again, Robin is coming to realise they have no need to be. Regardless of what they might know about her, or not know, their togetherness, their shared sense of purpose is enough in and of itself to keep her shut out.

Saira finishes the dance tune with a vigorous upstroke before launching into a minor key lament. After a couple of seconds Robin recognises it with a jolt of surprise as the grand passacaglia that forms the climax of Biber's cycle of rosary sonatas. And Saira is good, she can really play. The raw edge of her tone, the abrasive strength of her attack could come across as unsubtle but for Robin it is powerfully authentic, and there is something even here, in the music's striving to convince, that leaves her unable to rid herself of the idea that the whole scenario – the house, the music, the table laden with cheeses and home-baked bread – is a deception of some kind, a performance, that the moment she leaves the stage the players will disperse.

There are people who think you're dead, she says to Frank suddenly. She sips the whisky, feels the burn. Her teeth are chattering. People who care about you. Have you any idea what it's been like for them, you running away like this?

She is speaking softly so the others can't hear, her sibilants spitting like dry kindling over smoking embers, already on fire. She finds she is angry beyond what she knows is reasonable or professional. The whisky is making her head spin and she tells herself it's that, though she knows it's really Rachel she is thinking of, Rachel she is angry for. She pictures Rachel's narrow hands and gold nail varnish, Friedrich's Winter Landscape in its chipped gold frame. Feels tears starting at the back of her eyes, thinks for God's sake don't cry, not now.

What are you doing here? she says, more gently. You might think it's none of my business but it is my business. It's my job to find out. She hopes the music and the chatter will go on long enough to keep their conversation private. The search, the chase, the pointless trip to Scarborough, all those nutty alien forums, only to discover Frank has been holed up with his chums all along, large as life and twice as clueless, bumming about in the Highlands a fucking phone call away. The situation is so laughable it feels like a dream, a series of random unrelated events jammed together in sequence to try and fake a story.

Frank looks taken aback by her vehemence. Chastened. Chagrined.

Eddie told me you were coming here because of the journalist, he says. Miles someone.

Miles Shipley is dead. He died in Scarborough. Did you know that?

Frank shakes his head. I never even spoke to him. Eddie told me I shouldn't. He seemed OK on the forums but Eddie thought he might be dangerous.

Dangerous how?

If he was working for the other side, Eddie meant. He said he'd been trying to hack my computer, that I should get a new one.

And do you do everything Eddie tells you? she says. She is thinking about the photographs, the folder of images the police had found in Shipley's hotel room, the same images later retrieved by Milan Harwicz from Frank's back-up machine. Shipley's laptop had been wiped, Milan had told her, so who had been hacking whom? Jesus. She watches Saira from the corner of her eye, hair swinging back and forth like an ashen curtain as she leans into the music. She plays so well, one hell of a downstroke, the edge of every note is bleeding raw.

You don't understand, Frank is saying. Eddie's looking out for us, that's all, Protecting us. He pauses, looks down at his hands and Robin sees they are shaking. Have you spoken to Rachel? he adds, is she OK? and there is something in the way he says it, in the way he seems suddenly, so fragile, so exalted, a saint in jeans and trainers, that makes Robin want to reach out and grab him, shake some sense into him, never let him go.

As though he were a prophet, she thinks, as if it were up to us, to all of us to shield him from reality, to prevent him breaking apart, to preserve his worldview, to hide the truth if such a thing were possible, which it is not.

She realises then that this is what it must feel like to be Rachel. She feels a shudder pass through her and then once again behind her eyes the hot press of tears.

Rachel has been trying to find you for months, she says quietly. She's terrified something has happened to you. The police don't give a monkey's because you're an adult. Supposedly, she adds, testing the cruelty in her words and finding it wanting. Will you let Rachel know you're safe at least? You owe her that, surely?

I'm protecting her, Frank says, the words so simple, so matter-of-fact they seem designed not to dispel her anger but to cast aspersions on it and on her, on the whole disreputable enterprise of her arrival here. Like on the forums, Robin thinks, all that certainty and self-righteousness, no room for doubt. Mutual reinforcement as mental Teflon; the harder you throw yourself against it, the easier you slide off. No entry beyond this point, believers only.

I am so, so done with all this shit.

How are you protecting her? she says, wearily, trying to stay gentle and to keep reasonable if only because she knows that is what Rachel would want.

Our work here is important, Frank says. Important for everyone – including you, including Rachel. There are people who would try and close us down if they could. They might try and get to us through our families – Eddie warned us about this. He says the less Rachel knows the safer she is, and I believe him.

Is he here? De Groote?

He's away this evening. He should be back tomorrow, though.

What does he do here, anyway? He's not a scientist.

He helps us organise. Frank shifts in his seat. Eddie's a brilliant writer. He knows how to inspire people. Most of those who come to us are here because of him.

So he spreads propaganda?

It's not like that. This is important, more important than anything. Once you've been to the site you'll understand.

I'm tired, Robin says. If you're planning on taking me mountain-climbing tomorrow I need to get some sleep. She smiles. You're not going to disappear on me again, are you?

Why would I?

Oh Frankie, Robin thinks. Her heart is pounding. She catches the eye of Kemal, the soil scientist. Kemal nods at her and taps the whisky bottle, raises an eyebrow. Part of it is missing, filled in with scar tissue. It looks like a burn mark. Robin thinks about accepting his offer of more Glenmorangie then shakes her head. More than anything she wants to lie down on the bed in her dingy hotel room, switch on the TV. She can get whisky from the hotel bar if she wants, it will still be open. She can already taste it going down, the burn and then the rush. The blunting of fingertips, the blurring of time to an endless continuum, no sense of past or future, only now.

Call Rachel, she says to Frank. I'll see you tomorrow.

Outside, it is still light, that strange bleached northern twilight she remembers Dunbar describing, waxing on about every now and then when he was drunk mainly, those endless madcap summers on the estate. It is curious, how unmoored she feels, how unstitched not only from time but from her reasons for being here. She should be feeling triumphant, vindicated. More than that she should be phoning Rachel, letting her client know her hopes, her trust, her expenditure have not been in vain.

Instead, there is a blankness, a lack of belief. Because you're knackered, she tells herself. That's all it is. She returns to the hotel and when she turns on the television she finds they're showing Apollo 13. Robin feels like laughing, like pissing her pants with laughter, such perfect irony, irony so perfectly unsubtle it is itself like something from a movie. She remembers seeing the film with Dianne when it first came out. She is surprised how good it looks, the tension still powerful, still present, even though the mission, the crisis, the whole iconic shitstorm had played itself out in front of millions more than fifty years ago.

There is nothing about those days that has not been explored, yet there on the poxy fourteen-inch screen the story of the mission that failed feels so jarringly new it is as if the budget technology, the smallness of the room is adding to the illusion of information only recently unearthed.

The legend of Apollo 13 is like the myth of Dunkirk: an almost-catastrophe cemented in the historical record as a hymn to heroes. Robin sips her whisky, thinks about the real Jim Lovell and the moon-men before him, about a documentary she happened to see part of, around the fiftieth anniversary of the first moon landing in which one of them – she forgets which – spoke of the mental isolation he had experienced on returning to Earth.

When you're up there you see the world for what it is, the astronaut had said. A planet spinning in space, more beautiful and more vulnerable than you'd ever realised, than anything in your life has prepared you to imagine, and no matter how many interviews you give, how many TV shows you go on, there's no way to explain how it feels to see the world that way, not as streets and cars and cities but as a part of the universe. We're like soldiers I guess in a way, soldiers who've been to war and don't know how to fit back inside their normal lives when they come home. And people aren't that interested. They say they are, but they're not, they'd rather go to McDonald's or watch the ball game on TV than hear about what it's like to fly to the moon. And you have to ask yourself every day how you're supposed to keep living like that – living the old life, the life most people live – when the most important thing you'll ever do is already in the past.

Life after space had seemed paler, less consequential, an unacceptable counterfeit for the real thing. The documentary had revealed how a number of the astronauts ended up living with depression and alcohol dependency. Robin sets down her glass, wondering if the doctor she had spoken to not long after resigning her job had been right when she tried to tell her the disorientation and rage she was suffering – the breakup with Ash – was at least partly to do with losing the comradeship and support of her colleagues on the police force.

This was a way of life you chose for yourself, the doctor had said, a way of life you valued. Stepping away from that is like losing a family. There are bound to be consequences.

Alec Dunbar was a shit, a bully, a murderer, but he had seen her. Better than Ashley and better than Dianne, he had understood what she was like. Robin hates the knowledge of this, the mute fact of it, but she cannot deny it. She wonders if this is what her being here in this shitty room is all about in the end, this crazy search for the solution to a mystery that does not exist. Not just the buzz but the sense of meaning, the sense of completion. The sense that facts were more than isolate facts, that they added up to something. Even if what they added up to was like saying she believed in aliens or the man in the moon.

She thinks of the woman at Crombie House, Eddie de Groote's girlfriend. Saira with the ash-coloured hair, playing the Biber passacaglia like it was an ancient folk tune. What are they doing here, these people? Robin reaches for the whisky tumbler and finds it is empty. She has still not phoned Rachel and now it is almost midnight, too late to call. She cannot understand how she is still awake.

Robin closes her eyes, thinking how going to sleep is like being launched into space; you never know how the mission will turn out, and there is no cast-iron guarantee of coming back. No one thinks about sleep this way, but that's how it is. You just trust that you will. Come back, that is. You shut your eyes and hope.

Eddie taught me to drive, Frank says. He gave me lessons then took me to do my test in Inverness. I passed but I still don't like driving in towns. Inverness isn't too bad for traffic, but I don't drive there unless someone needs me to. I'd rather go on the train. This is all new, he adds as he makes a left turn off the high street and on to what looks like a local authority housing estate. New since World War Two, I mean. If you look at old maps you'll see there was nothing here before that, just fields. The men used to walk up this road on their way to work at the quarry. The town's pavements are built from the limestone they mined there. The quarry closed down in 1912. Most of the site's filled in now, but you can see where it was.

The flatbed shoots across the bypass then diverts on to a smaller, narrower road, climbing steadily through open fields and small stands of trees. Robin's mouth is dry and her head aches, but the sky is cloudless and sunlit, the air scented with autumn. In spite of her hangover she feels calmer than she has felt since leaving London. She likes Frank, she realises. He is easy to be with, probably because unlike most others he appears not to judge people. There is an openness about him – to experience and to stimuli, to ideas – that makes him charming but also vulnerable.

She thinks briefly of Rachel, eyes darkened from sleepless nights, the grief etched into her face like workday grime, like the scars of harsh living. Small wonder she has been so afraid for him. With someone like Frank you would be constantly afraid, constantly fearful that he might be hurt in some way. The thought comes to Robin that now Frank is found there will be no reason for her and Rachel to remain in contact. No reason for them to see each other again or to speak even, to wonder what happens next.

It has been twelve hours and Robin still has not called her. Robin tells herself she has a duty to see how the land lies, not to rush things. Twelve hours is nothing, when you stop and think about it. There is plenty of time.

We have to walk from here, Frank is saying, it's not too far. They have arrived at the edge of the forest, at what appears to be a car park, though aside from themselves the levelled space is empty. Frank brings the truck to a standstill beneath the trees. The scuffed, pine-needled dirt is swarming in boot prints – dog-walkers, hikers, ramblers, Robin notes them automatically – yet the place seems strangely quiet, almost oppressive in its stillness, in the darkness of its undergrowth, in the dense, khaki-coloured overhang of the tree canopy.

The forest is very old, Frank says, and Robin wonders if he senses her disquiet. There's been forest here for thousands of years. Scots pines can live for centuries – they're one of the oldest types of tree, Saira says. That's why they're so useful.

How do you mean, useful?

Because they respond to changes in their environment over a long period. Trees are sensitive in that way, they take note of things. Trees are like recording devices, you just need to learn how to read them properly.

They follow the path from the car park into what a Forestry Commission signboard describes as a temperate rainforest: Scots pine and mountain ash, once the property of the local laird, reserved for his pleasure, his hunting, his shooting, his sports and recreations. Many of the trees here are young still, flanked in dense undergrowth, though there are some, gnarly and fissured and twisted at the base Robin guesses have stood in the forest for centuries, that were here when Bach was still alive, and the thought of this, the wonder of it is so present in her, so urgent that when moments later Frank starts to speak of Bach and of his music it seems inevitable that he should do so. As if thought itself were a wire and Bach the current, travelling like lightning from her mind into his.

I've been thinking about it a lot, Frank says, as if in answer to a question Robin has not asked. When you look at the dates it makes sense. When it comes to Bach it's about the only thing that does make sense.

Tell me, Robin says, because she is interested, and because it seems easier to let him run on than asking questions.

Before Bach there was plainchant and then there was polyphony. People think mediaeval music is difficult to listen to, that it's too complicated to understand because there's so much going on at once, so many different voices. Most people prefer tonal music because it's based around melody. The musical language Bach invented caused a revolution because it developed the idea of counterpoint, but based around melodies ordinary people could learn by heart, that they could sing along with. That was when music started to become democratic. People began singing and playing music in their homes, they began writing it down, instead of just listening to it in church. No one ever asks where tonality came from, though. Scientists don't ask that kind of question because music doesn't save lives or kill people like medicine or war. The people of Europe were still recovering from the plague when Bach first started writing. The entire feudal system was collapsing. People were talking about revolution, not music.

Order out of disorder, Robin says. I once read somewhere that Bach's music was like a phoenix, rising from the ashes of old Europe. After the Black Death and the Thirty Years' War, the music Bach wrote became part of the healing process.

Yes, Frank says excitedly, that's true – but where did it come from? Tonal counterpoint, I mean, the tonic scale, the harmonic structure, the stable chord progressions? Mediaeval polyphony just isn't like that – Renaissance music is based around chromatic harmony. It's more flexible, more liquid, much closer to atonal music when you think about it, which is why people find it harder to listen to, even if they don't realise why. Mostly they prefer baroque music – because it's more ordered, more predictable. Even if you don't read music you can usually guess which note is coming next, almost like it's running on railway tracks, and the human brain likes that. They've done experiments – studies that prove the brain makes connections faster after listening to Bach than it did before. Bach's music is like fuel for the brain, and all because of the way Bach uses counterpoint. When you look at the art and music that came out of the Renaissance it's like a grand proclamation of heresy, of rule-breaking and difference. But then you have Bach, who rebuilt Western music to a completely new design. Then comes Haydn, who followed him, like the polite, rule-following grandson of Bach, the kind who wears a suit and tie to work. The whole of Haydn is a kind of politeness, like watered-down beer.

Schoolmaster's music, Robin says. Talking about music, Frank seems transformed. Fluent and forthcoming, his awkwardness vanished. He is a different person.

Yes, but Haydn doesn't matter, not really. It's Bach that matters, because his music is unique, because he is a genius. But I don't think he discovered tonality. I think tonality discovered him. Either that or he was given it. Tonality is like code – a complex program that is all the more ingenious because it's universally applicable. Everyone understands tonal counterpoint the moment they hear it. It's as if the human brain is hardwired to receive it.

You're telling me Bach's music is alien? Or of alien origin?

Not really. Bach's music was written by Bach – you can't take that away from him, or from us. But I do think Bach was influenced – influenced at a subconscious level. By something in the atmosphere maybe, or by radio waves. Some kind of small change in Earth's environment no one could detect, especially not back then, but that would affect everything on the planet. Did you ever do that experiment at school, the one where you put a daffodil in coloured water? The daffodil goes purple because it sucks up purple water. It changes without knowing it's contaminated, and because it has no choice. The ink is in the water, and if the flower doesn't drink the water it will die. I don't think Bach's music is alien, but I do believe it is a sign that the world had been changed.

Frank falls silent and exhales, his shoulders slump. He seems worn out by the effort of communicating, of speaking so unguardedly for so long. Frank is a man in his thirties, yet in the way he holds himself, his diffident posture, his shying away from worldly contact, steeling himself against it almost, he keeps reminding Robin of the teenage kid he once was, listening to David Bowie alone in his bedroom, aching with love for Rachel, terrified of falling headlong out of this world.

He will still be a kid at fifty, sixty, a creaky gnome of a man at seventy, ironed flat by time's passage yet curiously impervious to it. Ageless, because Frank Landau has never been young in the first place, not properly, not like most people. Where most people are like mirrors, Frank is like glass, deficient in the innate human capacity for solipsism. He understands that he is soluble, a part of the universe, not the other way around.

They walk out of the forest, emerging on to high moorland, heathered upland striated with granite. Robin is flooded with the sense of the infinite, of the boundless unassimilable space she remembers from her train journey through the Cairngorms. This is Tain Hill, Frank says, and that's Pulpit Rock. He points. At the top of the slope stands an enormous granite boulder with a flattened crown. Three steps are carved into its base, making of the boulder a sermon-stone, a preaching place, a granite soapbox. Whoever commands the stone commands the forest, the valley and the pathway, the firth beyond. Robin finds it easy to picture scenes from centuries past, the assembled worshippers, the maverick preacher, the devilish shrieking cant of the winter wind.

Fiery with sunshine or thigh-deep in snow, the place is a hinge-point, a weird meridian, a turn of the screw.

The townspeople used to come here for midsummer matins, at Easter too if the weather let them, Frank is saying. You can read about it in the museum. Not far to go now, he adds. They skirt the rock and head into the forest again, and Robin distinctly feels a change in the atmosphere. The air in this part of the woodland is stiller and warmer, almost soupy in consistency, the greenish light beneath the trees dancing with motes.

That's the midges you can see, Frank says. You get them here a lot, they like the moisture.

They keep following the track down the hillside until Frank turns suddenly into the underbrush and starts tramping across the leaf litter, heading for a spot some twenty metres from the pathway. The ground is level and dry, and there is a stand of trees that look no different from those that surround them, though there is something in the way they are grouped together that reminds Robin of dancers, or of the

Burghers of Calais as sculpted by Rodin, arms about each other's shoulders, a union of souls.

Much later, when she thinks of the burghers once more and looks up their history she discovers they were saved from execution by Philippa of Hainault.

You can see it here, come and look, Frank says. He is speaking softly, almost whispering, standing beside one of the trees, his hand hovering some six inches from the bark, which Robin had taken to be dappled with sunlight but as she steps closer she realises the greyish-green patches of light are part of the tree.

As if the trunk has been painted with fluorescent pigment. She feels disquiet go rippling through her, that coldwater shudder.

You can come closer, just don't touch it, Frank says, you don't want it on your skin. He is gazing into the tree bark as if into a looking glass. Lichenologists say it's minerals in the soil. An anomalous build-up of silica, they call it. It's like they're not interested, like they don't want to know. Like they feel if they ignore the problem it will go away.

The lichens are delicate as lace, as cut paper, as snowflakes viewed through a microscope, an ice-city in microcosm, all those minarets and skyscrapers, a million tiny houses beneath the stars. As Robin examines them from different angles their colours seem to change, shifting from green to grey to silver then back again to green. Then she blinks and the shine is gone, the growth is simply lichen, a grey-green fuzz.

They must have come down close to here, Frank says softly. Over in the quarry, probably. One of the pits got flooded – they called it Libbet's Pond. It's gone now – it dried up decades ago – but the water would have been tainted by what was underneath it.

Saturated with oxidised minerals, metallic salts leaking from the alien craft buried deep in the silt. This whole area is contaminated – you can tell from the lichens. Whatever it was that fell out of the sky, it's already a part of our ecosystem. We couldn't get rid of it now even if we tried.

They return to the car park.

It's my job to interpret the data, Frank is saying. To work out a schematic for the evidence our scientists are gathering that will help us understand how advanced the changes are. How substantially our ecosystem has been colonised. I'm good at seeing patterns – at interpreting code. It was Eddie who found me, Eddie who asked me to come here. He didn't force me if that's what you're thinking. No one did. I'm here because I need to be.

How did Eddie find you in the first place?

We met on LAvventura. Does it matter?

Not if you don't mind being spied on.

Eddie was never a spy. He was just – looking out for the right people, people he knew could help. I could leave here now if I wanted – I'm not a prisoner. Why would I want to leave, though? This is the most important work I could ever do. There is nothing on Earth that matters more than this.

Not even Rachel? She came all the way up here to look for you, you know. She asked around everywhere.

I wasn't going out much at first. Frank hangs his head, looking so lost Robin feels again like shaking him. His thin neck, his untidy hair, those ratty jeans. Has she met someone else?

No, she hasn't. She's still working in the supermarket. She thinks you've been kidnapped. Or murdered.

Eddie said that maybe I shouldn't contact her for a bit. In case she tried to persuade me to go back. He didn't say I couldn't, just that it was a bad idea. He said—

He said what?

He said I could be a danger to her, Frank mumbled. Because of my dad being in the program. Eddie said there would be people keeping tabs on me but I know that anyway. The n-men—

That's bullshit, Frank, there's no one. No spies, no n-men or whatever you like to call them. Eddie's trying to manipulate you.

Frank shakes his head. If the government found out what we're doing here, they'd come and destroy our work. They'd put us in prison, like they did with those hackers. The more people know what's really going on, the harder it is to keep ourselves secure. That's what Eddie says, and he's right. They'd fence off the forest and burn down the trees. It wouldn't make any difference, not in the long run, but that's what people do when they're scared, they destroy things.

Rachel isn't people, Frank, she's Rachel. She has a right to know – that you're OK at least, that you're not in danger. If you don't tell her, I will, Robin adds. She finds she is trembling, on the verge of tears. She keeps remembering the lichens, the shining tree bark with its microscopic city, the shimmering pondwater light beneath the ancient trees.

I think you should tell her, Frank says. You can tell her I'm fighting the war. She'll understand.

Don't you think it's a waste, all this? A waste of your talent?

Do you think Bach wasted his talent, writing music for a God you don't believe in?

That's not the same thing.

It is, though. Have you been to the museum yet?

How can I have? I've been chasing around the countryside with you.

There's a painting in there at the moment. It's on loan from a museum in Amsterdam. The Nunc Dimitis, by Jehan Fouquet. He painted it in 1450. You should see the colours. When Fouquet painted the old man Simeon cradling the infant Jesus he was thinking about the end of an era, the passing of one time into another, the beginning of a new chapter. It's as if he knew things were about to change, as if they all did – all the artists and writers and musicians. The common people sensed it too – think of the Crusades. It's the same now. That's why they made us wear masks – it wasn't really about the virus, it was because of the code, the same code that infected Bach and inspired his music. You can't stop alien code with a mask though, it's already in the soil.

Robin feels queasy suddenly. She tells herself it's the whisky, the hangover from last night still, though she knows it is not, it is the breach in logic, the disconnect, the weird, unassailable schism between Frank's version of reality and her own. The way he can be talking so passionately, so knowledgeably about art and music one minute, spewing nonsensical conspiracist garbage the next. The way he seems normal but is actually broken beyond repair, sliding slowly and sickeningly into the no-man's-land between madness and genius.

And the painting, the Nunc Dimitis, Ich habe genug? If she were to tell Frank what music she'd been listening to on the train on the way up here, he would take it in his stride most likely, say it was proof they were on the same wavelength, that all this stuff was connected, that they'd been destined to meet.

Robin doesn't want to hear it. She rubs her eyes with the back of her hand, looks away up the path. We should be getting back, she says. She wants to be rid of this place, the reality and the memory. She wonders if she has made things worse by coming here, by stoking Frank's delusion. Probably not, but even so. She has handled things badly.

They climb into the pickup. Do you want to come back to the house? Frank says. Eddie should be back by now if you want to talk to him. I know he wants to meet you.

I'll come after supper if that's OK. I want to have a shower first, change my clothes. Maybe go to the museum, she says, as a peace offering more than anything, though half an hour after Frank drops her off at the hotel she finds herself going in search of it. She wants to see the painting, the Nunc Dimitis. The museum is less than five minutes' walk away. Most of the exhibits are centred upon local history. There are photos of the quarry from when it was still being mined, sepia-tinted images of women in headscarves carrying lunch pails, men in dirt-spattered work clothes leaning on shovels.

The town in the photographs appears eerily unchanged. Robin finds Tain's likeness to itself disconcerting, as if the town she is in is not real, a facsimile of some kind, though she knows this is nonsense, an overreaction to a stressful day.

The painting by Jehan Fouquet is in a side-room, protected by a glass screen and a warning to visitors not to step beyond the guide rope. The canvas is small, less than two feet in height, yet it glows with the bright intensity of a stained-glass window. The blue of Mary's robe, the green of Simeon's shift – the hues look newly minted and so in a way does the painting, the company of angels in human guise mixing with the gawpers in the temple like common gossips. The sharpness of the scene, the inherent knowingness. Tempting to the eye, like a glossy cover shot, more like an image from a tabloid newspaper than a religious icon. Leaves you dying to know what is really going on.

Robin stares at the old man, Simeon. Half an eye on the pretty young virgin even as he holds out his arms for the Christ child; not so done with the old world yet then, my son, not done until you're dead. One of the angels is holding a trumpet, a flash-fire in gold, though they seem more interested in what one of their fellows is whispering than in rousing a sacred aria to mark the occasion.

The world of the painting is vital and untrammelled and faintly bawdy. Instead of resorting to stock images of piety and devotion, Fouquet has tried to tell the story of what took place in the temple as it actually might have happened. In every sense that matters, the work is modern. Robin remembers what Frank had been saying earlier about Renaissance art, the way it seemed to embrace freshness and vigour and violence as a true reflection of a world on the cusp of change. A world still open to magic and aware of its frailty, a world existing in the cosmic firelight of Armageddon.

Robin eats supper in a wine bar on the High Street: steak-and-ale pie with chips and then a double Macallan, which she hopes will not turn out to be an error of judgement. She does not want to be drunk or even in that ballpark when she meets de Groote, though part of her doubts the elusive Eddie will even be there. The situation is ridiculous, a set-up: the town at the back end of nowhere, the so-called study centre, the violinist girlfriend, the eternal teenager who believes his dad is a supersoldier, a patch of greyish fungus growing on a tree and Edmund de Groote the mysterious fixer at the heart of it all?

Choosing not to believe in something you know to be true is an act of self-destruction, Jeanne Vanderlien had said, but can Robin honestly say she believes a word of what Frank has told her? Her gut says there is something here, something she should not ignore, but surely that is the whisky talking, the twenty-five-year-old single malt that cost her as much as the meal itself but that seemed worth the money, not just worth it but necessary as an act of self-protection. The Macallan says yes but her head says no, and Dunbar – Alec Dunbar says screw you Clay, what did I tell ye, no drinking on the job and that's coming from a man who's lost more brain cells to alcohol than ye had in the first place. Drinking on the job clouds your judgement and here ye are lassie, the living proof. I's sorry for what went down between us, ye had the makings of a fine detective, youse a been the last person on the squad I'd hae wanted to lose but alien invaders? Jesus Claymore, get a feckin grip.

Screw you, Dunbar, Robin thinks, imagines, sees the old bastard, her mother's killer, how he'll be in twenty years' time, rug across his knees in a communal lounge, gas fire turned up to eleven and the flush in his cheeks to prove it or is that just the whisky, a book face-down on the armrest, cracking the spine.

Jack House's The Square Mile of Murder, a fake book for a fake legend, as Dunbar used to call it. Every bugger knows the old hack made half of it up but still it's a pleasure I like to revisit every couple of years. Ma comfort read, lassie.

Screw you, Dunbar.

Screw you.

She can cry screw you all she likes, but Robin still misses him. Alec Dunbar may have murdered her mother but he is still family.

I'm glad you decided to come, de Groote says. Frank tells me he's shown you the site. What did you make of it?

I have no idea. I'm not a botanist, a mycologist, whatever. I don't know what to think.

Lichens are neither true fungi nor true plants. That is part of what makes them remarkable, or so I understand it. I'm no expert either.

But you make it your business to facilitate the work of those who are. You and your family.

I realise my family has a history, but so do all families. I cannot escape the past. But I can at least choose to spend my inheritance wisely, where it is needed, on what I consider to be important. The pursuit of science—

Don't you mean pseudoscience?

Also, I like this town. De Groote continues speaking as if Robin's interruption is of no account. I like being here, out of the way. I am considering moving to Scotland permanently. With the help of technology it is possible to work from anywhere in the world these days, even more so since the virus. Do you still remember where you were the winter it began? I was in Hong Kong, for a film festival. When I think about that week now it seems to stand out, lit in neon, as if the colours in the world were brighter than in the weeks to either side. The strangest thing about history is that we are rarely able to perceive how it is being made, especially when it is happening to us.

Most people have a story like that, like with 9/11.

Do you have a story?

Not really. It was March and I was in London. The weather was filthy. My boss was being a bastard and I was beginning to suspect my partner was having an affair. I remember it was almost a relief at the time, to have something more important to worry about.

Yet you felt the world shift, nonetheless, you experienced a change.

I was about to lose my job.

Yet you invented a new one – a new idea of yourself. You evolved.

De Groote is almost comically urbane: the grey turtleneck, the designer jeans, the expensive-looking long-line blazer with the navy fleck that matches his eyes. He looks exactly what he is – a cross between a European intellectual and the son of a gangster. Robin feels exhausted suddenly. Has Frank explained to you about his Bach theory? de Groote is saying.

He gave me the basic idea. He seems to think Bach's music contains the blueprint of an alien code.

Do you know about the music festival in Tromsø, Norway, where they sent thirty-three different musical extracts into space, sequenced in binary code? This happened in 2017, through the ESCAT radio antenna. The broadcast included instructions on how to reconfigure the binary back into music. Music already is an alien code. Every act of listening is an act of translation.

I don't suppose they heard back, though?

It is too soon to know. Would you like to see our music room while you are here? Saira likes to practise there. I think you will like it.

He leads her through to a room overlooking the garden. Narrow French windows, a glass-fronted bookcase overflowing with scientific journals and what must be several hundred issues of the Fortean Times. Against the far wall stands an upright piano in a walnut case, the kind of modest, unassuming instrument you might expect to find in the rooms of a Methodist minister or provincial schoolmistress. De Groote seems too big for it, knees jammed up under the keyboard, bony wrists protruding, hawk-like, from his rolled-back sleeves.

I would like to play you something, he says, BWV 528, which as you will know is the trio sonata in E minor. Jeanne tells me you are as crazy about Bach as Frank is. I find it interesting, and also revealing, how alike you are, the two of you. And yet you say you never met before you came here.

He begins to play the andante, his hands like steel traps, his shoulders hunched forward like he is walking into a forest on the eve of a war. Robin finds herself counting the beats, the beats that strike the hours, the melody slow with the black-caped solemnity of a funeral procession, and she thinks of all the dead, the dead of the plague, the dead of Culloden and the famine that followed, the dead of the towers, of the Lockerbie bomb and the dead of the virus. She feels a tear slide down her cheek. De Groote is a fine pianist. She assimilates the fact without surprise. She wonders if this is a trap of some kind, though what that trap might be is not at all clear to her.

You do not play yourself? de Groote is saying.

No. It was my mother who played. She studied composition and harpsichord at Goldsmiths.

Her words seem to fall into the room, echoing off the parquet like the final perfect cadence of the andante. She feels the shock of them striking her eardrums, words she has never uttered aloud, not even to herself.

That I did not know.

She died.

Recently? De Groote raises his eyebrows.

A long time ago now. Robin can feel de Groote's curiosity, an appetite for knowledge he is used to satisfying instantly and at others' expense. Robin finds she is not of a mind to accede to his silent demand. Where did you study? she asks him instead. She does not care about his answer. She wants to change the subject.

Oh, nowhere really. Music is simply a hobby for me. Maybe if I had been more disciplined when I was younger I might have made something of it, but we so rarely know our minds when we are young. He shrugs.

I think you knew already. About my mother, Robin says suddenly. Or else your father did, or your uncle. One of you knows, anyway.

De Groote stares at her steadily, unblinking. One of us?

The de Grootes. You know what happened.

And what if I do? de Groote says softly. Do you?

My mother's name was Marianne Lees. She was shot dead in a kidnapping that went wrong. She wasn't the target but she was killed anyway.

You see, you don't know. Or you don't know the whole truth.

Those two boys were sent to carry out a punishment and that is what they did.

They were supposed to punish Mark Denisov's father, you mean? I know that already.

Mark Denisov was no one. Your mother did not realise, perhaps, how anger when combined with power can lead to rash actions. Mark Denisov is not your father, and he was not the real target, although I think you have guessed that. What you do not appear to know is that whatever you accuse me of being, you are also. If I were to call you my sister that would not be strictly accurate in the genealogical sense, though if you are prepared to be more liberal in your interpretation – more inclined towards metaphor – then you will see how we are related. How everything we have accomplished is related.

You are saying that my father—

That we are family, yes. Your mother had a brief relationship with an uncle of mine. Or maybe a second cousin – unlike some of the older generation I am not obsessed with such minutiae. As I understand it, Mark Denisov became involved with Marianne after meeting her at a party he was invited to at your father's home. Only a character in a Greek tragedy would be more foolish. Your mother's death was payback, a matter of honour. Your father was not the kind to let sleeping dogs lie.

I don't believe you, Robin says, though she knows her words are more a form of protest than a statement of fact. That she, Robin Clay, is herself a de Groote seems beyond ridiculous, the kind of twisted, farcical luck only Alec Dunbar would find amusing. Even if it's true it doesn't matter.

I agree with you. It is of no account to anyone, not now. I thought you might be interested, that is all.

Did you kill Miles Shipley?

You know I did not.

I know you were in Scarborough at the conference the day he died. I know you were probably the last person to see him alive.

I am an academic and a film critic. I would not know how to kill someone even if you paid me a great deal of money to do so. Yes, I was in Scarborough. And yes, I met with Miles. He claimed he wanted to interview me about my interest in fictional narratives of alien abduction. As it turned out he was more interested in the factual narrative of Frank Landau's kidnapping, as he referred to it. He was rather aggressive, at least to begin with. He threatened to expose me as some sort of cult leader. I managed to persuade him that he was wrong, that Crombie House is a genuine research facility and that Frank was working for us of his own free will. I said I was willing to give him as much information as he wanted, provided that he promised to keep the location of Crombie House and the exact nature of our research off the record. He said he would think about my offer, and we agreed to meet for lunch the following day. When I left his hotel room at around nine o'clock he was very much alive. He even offered me a glass of wine. I told him he looked exhausted, that he should get some rest. It did not occur to me that he might be ill or I would have advised him to consult a doctor. He said he never slept well in hotels, and those were the last words we spoke to one another. The following morning I learned he had died of a heart attack — two of the room attendants were talking about it and I happened to overhear. My conference schedule was finished. I couldn't see the point of staying on any longer and so I left.

Do you really believe all this stuff – about the war, I mean?

It is Frank who calls it a war, and Jeanne-Marie Vanderlien, but Jeanne is an old woman now, and you know what old people are like – for them, war is as much about their personal memories of past wars as about war itself. I do not know what I think yet, because I do not know enough about what is really going on. I want to discover more facts before I decide my place in this. My uncle – not your father, another one – calls me the Student Prince, perpetually in pursuit of a fantasy, perpetually in debt. But then my uncle is what you might call a de Groote of the old school, stubborn as lichen and ruled by money. When I tell him that cash is a capitalist construct he says he does not see me complaining when this capitalist construct buys me lunch. Then we both laugh. I think he prefers me this way, actually. It gives him something to complain about.

Are you afraid? Robin asks as she leaves.

De Groote shrugs. It would be like being afraid of thunder – there is nothing you can do to stop it, so what would be the point? Better to be a storm chaser. There is something thrilling about lightning and tornadoes, don't you find? And the summer skies up here are peerless. Bergman skies, I call them, a glimpse of eternity. The skies are part of the reason I think of coming to live here.

If you walk down the hill past the station and over the railway bridge you will find a pathway that cuts across the links towards the Dornoch Firth. Turn left and you will arrive at the golf club and presently the town. Turn right and you will find a steel suspension bridge that links the mainland with a marshy outcrop jutting out into the water. This is the Alexandra Bridge, manufactured by the Rose Foundry of Inverness in 1902. The bridge is for pedestrians only – there is a warning sign, maximum load two persons – and a metal plaque commemorating the refurbishment and reopening of the bridge by the Princess Royal in July 2016. I can remember Princess Anne getting married and so can Dianne. She invited some friends round to watch the wedding on TV, people she worked with in social services. See how they pile into her living room, drinking Cinzano and munching Ritz crackers and laughing their heads off. Dianne has not laughed so much since, or not so often, girlishly and without restraint. I remember especially Princess Anne's wedding dress, understated and rather prim and with a high lace collar. She looks like a queen in that, says Dianne's friend Billie. Not like one of your Disney princesses, like a queen in an old fairy tale.

On the day Princess Anne travels to Scotland to open the bridge named for her great-great grandmother Queen Alexandra, Lucian Cherish has been dead for less than a week, the EU referendum happened less than a month ago, a fracturing of time, the dawn of a new era. Robin stands still for a moment to read the plaque and imagine the scene – the quiet town, the gathering of onlookers, the polite clapping – then walks across the bridge and stands on the damp grass looking out over the water. She is entirely alone there. She can hear the cries of herring gulls and curlews, oyster catchers and rooks. She is thinking about her father, Derek Clay, who began teaching her to recognise bird calls the weekend they went camping on Mersea Island. It'll be an adventure, he said, just the two of us, though from what

Robin remembers the trip had been organised because of Dianne. Either she hadn't been well or she and Derek had had a row, she just needed some time to herself for goodness' sake . . .

The tide is out and the sky is huge, its silvery flanks striped with cloud, the gently flexing sides of an enormous tabby cat. The mudflats, silvered with tidewater, swarm with waders. Robin is five hundred miles from Mersea Island yet still she can recognise the earnest, aching keening, the east coast refrain. She has come to the end of the road and there is only bleakness, only solitude, the slipping away of autumn into winter.

Edmund de Groote is right though: the evening light is so intense here, Bergman skies, the clouds with their sun-pinked fingers, the last, the last of everything.

The mist rises up; the mudflats shimmer. She has come to the end of the road and there are no clear answers.

She knows she has to call Rachel, that any further delay would be irresponsible, a betrayal, not only of her professional integrity but of Rachel herself, of the closeness, however unsuitable, that has sprung up between them. Now the decision is made she cannot give herself the excuse to put it off further. She takes out her phone. The moment Rachel picks up she gives her the news.

He's here, Robin says. Frank is here in Scotland. But I don't think you should come.

She hears a massive outrush of breath and then Rachel is crying. She is asking if Robin is sure, if she has spoken to Frank, if he is all right.

What do you mean, don't come? she says, and Rachel is laughing now, not crying. Of course I'm coming.

*

There is a version of this story in which Robin manages to persuade Rachel that she should wait, that she should put off making a
decision until Robin has had the chance to explain things properly.
Robin leaves Tain first thing the following morning and heads over
to Rachel's place the moment she arrives back in London. They
talk for hours. Frank's not going anywhere, Robin says. There's no
harm in waiting a few days. I'll go back up to Scotland with you
if you want, she adds, taking Rachel's noncommittal maybe as an
indication of how already in these first few seconds Rachel is slipping
away from her; their time together has only ever been about finding
Frank, about Frank full stop.

Rachel is not happy about having to wait but in the end she does
listen, her restless pacing gradually slowing as Robin continues to
describe Frank's current circumstances, all the ways in which he needs
help, the reasons why Rachel – really – is the least qualified to give it.

Frank isn't well, Robin says. This isn't just a phase he's going
through, it's something deeper. You have already given twenty years of
your life to him. You need to think about yourself, about your future.
What you want your life to be, what you need to be happy. You owe
it to yourself, Robin says. Some fates are dead ends.

Rachel cannot stop crying. She is insisting she has to look up the
train times, pack her stuff, but in the end and after much argument
she agrees to put off her journey until the following day. It is late
already, she couldn't get further than Glasgow tonight in any case,
and everything will seem clearer in the morning. Robin insists Rachel
really should eat something and so they send out for takeaway. By the
end of the evening Rachel finds herself agreeing that she should not

make the journey, not yet at least, that she will write to Frank instead and see what happens.

She writes Frank a letter – Robin has told her Frank has stopped using email because he is increasingly nervous about being hacked – asking if it would be all right for her to come and visit him at Crombie House. I respect what you're doing, she writes. I just miss you so much, Frankie, I've been so worried. I need to be sure you're really OK.

There is no reply. After three months Rachel writes again, a chatty letter this time, just day-to-day stuff. She tells herself it is better not to pressure him, but there is still no reply. Rachel calls Robin in tears and tells her she has decided to take Robin's advice, to put her time with Frank behind her, to move on with her life. When they meet up later that week, Rachel is wearing gold sandals, gold bangles on her wrists. Her hair is piled on top of her head, secured with pins whose coloured-glass heads sparkle like gemstones beneath the lights. And yes, they spend the night together, which feels inevitable by that point, something of a relief for both of them, yet in the days and weeks that follow neither can escape the feeling that it was a mistake.

They keep in touch by email, on and off. Rachel begins her teaching course, wins a placement at a highly rated secondary school in Hither Green. She loves the work and she is good at it. Rachel's friend Claris can't help saying I told you so, but she is pleased as punch you can tell, and they celebrate Rachel's first proper teacher's pay cheque with a night on the town. Eighteen months later, Rachel goes on a date with Martin the new history teacher and they hit it off immediately.

This future has everything: marriage, children (Rimini, Celia, Vernon), birthdays, holidays and Christmases, the kind you still remember when you are old. There is no space in this future for Robin because she doesn't make sense there. Rachel asks herself what it was exactly between them and the only logical answer is probably nothing. It was so long ago in any case, another life really, and if there are moments when Rachel wonders whatever did become of Frank Landau (her Frankie), moments when she feels the ache of him, the once-in-a-lifetime closeness, the sense she failed some crucial test, then they are few and far enough between not to be a hindrance or a shadow on the life she has chosen.

Of course there is another version of this story in which Rachel will not hear of delaying her journey north. She flings some stuff in a rucksack and goes straight to the station. Robin is waiting for her at the other end, and after an hour's debrief in the hotel bar they go together to Crombie House. Do you want me to wait? Robin asks, but Rachel shakes her head.

I'll call you later, she says, and then she rings the bell. Robin does not stay to see what happens, to see Saira open the door and welcome Rachel inside as she carelessly yells Frank's name into the depths of the house. She does not witness their reunion, cinematic in its intensity. Frank seems younger than ever, beautiful in his waifishness, those ratty old jeans. Rachel is hugging him to her – Frankie, my Frankie – and her eyes are like gems. She is wondering how she could have doubted, not that it matters, because finally she and Frank are back together and everything is going to be all right.

She meets Kemal and Rory and Abigail, another coder named Wilson and his girlfriend Sheena. Frank introduces her to Eddie, who takes her hand. Welcome to the asylum, he says with a smile. His eyes remain watchful, his stance is tense though not prohibitive and he is thinking maybe it's a good thing after all, her coming here, at least we'll have no more journalists or private dicks.

Rachel is thinking how nice they all are, how normal, why the secrecy and months of confusion, all for nothing? She is certain things really will be OK now, though in a day or two, a week maybe she will begin to see the shine come off, the first cracks appear, the truth behind the facade. Frank is like he was before; if anything, he is worse. His obsessions have grown and deepened, have taken control. He speaks constantly of the war, and he has acquired some other strange beliefs now on top of that: that it is wrong for him and Rachel to be intimate, that there is no question of them living together, that too many outward signs of their closeness will put Rachel in danger.

I'm not always in this body, Frank says to her. He touches her hand then pulls away, his shoulders hunched over crowlike, his face distraught. There are dangerous people about, Rach, and they're coming closer.

Rachel feels the familiar approach of despair, the sense that everything is sliding away from her, that she has been in this place before, too many times. Yet this is a state of mind she is used to and knows how to deal with. She makes enquiries about starting her teaching course in Inverness. There is a shortage of maths teachers in the Highlands so this is no problem, quite the opposite. She is asked if there is any chance at all she could begin straight after Christmas.

Fast forward a couple of years and Rachel feels settled here. She buys a cottage in the town, a tiny place but hers. She feels proactive, balanced, sensible and above all at peace. She has a job, doesn't she?

She has colleagues, friends and neighbours. She grows to love the little grey town with its northern climate, its Bergman skies. She joins the local choir, sings Handel and Bach. Most importantly of all, her Frankie feels secure and he is nearby.

Rachel makes a life for herself. Not the life she imagined, perhaps, but a life nonetheless. As Frank grows into middle age he seems less troubled, less anxious, and soon there will come a time when Rachel will ask him again if he would like to move in with her and Frank will say yes.

And in the meantime there is Robin. Her first visit is very emotional. Rachel is still in a rented flat at that point, still confused and upset by Frank's behaviour, what she sees as his rejection. She and Robin end up in bed together (one too many Macallans, Rachel tells herself afterwards) and there is rapture in it (like the dawn sky, the dawn sky rent asunder by the rising sun) and for some days afterwards Robin lets herself believe they can make it work. But then once she is back in London Rachel goes silent. She does not pick up her phone or answer her emails, and when finally she calls she tells Robin she feels awful about what happened but her place is with Frank.

Robin says she's sorry too and yes, Rachel is right, it is never a good idea for detective and client to become overly entangled.

Robin will still visit, for a couple of years at least, coffee and scones with the stove going, Caspar David Friedrich's Winter Landscape hung in the chimney alcove, those heady Bergman skies.

One thing Robin is certain of in either scenario: she has no desire to seek out her birth father, Oscar de Groote. So far as her present life is concerned, he is irrelevant; as regards the life he took away from her, he is so far beyond the pale as to be invisible. Family is her and Dianne, same as always. Some fates are dead ends.

Five years or so after the Frank Landau episode, she is working a case (somebody's husband, somebody's con man) following up a lead when she happens to encounter a journalist named Kevin McNaught. The strangest thing is that he once knew Miles Shipley. They find they have plenty to talk about, even after the con man is arrested and sent down for eight years. Kevin McNaught is divorced (his ex-wife took her romantic interests elsewhere, is the way Kev puts it) and a workaholic, but there are worse things than workaholics – Robin should know because she's one herself – and at least when they are together Robin has no doubt that she is truly seen. Kev likes fusion jazz and electronica, Xenakis and Glass, and when Robin plays him Gubaidulina's In Tempus Praesens he likes that, too.

They are alike, the two of them, and it is this likeness more than anything that draws them together. Gradually they begin to believe they can make a life that suits them both equally, that happiness is possible.

At some point (she and Kev have been together for almost ten years) Robin stops sending postcards, Christmas cards, birthday cards to Rachel Gabon. She hasn't heard from her for a while now, and some fates are dead ends.

She wonders how they are, the two of them, and how the war is going.

ACKNOWLEDGEMENTS

THIS BOOK BEGAN LIFE well before 2020 but was radically altered by it; one might even say that *Conquest* stands as my personal diary-in-code of that extraordinary year. The chapters Tainted Ground and Night Terrors draw on real-life cases; the relevant information pertaining to these is in the public domain. Translations from the German are my own.

I would like to thank my agent, Anna Webber, and my editor, Jon Riley, for their unstinting support and belief in my work through the weirdest of times. Huge thanks also to the good people at United Agents and riverrun books for keeping the faith and keeping things moving.

Thanks to my mother, Monica Allan, for being with me on this journey, and boundless love and gratitude as ever to my partner Chris Priest for not being fazed by my fascination with putative alien spores or my passion for music. The truth is out there.